A MUSEUM MYSTERY

PRIVY TO THE DEAD

SHEILA CONNOLLY

WHEELER PUBLISHING
A part of Gale, Cengage Learning

GALE
CENGAGE Learning·

Farmington Hills, Mich • San Francisco • New York • Waterville, Maine
Meriden, Conn • Mason, Ohio • Chicago

GALE
CENGAGE Learning®

LIBRARY OF CONGRESS CATALOGING-IN-PUBLICATION DATA

Names: Connolly, Sheila.
Title: Privy to the dead / by Sheila Connolly.
Description: Large print edition. | Waterville, Maine : Wheeler Publishing, 2016. |
© 2015 | Series: Wheeler Publishing large print cozy mystery | Series: A museum
mystery
Identifiers: LCCN 2015041189 | ISBN 9781410486608 (softcover) | ISBN 1410486605
(softcover)
Subjects: LCSH: Pratt, Nell (Fictitious character)—Fiction. |
Murder—Investigation—Fiction. | Large type books. | GSAFD: Mystery fiction.
Classification: LCC PS3601.T83 P75 2016 | DDC 813/.6—dc23
LC record available at http://lccn.loc.gov/2015041189

Published in 2016 by arrangement with The Berkley Publishing Group,
an imprint of Penguin Publishing Group, a division of Penguin Random
House LLC

Printed in the United States of America
1 2 3 4 5 6 7 20 19 18 17 16

ACKNOWLEDGMENTS

For several years I worked at the Historical Society of Pennsylvania in Philadelphia, and had the privilege of spending time with its marvelous collections. Most people will never know the thrill of handling documents written by eighteenth-century presidents, or holding the Bible that belonged to William Penn and is now used to swear in Pennsylvania's governors, but I did. Even the more mundane items, like ledgers from nineteenth-century businesses and household account books, give glimpses into daily life a century or two earlier, and I'll admit to browsing now and then, just for pleasure.

All of these diverse items preserve the past that we share, and when I write about the fictional Pennsylvania Antiquarian Society, that's what I try to convey. But sometimes artifacts can tell us a different story, and that's what happens in this book. Something was found where it shouldn't have been,

5

and it points to an event that had been concealed for a century, and that led to the death of a man in the present.

This book wouldn't exist without a casual comment from Daniel Rolfe, longtime head of reference services at the Historical Society. When I visited him there a couple of years ago, he mentioned that in the course of a recent building renovation, a deep hole had been found in the basement of the building, and nobody knew what it was or why it was there. Of course my ears pricked up, and I was careful not to ask what was found in the pit, so that I could exercise my own imagination. In this book, what emerged from that pit is my own invention.

Many thanks go to Page Talbott, a longtime friend who became president of the real Historical Society after I started writing this series, and to former colleague and present friend Sandra Cadwalader, who knows more about HSP and Philadelphia (past and current) than anyone I've ever met. I am so relieved that neither one takes offense when I attribute evil deeds to anyone associated with the institution. I have the greatest admiration for the place and its employees, and I'm proud to have been a part of it for a time.

As always, a big thank you to my agent

Jessica Faust of BookEnds, who made this series possible, and the efficient and supportive staff at Berkley Prime Crime. I also owe thanks to Sisters in Crime, its New England chapter, and its online Guppies chapter, for their unflagging support. I couldn't do this without you!

CHAPTER 1

As I looked around the long table, I realized it was the first time I had ever seen the board members of the Pennsylvania Antiquarian Society look happy all at once. I was tempted to take a picture, just to remind myself of the moment when darker days returned, as no doubt they would.

The group had good reason to look happy. We were fully staffed, with the recent addition of a new registrar to complete the roster of management positions; we had a wealth of material to keep our staff busy cataloging for years; and we had earned the gratitude of the FBI for agreeing to sort through the bits and bobs of art and artifacts that their Philadelphia office had confiscated over the past several years. And we had just received a nice — make that a *really* nice — financial contribution from big-name local developer Mitchell Wakeman, who had asked me to help him smooth the path for his planned

development project in the suburbs. Luckily he hadn't blamed me when we had stumbled over a body along the way, but I'd shown him how to use the information we'd uncovered in solving the murder to strengthen the project, unlikely though it seemed. He had been appropriately grateful and had presented the Society (of which I, Nell Pratt, was president) with a pot of money, with the restriction that it must be used for physical improvements to our century-plus-old building, rather than collections or staff salaries. It was a reasonable request; he was, after all, a mogul of the construction industry, and we really did need those physical improvements. We had already moved from the planning stages to the physical preparations, and we were ready to start the construction phase.

I'd been pleased that I could introduce both the project designer — Kemble and Warren, a long-established firm with an excellent track record — and the contractor for our renovations, Schuylkill Construction, which had come highly recommended by Mitchell Wakeman at the fall board meeting. I hadn't expected any problems, and there weren't any. The companies involved in the project had taken part in a number of similar projects for local art or

collecting institutions, so the staffs there understood the challenges of working around delicate collections and finicky researchers. We wanted to accomplish the overhaul with a minimum of disruption to patrons, and without closing the doors. There were sections we were going to have to restrict access to for a time, but all things considered, the plan was the best we could hope for. We'd make the best of the inevitable disarray by giving our annual holiday-season party a construction-related theme — paint-spattered tablecloths and mock hard hats for all. By spring we'd be all prettied up, structurally and environmentally sound, and ready to throw a big unveiling party.

"We've already given approval of the design aspects by Kemble and Warren. Now we are voting to approve the final work plan as presented by Schuylkill Construction. All in favor?" I asked, standing tall at the head of the table. *Aye*s all around. "Then the project is approved, and work will begin immediately," I announced triumphantly. Actually, work had already begun. As a collections-based organization, for more than a century we had accumulated a lot of stuff, not all of it with historic importance. For example, the basement was loaded with

wooden filing cabinets and computer terminals so old that the companies who made them had long since gone out of business. A Dumpster now occupied a permanent place next to the loading dock in the alley behind the building, and we filled it regularly these days.

I turned to Joseph Logan, head of Schuylkill Construction, who'd been invited to witness the final board vote. "Thank you, Mr. Logan, for all the work that you've put into this so far. We look forward to working with you — as long as you stick to the schedule."

Logan smiled. "Don't worry — it's all under control. And you've got a great building here, so I don't expect to find many problems."

I knew full well that digging into any old building usually resulted in at least a few unexpected problems, but I had faith that they would be minor ones. At least, I hoped so. Hadn't we had enough problems in the past year? We should have earned some good karma by now.

"Any new business?" I asked the group.

One of our older, more scholarly board members raised his hand. "How do you intend to prioritize projects going forward, when we have our own cataloging to do,

plus the FBI materials, and now our space will be reduced?"

"Our vice president of collections, Latoya Anderson, has worked out a schedule to deal with that, and I have every expectation that she will run a tight ship," I told him. "Of course, our own collections come first — there's no particular timeline for the FBI materials. I didn't ask her to attend this meeting because I wanted to focus on the construction aspects, but I can have her forward you a copy of her plans. Anything else?"

"How do you plan to handle dust spreading through the building?" someone else asked.

"Fair question. When we reach the stage of adding modern ventilation, we will address protecting the collections then. That's why we've hired people who have worked under these conditions before, and they all have excellent reputations."

"Wouldn't it have been better to remove the collections to an off-site location?" he asked.

I swallowed a sigh; we'd been over all this before. "We did consider that, but off-site storage presents its own problems — we'd have little control over the physical conditions, and security is not always what it

should be, no matter what promises the storage companies make. We're talking about some priceless documents, among other things, and we'd rather keep them here, even if it means shuttling them from one location to another within the building."

I scanned the group, and saw most of them making twitchy ready-to-leave motions. "And remember, when we're done, we will actually have increased our storage space without expanding the building's footprint, thanks to installing compact shelving wherever possible. I can't tell you exactly by how much, because the contractor is still assessing the load-bearing capacity of some of the areas, but I have been assured that it will be substantial."

Lewis Howard, the venerable board chair, stood up. "Thank you, Nell, for all the good work you have put into making this happen. If there are no other issues" — he looked sternly at the other people around the table, and nobody opened their mouth — "then I declare this meeting adjourned. Good night, all."

The board members gathered up their folders and coats and hurried to the elevator. I thanked the architect and the contractor, who told me they'd be back early the

next morning for a final walk-through before the physical work began. Finally I was left alone with Marty Terwilliger, a longtime board member (practically hereditary, since both her father and her grandfather had been very actively involved at the Society) and good friend, both professionally and personally.

"Good job wrangling the board, Nell," she said.

"Thanks. It did go well, don't you think?"

"I do. Of course, they had nothing to complain about, since you brought in Wakeman's pile of money. Which you earned, since you helped save his butt on his pet project."

"In a way, I'm glad he restricted how it should be used. He had a pretty clear idea what we needed to do here, and it saved a lot of squabbling among the board members."

"He's a smart man, and an honest one. If you throw a big bash, make sure you invite him — and that he comes."

I'd certainly ask, although I knew that Mitchell Wakeman didn't like socializing much. "Of course."

Marty glanced at the clock on the wall and stood up. "I'm heading out. You ready? We can walk out together."

15

I nodded. "Let me grab my stuff." I went back to my office down the hall, picked up my bag, put on my coat, and rejoined her in the hall after turning out the last few lights.

"How're you and Jimmy liking the new place?" Marty asked as we headed out. "Jimmy" was FBI Special Agent James Morrison, who had somehow gotten sucked into several crimes that I was also involved in, and since we were both single and intelligent and reasonable human beings, the inevitable had happened and a couple of months earlier we had bought a house together. Marty had a proprietary interest in our relationship because James was some kind of cousin of hers (one of many in the greater Philadelphia area) and because she'd introduced us and seen us both through some traumatic events. She was a snoop, but a polite and well-meaning one, and she was willing to back off if asked.

For the past decade, I'd been living in Bryn Mawr, in what had once been a carriage house behind one of the big Main Line houses. It had been cheaply converted before I bought it, and I'd spent a couple of years improving it. It was small, but it had worked for me.

And then James had happened, and the carriage house simply wasn't big enough for

two. And he didn't want to live way out in the suburbs. When we first met, his own place was a Spartan apartment near the University of Pennsylvania, in a converted triple-decker. As in my case, it suited him but it wasn't intended for two adults with decades' worth of stuff. So we'd taken the plunge and bought a Victorian in an area that wasn't quite city or suburb but the best of both.

"You know, I'm really not settled into this commute to Chestnut Hill yet. I don't want to drive every day. I'm still trying to figure out the daily train schedule — I had the one to Bryn Mawr memorized, but this one is new to me. I catch a ride with James when I can, but his schedule is kind of unpredictable." We'd been living in the house only a month, once all the closing formalities had been completed and we'd written checks with a horrifying number of digits on them, and we still hadn't established any kind of routine. But if that was the worst of my problems, I wasn't going to gripe. "Eliot waiting for you tonight?"

Marty and Eliot Miller, the Penn professor she'd been seeing, were moving more slowly than James and I were, and still maintained their own domiciles. Marty lived in a lovely nineteenth-century row house in

17

a convenient Center City location — the better to walk over to the Society when the spirit moved her, which was often — and I had no idea where Eliot lived. He taught urban planning at the University of Pennsylvania, though, so I figured he probably lived not far from campus. Marty and I hadn't discussed their long-term plans, and she was volunteering little information, maybe afraid she would jinx the fledgling relationship. She had a couple of failed marriages on her résumé.

"Not tonight — he had an all-hands faculty meeting, and I had this, so we decided we'd see each other tomorrow. How's Lissa working out?"

Lissa Penrose was one of Eliot's advisees as she worked on a graduate degree. "Great. I've asked her to review the history of this building. She'll be working with Shelby, too."

Shelby had taken over my previous position as director of development at the Society when I'd been abruptly elevated to the position of president, and we worked well together. Her dash of Southern charm had proved to be an asset when wangling contributions from our members. She had submitted a brief report on contributions and attended this meeting for purely cere-

monial purposes, as a senior staff member, but had disappeared quickly while I was still saying my farewells to the board members. "I'm hoping we can put together some material on interesting building details, to use for fundraising."

We closed up the building behind us, making sure the security system was armed, and said good-bye at the foot of the stairs outside. Marty headed home, and I crossed the street and retrieved my car from the lot. At least this parking fee I could charge to the Society. At this time of night there was little traffic, and it didn't take long to reach home.

Home. I had trouble wrapping my head around that. The house was gorgeous, and I still tiptoed around it waiting for someone to tell me I wasn't worthy of it and throw me out. It had a parlor. It had five bedrooms. It was ridiculous for two people, but James had fallen for it on sight, and I had, too, when he showed it to me. And we could afford it, mostly. Neither the government nor mid-sized nonprofit organizations pay very well, but we were managing, albeit with not much with the way of furniture. But now it was . . . home.

I parked in the spacious three-car garage, then made my way to the back door, which

led into the kitchen. "Hello?" I called out. "I'm home."

I could hear James galumphing down the stairs (original woodwork! Never painted!), and then he joined me in the kitchen (which had a modern stove that terrified me with its array of knobs and digital indicators). As he approached I marveled once again that this tall, dark (well, greying a bit), and handsome — and smart and successful — FBI agent had fallen for me. "How'd it go? Have you eaten?" Rather than waiting for an answer, he gave me a very satisfying kiss. I was definitely enjoying coming home these days.

When he finally let me go, I said, "I'll answer question number two first: no. What is there?"

"Check the fridge. I think there are still leftovers."

"I'm afraid of the fridge. I keep thinking I'll start looking in there and I'll never find my way out again." I walked over to the gleaming expanse of stainless steel, opened the door, and peered in. "I see . . . Ooh, Chinese. How old is it?"

"Three days, maybe?"

"Good enough." I dumped a half-full carton of lo mein into a bowl and stuck it in the microwave. "As for the first question,

fine. No surprises. The next couple of months will be chaotic, but we'll survive. Wine?"

"Way ahead of you." James handed me a glass of white wine, and we clinked glasses.

"Ahh, that's good." I sighed after downing a healthy sip and kicking off my shoes.

He carefully took my glass and set it on the shiny granite-topped island — and repeated his earlier greeting. It took a couple of minutes before we peeled our-selves apart. "Welcome home, Nell," he said softly.

"You must have missed me. How was your day?"

"Very ordinary, thank you. That's a good thing. No crises, no disasters. I filed a lot of reports."

"And here I thought that working for the FBI was exciting," I said, pulling the hot food out of the microwave. "Where did we hide the chopsticks?"

"That drawer? Or maybe the one over there. I haven't seen them lately."

Our few pitiful utensils looked like or-phans cringing in the vast spaces of drawers and cupboards. It didn't take long to look. "Got 'em. I assume you ate? Because this is all mine."

"I did, and it is. Enjoy."

When I'd all but licked the bowl, I drained the last of my wine. "Much better."

"By the way, the faucet is still dripping in the bathtub."

"Hey, you're the big, strong man — you're supposed to know how to fix it."

"You're the historian," he countered. "This is definitely Victorian plumbing, therefore old, therefore your territory."

"Uh-huh," I said dubiously. "Well, let's go look at it together, and maybe something will occur to us."

On the way upstairs, something did occur to us. It was a while before we reached the bathroom.

CHAPTER 2

The next morning, James and I sat at the little round table (his — my larger table took up only a fraction of the space in the formal dining room next door) at one end of the kitchen, reading sections of the paper, drinking coffee, and munching on English muffins.

"What's the schedule for today?" I asked.

"The usual, I hope. We don't usually schedule 'crisis today' on our calendars, you know," James said, smiling. "You?"

"The construction team has finished the clean-out and is going to do a walk-through today, before they start making any physical changes, and I want to tag along."

"Is that part of your job description?"

"I have no idea, but I feel responsible anyway. Besides, I like to see the bones and guts of old buildings."

"There's a lovely image. Listen, about this weekend . . ."

23

My ears pricked up. "Yes?"

"We need to think about furniture," James said.

"What do you mean?"

"Look around. Your stuff looks fine, but my IKEA-type pieces look like fish out of water in this place. And there isn't enough of any of it. We've got an average of two-point-two pieces of furniture in each room — and some of those rooms could host an army. If we invite anyone over, they'll have to sit on the floor."

I couldn't disagree. And if we didn't fill in a few things, this place wouldn't really feel permanent. Apparently I was missing a nesting gene, because I hadn't really noticed until now. I was surprised that James had, but, of course, FBI agents were trained to be observant.

But then, I'd never really paid much attention to furniture. Most of my own furniture I'd inherited from one grandparent or another, and there had been more than enough to fill the small carriage house. I hadn't realized how sparse it would look in a different, bigger space until we moved in and discovered that we could hold bowling competitions in the front parlor on the lovely parquet floors. And those five bedrooms? We'd each brought along double

beds — two of mine, one from James — but what we really needed together was a queen or a king, since neither of us was exactly slender (although I had to admit, James was more fit than I was). The doubles would work fine for guest rooms, but that still left our loosely defined "offices" with nothing but boxes in them. James was right: we had to do something. But what?

"You have any ideas?" I asked.

"Go to a furniture store and look?" he suggested, with a gleam in his eye.

"We have a lot of rooms to fill, or at least start to fill," I reminded him, "and not a whole lot of money. I suppose that rules out antiques."

"Well, there are auctions, and some big antiques fairs. I don't have a lot of experience, but I'd guess that's kind of a long-range issue. Basically, though, I want this place to feel like home. *Our* home. And that means we have to choose things together."

I loved the thought that we had a long range — I was still getting used to that. One more reason to love the man. He was brave, steadfast, and true; he served his country loyally at the risk of his own life; and he wanted to look at furniture with me. Life was good.

"I'm almost afraid to bring this up," I said,

"but we could ask Marty for advice. She has some nice stuff."

"She does, and some of it is worth more than this house, although you wouldn't know it from the way she treats it."

I'd been to Marty's home more than once, and even to my eye she had some impressive antique pieces. I assumed they'd been passed down through the family, which extended back centuries in Philadelphia. I gave him a big smile. "Okay, let's start looking this weekend. If I see Marty, I'll ask her for advice on where we should look. And I know we've got some members with expertise in that area — although they know more about eighteenth-century stuff than modern, and as I said, I'm guessing that's well beyond our wallets at the moment. Oh well. We should make a list and set a budget. How does that work?"

"Sounds good to me." James stood up and carried his cup and plate to the sink. His mama had trained him well. He even did his own laundry. "Want a lift to the city?"

"I'd love one."

It was nice to arrive at work at a reasonable time, and to be delivered to the Society's door (or at least the nearest corner — the street ran one-way opposite the direction to James's office). It was also nice to

walk into the building without worrying about which disaster was looming. I had been honest with the board the night before: things were good, as good as I could remember them being in the five or more years I'd worked at the Society. I hoped it would last.

Upstairs on the administrative floor, I found I had arrived before Eric Hampton, my indispensable administrative assistant. I hung up my coat and made my way down the hall to the staff room, where I filled the coffeemaker. We'd made a pact when he started working for me: whoever arrived first made the first pot of coffee. I thought that was fair, although Eric was better with the temperamental coffeemaker than I was; it had begun to make ominous gurgling noises, and I wondered if it was time to upgrade to something more modern. Maybe one of those single-serving-type things, so nobody would have to argue about who had emptied the last of the pot. Why not? I was feeling flush, on behalf of the Society. That's what having a seven-figure balance in the bank did to me.

Ben Hartley rolled in as I watched the coffee dribble into the pot. Ben was our most recent hire, the new registrar. He'd been badly injured in an auto accident several months back, before he started at the

Society, and he was still coming to grips with the day-to-day realities of being confined to a wheelchair. "Morning, Nell," he said.

"Coffee'll be ready in a minute. You're in early," I commented.

"I was up, figured I'd come in. Sometimes I have trouble sleeping — it's hard to find a comfortable position. Better now that the weather's cooling off."

The machine sputtered, signaling that coffee was ready. "Can I pour you a cup?" When Ben nodded, I filled a mug and handed it to him, then filled one for myself and added sugar. "Are you ready for the construction to begin?"

"I plan to stay out of the way as much as possible. But Latoya and I have worked out a schedule for keeping one step ahead of the work crew without misplacing half the collections."

"Good! Because that's what I told the board last night," I said. "I'm hoping everything goes smoothly, but you never know. In the meantime I'm sure we'll field complaints from angry patrons who can't get access to that one document they've waited years to lay hands on, but it's a small price to pay, as I'm sure they'll agree — eventually. The good news is, the renovations are

already paid for. Do you have any idea how rare that is in the nonprofit world?"

"I can guess," Ben said. "You did Wakeman a good turn, and it paid off — literally, in this case."

And changed a little piece of history along the way, I reminded myself. That made me feel good, too. "Every now and then the gods are kind. Well, I'd better get my day started. I'm supposed to walk through the place with the architect and the contractor one last time, to see what they've got planned. See you later, Ben." I topped off my coffee and went back to my office, where Eric had just arrived.

"Coffee's ready, Eric," I told him. "Oh, could you do some research on current coffee systems? The one we've got has been here since before I started working here, and I think coffeemaking technology might have improved just a bit."

"You don't like my coffee, Nell?" Eric smiled.

"Hey, I love your coffee, especially when you bring me a cup. I'm so happy you don't mind doing that. But I just thought we could check out the new technologies. Maybe even get a new fridge for the staff room. Wouldn't that fall under the 'physical improvements' mandate?"

29

"Whatever you say, Nell. Oh, Scott Warren left a message saying he'd be here at ten for the walk-through. Does that work for you?"

"Unless you tell me something different. You haven't seen Marty Terwilliger yet this morning, have you?"

"No, ma'am. You need her for something?"

"I'll give her a call later, if she doesn't come in. This isn't about Society business anyway." I went into my office and surveyed the scene: a beautiful antique mahogany desk I was terrified of spilling something on or scratching, and a damask-covered settee and flanking chairs. All these were for show, designed to impress people with the president of this venerable institution's importance and good taste. The filing cabinets were more practical, as was the sleek laptop computer (the connected printer was out near Eric's desk, so as not to mar the elegance of the ensemble). At the moment what pleased me most was the absence of any important "must do immediately" papers and messages cluttering up the desk. It looked serene.

But I found enough to keep me busy until Eric popped his head in and said, "Mr. Warren is here."

"Can you bring him upstairs, please? I

want to talk to him before we start rambling around the building." The administrative floor was off-limits to the general public, so anyone without an elevator key had to be escorted upstairs.

"Will do," Eric said and darted down the hall. He returned a couple of minutes later with Scott Warren, one of the senior partners of the architectural firm he had helped found. He was an attractive man, older than I was, with an unassuming manner — and I appreciated that he treated me as an equal yet was also happy to answer any construction-related questions I had.

"Hey, Scott. You want some coffee?" I welcomed him.

"No, thanks, I'm fine. You ready for the tour?"

"Sure. By the way, I just wanted to thank you and your construction contractor for delivering all the documentation for the board meeting early enough so the members might actually read the material — they don't always, you know. And you made it clear and simple. Well done! As you saw, the final approval sailed right through, and we're ready to go."

For a moment he looked like he wanted to hang his head and say, *Aw, shucks.* But instead he said, "It's a pleasure to work with

the people here, and it's a great old build-ing."

"Before we start, can you give me the high points one more time, so I know what to look for?" I asked.

"Of course," Scott said politely. "As you know, with the help of some of your people we've had the construction crew clear out the non-collection items —"

"Otherwise known as trash," I interrupted, smiling.

"Exactly," he replied, matching my smile, "and we've completed all the stress analyses. We've mapped out the new ventilation system and how it will integrate with what is in place. The roof replacement will hap-pen first, since you've got a lot of leaks as it is, and we want to seal up the building bet-ter and reassess before we can fine-tune the ventilation. Only after all of that has hap-pened will you need to start moving collec-tions around so that the compact shelving can go in."

"I know that compact shelving won't work everywhere. What increase of shelving space can we expect?"

"Probably twenty percent, give or take."

"I love it! We get that much more space without altering the building — it's win-win."

Scott nodded. "I agree. You ready to see it now?"

I stood up. "Yes. It's been a few weeks since I've visited everything, and I can't wait to see the place stripped down. You've taken pictures, I assume?" I wanted to be sure that the Society had a complete record of what had been done to the building, in case future generations needed to know.

"Of course. We always document each step of our projects."

"Then lead the way!"

CHAPTER 3

As we walked down the hall, Scott asked, "Do you want to start at the top or the bottom?"

"Top, I guess," I told him. "Although you don't have to point out all the leaks — I know them all too well." There were some areas of the stacks on the top floor that were draped with plastic, to keep the collections dry, and it broke my heart every time I went up there. But that was going to change, thank goodness. "You mind walking up?"

"Of course not."

We took the side stairs up to the top floor, and meandered through the forest of shelves, which held a wide variety of items — books, of course, often old leather-bound ledgers from nineteenth-century companies long gone, but also boxes that held china and fabric items and various oddities that had been given to the Society over its long history and we'd never had the time or the

heart to get rid of (at least, not as long as any of the donors or their heirs were still living). It was an intriguing jumble, but its storage was unprofessional and messy — another thing that would change soon.

It was a blessing to have an excuse to overhaul everything in the building, even though it was going to be a heck of a lot of work. Collecting institutions like ours acquired stuff over decades or even centuries, but there were seldom enough staff members to manage said stuff, which meant that sometimes it wasn't cataloged fully and accurately or stored in an archivally appropriate manner. Mainly, something would arrive, the donor would receive a nice thank-you note, and unless the item was of significant historical interest (and to be fair, a few of those did pop up from the most unlikely donors), a brief note would be entered in our computerized cataloging system and the item would get stuck on a shelf, wherever there was room for it. Sometimes that remained the status quo for years.

Now that we were going to have to move these items, we'd have a chance to sort through all of the accumulation and redistribute much of it throughout the building. Some things we would likely dispose of,

discreetly. Other things we might discover needed conservation, which was beyond our staff's skills, so they'd be sent out for treatment. Yet more things would be consolidated, like with like, so we could more easily find them in the future. And everything would be cleaned along the way — that board member last night had been right to worry about dust, because we were looking at the dust of ages here. Maybe I should poll the staff for allergy sufferers and hand out dust masks. Or maybe I should trust the renovation team to have planned for all this and stop worrying.

I was happy that Scott Warren proved to have an interest in historical objects, and he didn't rush me through. We toured the top floor, then the portions of the third that weren't given over to offices. The second floor housed the processing area and fewer stacks; the ground floor was the public space, with the sumptuous reading room, computers for public access, and open stacks — we didn't plan any significant changes there. It was nearly noon by the time we made it to the basement, which was seldom visited by the staff, and never by the public.

I hadn't seen the lowest level lately. I'd had a regrettable experience with the former

wine cellar down there some time ago, but I'd surprised myself by asking that the architect preserve it as a memorial to the original planners of the building. Nowadays there was no call for fine wines for the gentlemen who had once run this establishment along the lines of a private club, and in the past few years it had served only as storage. The rest of the basement space had until recently held a jumble of retired furniture and files. But now the files had been properly archived, and most of the usable furniture had been donated to a local charity. Anything else had ended up in the Dumpster (under the watchful eye of a member of the collections staff). As I looked around I realized how large the space actually was, and how we'd wasted its potential.

"You're putting shelving in here, too, right?" I asked Scott.

"We are," he replied. "Since this is the lowest level, it can easily tolerate the weight of that kind of shelving. It's up to you to decide what you want to store down — it won't be public space, right?"

"Right, staff only. My staff and I will be discussing the best use for the space," I told him, "but I'm sure it will be a big improvement. We won't have a problem with damp, will we?"

"No, it's surprisingly dry. Well built, for its time. You know the history of the building?"

"I know where to find it in our records, but I haven't memorized it. What I do remember is that there used to be a nice large house here, but when the Society decided to expand they looked at the existing building and found that it was falling apart, not to mention inadequate for the growing collections, so they started fresh."

"Smart move," Scott said, with an architect's appreciation.

We'd been alone in the basement, but now a workman stuck his head in the door and addressed Warren. "Hey, Scott? There's something you'd better come see."

"Trouble?" he asked quickly.

"Uh, I don't really know. It's kinda odd."

I felt the slightest hint of a knot in my stomach. We hadn't even started construction. This could not possibly be a problem. Could it? Maybe we had vermin? Maybe toxic mold? I was still running through a menu of possible issues when Scott nudged me. "You okay? Let's go check this out."

"Of course." I followed the two men to a windowless room toward the back of the basement. As we walked, the man who had come to find us was saying, "So we hauled the last of the old cabinets and junk out

yesterday — first time we'd seen the floor. Then we notice this wooden cap thing in the middle of the floor. Tight fit, looks like it's been there forever. So we find us a pry bar and pull it up, and damned if there isn't a hole going down who knows how far?"

We'd reached the room in question, and it was easy to see the circular hole in the floor, about three feet in diameter. My first wild thought was to wonder if there was a dead body down there — clearly, I'd been through some rough times lately. I shook it off.

"Hey, Joe," Scott Warren said, and I recognized the construction foreman from the board meeting earlier in the week. "What've you got?"

"Always surprises in these old buildings, Scott. Looks like an old privy hole."

I found my voice. "Can you see anything down there?"

There were a couple of other workers clustered around the hole, and Scott moved forward to peer into the depths. "Anybody got a light? Flashlight, whatever?" Someone handed him a heavy-duty halogen flashlight, and he pointed it down the hole.

I found I was holding my breath. "What do you see?"

Scott squatted on his haunches. "Not

much. No water, so it wasn't a well, most likely. Probably an old privy pit."

Ick. "From the house that was here before?"

"Maybe. I imagine the builders would have expanded the footprint when they put up this building, so the pit would have been outside the earlier house you mentioned."

"What should we do?" I asked. I wondered why the pit hadn't been filled in and covered with concrete when the floor was poured a century ago. "Can you see anything down there?"

"Not much. Looks like trash from here, but it's maybe twenty feet deep. You want us to clean it out?"

I thought for a moment. "Actually, yes. If it's old, who knows what might have been thrown down there? One of our former members coauthored a wonderful book on the archeology of privies in the city. They found all sorts of interesting stuff in them. Well, interesting to an historian, anyway. Is it, uh, sanitary? Any health risk?"

"I doubt it. Anything, uh, biological should be long gone. Okay, then . . ." Scott turned to the work crew. "Can you guys clear it out? But keep whatever you find — don't just pitch it."

The guy who had announced the find to

us looked skeptical. "You want us to keep the trash?"

"That's what I said. Fred, make sure it gets set aside rather than tossed." Scott turned to me with a smile. "Sorry, Nell — we can't do a formal dig, with strata and all that. Are you okay with that?"

"Sure. I'm just being nosy," I said. "But if anything interesting turns up, maybe we can use it for our promo pieces. Thanks, guys."

Fred peered down into the hole. "Shouldn't take more than a couple of hours. You want we should seal it up when we're done?"

"Let me take a look at it when you've finished cleaning it out," Scott told him. "It might be a good chance to see what the underlying soil and rock look like. I'm surprised it wasn't affected when the PATCO line went in."

I knew the PATCO line ran along Locust Street, practically under the building. It was easy to tell when a train went past. "You got it."

Scott turned to me. "Seen enough, Nell?"

"I think so. Are you going to stick around for the rest of the day?"

"I've got to put in some time at the office, but I'll probably be back later in the after-noon."

"Then I'll walk you out, if you're ready to go."

We returned to the first floor and I escorted him to the lobby. Before he left, Scott said, "You know, we've talked about the dust, but it's going to be noisy, too. There'll be equipment out back to get the roofing materials up to the top. There'll be pounding. There'll be people hauling shelving and stuff through the building — and those shelving units are heavy. So you maybe should warn your staff and your patrons that things will be less than peaceful for a few months."

"Thanks for thinking about that, Scott, but we're already on it." We'd been warning our patrons for months through letters and our newsletter and our website, so they could plan around the construction, but that didn't mean they'd paid attention to the warnings. We planned to apologize a lot to disgruntled researchers. "And we know it will be great in the end. I'm looking forward to working with you."

"Me, too. See you later, Nell." As he went out the front door, I turned to go back to the elevator. I paused for a moment at the door to the reading room. There were perhaps fifteen people at the large tables lined up there, all silently reading or taking

42

notes, their books and laptops and research materials laid out around them. I sighed: they would not be happy about working in the midst of a construction site. But at least we'd stay open. Maybe we should keep boxes of earplugs handy, too. I turned and went back to my office.

I found Marty Terwilliger waiting for me there. Marty had an unnerving ability to pop in unexpectedly, and when I'd first gotten to know her, I'd sometimes wondered if she actually lived in a burrow in the stacks somewhere. She was at the Society early and late, and any time between. Since Eliot had appeared in her life, her appearances were less frequent, but her passion for the place — and in particular, the Terwilliger collections of letters and memorabilia donated by generations of her family — was undiminished.

"Hi, Marty. What's up?"

"You free for lunch?"

"I think so, unless Eric tells me otherwise." I turned to my assistant. "Am I free for lunch?"

"You are."

"That's fine. Marty, I'm all yours."

I gathered up my things and we went downstairs and strolled along the sidewalk outside, talking of nothing in particular.

"You have some ulterior motive, or is this really just lunch?" I asked as we crossed the street.

"Hey, I just wanted to catch up. You've been busy with your new place, I've been busy, and then there was the board meeting. Now it's clear sailing until the holiday party, right?"

"In terms of running the place, yes. I don't know how our patrons will react to the construction, but Scott Warren says we're good to go."

We went into the sandwich place a block away and ordered. "So how're things going?" Marty asked, once we were seated with our food.

"With the house, you mean? Good. Although things still feel unsettled."

"Still unpacking?"

"No, because we don't have that much to unpack. And that's a problem. We need more furniture. What few pieces we have look kind of lost in all the space."

"What're you looking for?"

"I have no idea. Something that doesn't look out of place in a grand Victorian house with nine-foot ceilings and oodles of carved moldings. Oh, and that we can afford."

"Those two may not go together," Marty commented, munching on her sandwich.

"I had that feeling. You have any ideas?"

Marty got a faraway look in her eye. "Maybe. Let me think about it. You looking for Victorian furniture, or earlier?"

"The real stuff? I don't think we're that picky, but if I could choose anything, then sure, probably Victorian. Why, do you have a warehouse full somewhere?"

"Not exactly, but I do have a lot of relatives, as you know."

I wasn't sure of her point, and Marty didn't elaborate. Was she thinking donations or loans? Or were we supposed to pay for the furniture? If so, who was going to set the price? I decided it wasn't worth pursuing yet. If Marty came up with some real items, then we could haggle. "Oh, guess what? We found something interesting in the basement at the Society this morning." I proceeded to outline the discovery of what I was mentally calling The Pit.

"Huh. A privy?" Marty asked, chewing.

"Scott said maybe. Hey, we could add a bathroom down there and call it historical, if we modified the plumbing discreetly."

Marty snorted. "Lots of history for that site, even before the Society bought the land. You never know what might turn up."

"Well, I told Scott to have the crew clean it out and save whatever they found, so we

could take a look at it. If it's just trash, it goes straight to the Dumpster."

As we ate we discussed the timing of the project and the events we were planning around it and other normal Society business, as appropriate between the president and a long-term board member. As we were finishing, Marty said, with unusual hesitation, "What would you think about asking Eliot to join the board?"

I considered. "Does that mean you think this thing you've got going will last? I think as a candidate he'd be great — his scholarly connections and his area of expertise would be big plusses for us. Who's planning to leave the board?"

We hashed over board prospects and plans, then walked back to the Society. Before we reached the building I asked, "Have you talked to Eliot about this?"

"Not yet. I'm just thinking about it. But you're good with it?"

"I am. Go for it," I said firmly.

"Maybe I will."

Back at the Society we went our separate ways. As I'd told Marty, I'd already asked Lissa to look into the history of the building. I was reasonably familiar with it, having used the boilerplate about it often when I was in development, but nobody had been

looking for surprises in the basement, and maybe Lissa could shed some light on the pit. When I got back to my office, I called Lissa, who answered quickly.

"You know we're using the Wakeman money to make physical repairs to the building," I began, "and we've been clearing out about a century's worth of junk before the construction crew starts — you might have noticed the Dumpster outside. The workers were finishing up in the basement today and they found some kind of pit in the floor. It had a wooden lid on it, and it had been covered who knows how long by some ancient wooden filing cabinets. I've asked the construction guys to save whatever they pulled out of it, just to see if it was anything more than a trash pit."

"I haven't seen any mention of a pit in the records so far. It's not a well?" Lissa asked.

"No water in it now, although it's possible. I don't have any idea about things like that. I know there were tunnels to the river under some of the older houses east of here, so I'm guessing the water level was below the level of the pit. But I'm wondering if it was originally outside the building, and in that case, if it might have been a privy."

Lissa said, "Ew," and I laughed. "Don't worry," I said, "if that is the case, it hasn't

been used for a long, long time. I think any . . . waste products are long gone. You know the Cotter book?"

"Of course!" Lissa replied eagerly. "*The Buried Past.* I'm glad to hear that you know about it, too."

"Mr. Cotter used to be a member here — he was a delightful man. If I remember correctly, he included a section on Philadelphia privy pits and what was found in them. You can skim through it again and see if there's any helpful information there. Oh, and look for the original plans for the mansion and for this building, to see where the perimeters were, and how they line up with our current plans. No need to rush, I'm just satisfying my own curiosity. And of course I'm always on the lookout for interesting little bits of information like this, to put in the newsletters or online. Although I'm not sure our patrons would be charmed to learn that they've been working above an antique loo — we might have to do some fancy rephrasing."

"I hear you," Lissa said, laughing. "Let me see what we've got. Surely there must be some plans for the building?"

"Ask our architect — he must have them, or copies of them. Start with him."

"Will do. I'll get back to you if I find anything interesting."

CHAPTER 4

James picked me up after work and we rode home together. As we pulled into the driveway, I noticed how dark the house looked. "We need to put some lights on timers," I told him. "Of course, that also means we have to get lamps for the inside."

"Don't we have some already?" James said.

"About one per room, which is not enough. Do we have an alarm system?"

"Yes, but it's not connected. Besides, we have nothing to steal."

"True, but anyone who broke in wouldn't know that, and they might get annoyed and start smashing things out of pique."

He parked and turned off the engine. "Pique?" He raised one eyebrow.

"What, burglars don't get piqued? How about pissed off?"

"That's a more likely response for a burglar, I think. What should we do for

dinner?"

"I haven't a clue. Do we have raw products in the fridge? Because I think we finished off the leftovers last night."

"We did and we do. Or vice versa." James went ahead of me and unlocked the back door, then graciously let me enter before him. I hung up my coat and bag, and went to the refrigerator to forage. Ah, chicken breasts and some shriveled mushrooms. I could work with that.

Less than an hour later we were settled at the table with wine and food in front of us. After a few bites of the improvised dish I had concocted, I said, "I had lunch with Marty today and I mentioned that we were furniture-challenged."

Curiously, James did not look happy at that news, but said nothing.

"What?" I demanded. "You brought it up."

"Upon reflection, I decided that I should warn you that furniture is a sensitive subject in the Terwilliger family," he finally said.

"Why?" I asked, bewildered.

"You really don't know?"

"No, James, I really don't know. What am I supposed to know?"

He sighed. "It all started with General John Terwilliger . . ."

"What didn't?" I muttered. "Okay, I know

51

he was an important figure in the Revolutionary War and the later eighteenth century, and I know he was Marty's however-many-times-great-grandfather. But where did the furniture come in?"

"That same John Terwilliger bought a grand house in Philadelphia when he married, and he furnished it in the latest and most expensive manner. You have all the documents pertaining to the fitting out of the house at the Society."

"Oh." He was right: I probably should have known. "Well, I haven't read every document we have, since there are a couple million of them, at least. I'm sure they must make interesting reading, but where's the problem?"

"There were, let us say, issues among various members, and when he died, the general's pieces were scattered among different branches. Some were even sold, and some people in the family are still a bit annoyed that they ever left the family, particularly when those pieces come up at auction now and then and sell for a couple million dollars."

"Ah," I said intelligently. "Is Marty one of the disgruntled?"

"It's not one of her hobbyhorses. Her branch managed to hang on to a few things,

and if you've seen her house, you've probably seen them. How did she react when you told her we needed furniture?"

"Kind of, 'I'll think about it.' When she asked, I said we preferred Victorian to match the house. Is that all right with you? Do you even like Victorian?" I asked. It was a question that had never exactly come up, although he was the one who had fallen in love with our undeniably Victorian house first.

"As long as horsehair isn't involved, I'm good with it. That stuff is literally a pain in the butt, plus it crackles. Frankly I don't care much, as long as I have something to sit on and light to see by. I give you a free hand. Although, since this won't in fact be free, what about that budget?"

I ducked the issue, since I had no real idea what furniture cost, old or new. "Maybe we should go to a Freeman's auction and see what the market is like," I suggested. "Of course, they're going to be high-end, but we can work down from there." Freeman's was a long-established and reputable auction house in Center City, and in my position I was aware of the auction house's standing in the furniture community. I'd never attended anything there, but I knew some of their staff were members of the Society. "I'll

have to check their schedule."

We finished dinner, tidied up the kitchen together, read for a bit, and went to bed. Another normal day, with no crises. I felt like I should make a note of it on the calendar.

The next morning seemed normal, too. The sun was shining, the trees on our still-surprisingly large lot were turning lovely colors (note to self: Buy rake or rakes? Better yet, hire a yard service?), and work was about to begin on the much-needed upgrade at the Society. James and I carpooled into the city once again, arriving nice and early. I couldn't help feeling pleased.

Until I walked into the building. Front Desk Bob, our gatekeeper (and a former cop) was already there behind the counter, getting ready for the day. When he saw me, he said, "You have a visitor," and nodded toward the corner by the front window. I turned to see Meredith Hrivnak, a Philadelphia police detective I'd had dealings with in the past. From her expression, I didn't think she was there to investigate her family tree. We'd first met after the death of a staff member at the Society. But if someone had died here again — heaven forbid! — wouldn't the police have called me at home?

54

Or rather, on my cell?

I plastered on a smile to hide my unease. "Good morning, Detective. What can I do for you today?"

"A man was hit and killed by a car outside your building last night." The detective was not known for sugarcoating her pronouncements.

My stomach plummeted. "How awful. Who is it?" *Please, please, not one of my employees.*

"Guy named Carnell Scruggs. You know him?"

I shook my head, relieved to say truthfully that I'd never heard the name before. "Of course, I'm sorry to hear about anybody's death by violence. But is that why you're here? To ask if I knew him?" I glanced at Bob, who gave a slight shrug. Apparently he didn't know anything more than I did.

"Thought you might be able to help us out. He was hit by a car traveling north on Thirteenth Street. Nice suburban lady heading home after a dinner with friends and only one glass of wine — and her blood alcohol level checks out all right. She says the guy came barreling out from between two parked cars, right next to that back alley of yours. You know, where you've got that big hulking Dumpster parked. What's

that for?"

"We're renovating some parts of the building, and we've been clearing out old junk. You think this guy was pawing through the Dumpster and got startled and ran?"

"Don't know yet. I'd like you to take a look at him."

"Am I supposed to, uh, view the body?" *Please say no,* I willed her silently.

"Nope. I've got his picture right here." She pulled out her cell phone and scrolled through it until she found the picture she wanted. Then she handed it to me.

I peered at the small image. The man appeared to be Caucasian, in his thirties or forties, with dark hair, neither long nor short. Ordinary clothes — jeans, a jacket, not particularly remarkable. Nothing that stood out. The tension seeped out of my muscles: I had definitely never seen him before.

"He one of yours?" Hrivnak asked.

"No, I don't think I know him. Why do you ask? You said you have a name for him, right? Can't you find out more about him that way?" *Without me?*

"Yeah, Ms. Pratt, we will be doing that. He had a driver's license on him, so we've got a name and address for him. We do know how to do our jobs."

I ignored her sarcasm. "Do you need to check inside our building, to see if he was here?"

"Don't see why. We already looked at your back door — no sign that it had been tampered with, so he probably wasn't running away from here. Your alarm system was on, right?"

"Bob here's the one who manages it, but he's very careful about that, so I'd guess yes."

"Then you're clear. For now. Oh, there is one thing that's a little weird."

"Weird how?" I asked.

"The driver of the car — like I said, she wasn't drunk, and from the skid marks she wasn't speeding — swears the guy came out from between those cars backward."

It took me a moment to process that. "You mean, like going backward, not facing the street?"

"Yup. What do you make of that?"

"He stumbled over something?"

"Backward? And traveled at least ten feet into the middle of the street? Try again."

"He wanted to commit suicide but didn't want to see it coming?" Wow, I really was grasping at straws — and by now I had an idea what she was looking for.

"Two strikes — you get one more."

"He was pushed," I said bluntly. Of course she thought it was murder. She was a homicide detective, and she wouldn't be here unless someone had guessed it might be murder.

"Bingo. I told the ME to look for signs of a struggle."

"Was there anyone around to see? Witnesses?" I asked.

"Nope. It was dark and the street was empty — as far as we know, that is."

"What about street cameras?"

"Focused on the street. Couldn't see the sidewalk because of all the parked cars. You got one on your back door?"

"No — we were going to add some outside with this renovation. We managed to get some installed in critical areas inside the building, but that won't help you."

"Were you the last person to leave?"

"I think Marty Terwilliger and I were — we were here late for a board meeting — but you can check with Bob on that, too. What can I tell my staff? They're bound to hear about this, and it doesn't seem right to just ignore the . . . accident."

"Looks like this Mr. Scruggs died after everybody here had gone home, but we'll probably interview them anyway, even if your Bob corroborates that he locked up on

schedule. Go ahead and tell 'em it was an accident."

Before she could think of something else, I said, "Okay. Well, if that's all, I'll turn you over to Bob." I looked expectantly at her. She gave me a cold stare, as if she suspected I was hiding something. Together we approached Bob again, and I explained what the detective was looking for. Since he'd been on the job once, he knew what to do, so I handed her off to him and scurried toward the elevator.

When I reached my office, Eric was already there. He greeted me, then he took a closer look. "You okay, Nell?"

"Better than I might be," I said. "I just heard that there was a car accident outside the building last night. Sadly, someone died, but it's not a staff member or anyone I recognized. The police aren't sure exactly how or why it happened, though, so they might want to talk to people here about when we locked up and set the alarm, but I'm hoping it's not really our problem." *Fingers crossed.* "I'll be in my office if anybody needs me." I went into my office, shut the door behind me, and sat down behind my desk, and realized I was shaking, just a bit. I waited for the shaking to stop, while I struggled to avoid thinking about

that poor woman driver, who could hardly be blamed if a body propelled itself into her path without warning. Then I called James.

He answered on the first ring. "Nell? What's up?"

"There was a fatal traffic accident outside the Society last night, on Thirteenth Street. Nobody I know, and he doesn't work here. I just thought you should know. I'm hoping it's just a coincidence."

"Oh, Nell, I'm sorry. Anything I can do?"

The sympathy in his voice was sincere, and it comforted me just a bit. "I don't think so. So far we're not involved, except for proximity. He was struck near our back alley. Nothing in the building appears to have been disturbed, although I'd better check that out." I hesitated before adding, "James, there was something odd about the way the man died. The detective said that he went into the street backward. I'm guessing she believes it's a suspicious death."

James didn't respond immediately. "You want to meet for lunch, or leave early?" he asked eventually.

Very cautious of him. "I think I'll stick around. I may have to field questions here. But thank you for asking. We can talk about it at home later. We may know more by the end of the day."

"Let me know when you want to ride home together."

"I will."

We hung up at the same time. I sat and stared into space. It was nice having someone to tell, someone who understood and would commiserate. Someone who wouldn't go all macho on me and expect me to fall apart at the sight of a dead person. James knew all too well that this wasn't my first body. But for once this death had nothing to do with me or the Society, and it would involve straightforward police work, and while Detective Hrivnak might be lacking in a few social skills, she was a competent police officer and would get the job done. I didn't have to be involved.

He went into the street backward? That didn't sit well with me, but I wasn't going to interfere. This was a city; strange things happened.

With a sigh, I turned to the neat stack of messages Eric had left for me the day before, but was interrupted by Eric himself, who stuck his head in my door and asked, "Anything I can do?"

"Yes, actually. Can you send out a quick e-mail to the staff? Just tell them there was a car accident outside the building last night and a man named Carnell Scruggs died,

and ask everyone to cooperate fully with the police if they come by asking questions. It may not even come to that, but I'd rather people knew what was going on."

I hoped any police activity outside wouldn't slow down the start of the construction. And then there was that hole in the basement, which was a nice distraction. I wondered if the crew had finished cleaning it out yesterday, and if so, what they had found.

I was about to pick up the phone and call Lissa when she showed up at my door. "This is really cool!" she said.

I could use a "really cool" diversion right about now. "Come on in and tell me all about it."

CHAPTER 5

Lissa was a relatively new contractor, a researcher-for-hire. She'd signed on to work on the Mitchell Wakeman project, which we had both assumed would be short-term. But she'd done a good job with it, and the resolution had ultimately resulted in the big bucks that were now paying for our renovations. Although the Society's budget couldn't support an additional full-time staff position at the moment, I'd been impressed by her work and wanted to keep her around in some way, so I'd suggested that we use her to work on single projects, as needed, with an emphasis on regional history and architecture. Since she was a graduate student with a flexible schedule, so far that had worked out well for everyone.

Researching construction details of the current Society building was one such project. While I knew a fair amount about it

from my development days, I certainly didn't know everything — and I don't think anybody had known about the hole in the basement floor, or at least, nobody had mentioned it in the records I'd seen (but who records the location of an old privy?). I was hoping that Lissa might be able to shed some light on it. I motioned her toward a chair in my office. When she had sat down, I said quickly, "Before you share whatever goodies you've come up with, you need to know that someone was killed next to this building late last night. I didn't know if you'd heard."

"You're kidding. No one from the Society, I hope?" she asked.

"No, thank goodness. The man fell into the path of a car, near our back door. I thought you should know. So, back to business. What've you got on the building?" I was eager to see what Lissa's fresh eyes would find.

"I feel like I'm cheating — a lot of this information was already in the files in the development office."

"I know," I said, "but I didn't have the time to go looking, and I've forgotten the details. Just give me the basic story, please."

"All right." Lissa straightened her stack of notes and began. "Okay, so you know this

site wasn't the first that the Society occupied, right? When the Society was much smaller, in the nineteenth century, the members rented space, which was okay until they received an amazing donation of William Penn's papers and things got a little crowded. When they started looking around, in the 1870s, there was a nice mansion here, maybe fifty years old, available for sale. Anyway, they had no problem raising the money to buy the site and the lot next door. It was still a mostly residential area, with trees behind. There are some pretty pictures of the old mansion, if you're interested. The Society added an assembly hall on one side and what they called a fireproof annex on the other, and that's where things rested for twenty-some years."

"Put together a folder on all this stuff, will you? Go on," I told her.

"Okay. Collections kept growing, and the place kind of overflowed again. Plus people were worried that except for that one addition, the building wasn't anything like fireproof. So they started looking for money for a renovation, and they were having trouble until they appealed to the state government. The governor at the time — named Dudley Pemberton — was sympathetic, since he'd been in your shoes, Nell,

before he ran for office. You have any plans along those lines?" Lissa said, smiling.

"Heaven forbid! I don't want to try to run anything bigger than this place, and certainly not the whole state! So I take it that's how they received the money?"

"Yep, and they turned around and added some new parts to the building in less than a year, if you can believe that. And that was just the first phase — there was a second one a year later, and they more or less tore down the old house and rebuilt it, incorporating the additions they'd already made. They wrapped the whole thing up by 1907."

"Wow, that was fast!"

"It was," Lissa agreed. "Anyway, most of the original mansion was demolished — I saw something that said they'd hoped to save more of it, but they found it wasn't structurally sound enough to support a larger building. But the foundation is original, which I assume includes at least part of the basement."

That, I hadn't known. Of course, I didn't spend a lot of time in the basement. As far as I could tell, no one did.

Lissa went on, "There are still bits of pieces of the original mansion scattered through the building — like a couple of fireplace mantels. And that gigantic staircase

that eats up so much room is kind of an homage to the old building. There are some wonderful old pictures of some of the rooms on the ground floor with leather-covered armchairs and reading lamps. You can just see the board members back then perusing some old tome, with a glass of sherry at hand."

"Those were the days," I agreed.

"Is that what you wanted to know?" she asked.

I thought for a moment. From what Lissa had just told me, it sounded as though the building as I knew it had been erected in stages, and in places had incorporated some of the older parts. What I was still wondering was, had the newly discovered pit been part of the original building, or had it lain outside the footprint of the mansion? *Was* it really an old privy, as the construction foreman had suggested? "Can you see what else you can find about that first building? Or anything more about the construction details in the early twentieth century?"

"Sure," Lissa agreed quickly. "Sounds like fun. I'll have to track down the Society's own records."

"Exactly. And happy hunting!" I said, then sent her on her way and turned back to the papers on my desk.

I'd barely had time to read the first page when Eric answered the phone and stuck his head into my office. "Bob downstairs says there's a police detective who needs to see you. Should I go get him?"

Again? "It's probably a her, and I'll go down." I stood up, straightened my shirt, and headed for the elevator. I had no idea what Detective Hrivnak could want with me now. Dare I hope she was going to tell me that they'd solved the killing and everything was hunky-dory? Yeah, right. Usually when the detective talked to me, it was bad news.

When the elevator reached the main floor, I squared my shoulders and marched into the lobby. "Detective, what can I do for you now?"

"We need to talk. Your office?"

"How about our meeting room down here? It's private," I countered.

"Fine."

I led her to the large room located beneath the massive main staircase, which was hardly ever used by the staff. The room I was taking the detective to had for a time served as the boardroom before board meetings had been moved upstairs, and I let Detective Hrivnak enter before me, then closed the door behind us. We sat.

"Do you have something to tell me?" I asked. No use in beating around the bush.

She sat back in her chair and looked at me. "Turns out the victim was a day laborer, worked for various construction crews around town."

I had an inkling where she was going with this, but I wasn't about to jump in. "And?"

"His latest job was working for your contractor, right here in this building."

I took a deep breath. "Are you telling me that the, uh, deceased, was a member of the cleanup crew?" The thought made me sad: I had probably seen him, but I hadn't noticed and didn't even remember him.

"Looks like it. We're still talking to people. Wakeman's footing the bill?"

I was surprised she knew about that. "That's right. Mitchell Wakeman made a contribution to the Society, and restricted its use to physical improvements, which in fact we need badly. The preliminary cleanup was finished yesterday, and we're supposed to be starting construction today."

Detective Hrivnak nodded. "I've already talked with your project manager, name of" — she stopped to riffle through a pad — "Joe Logan. He confirmed that Mr. Scruggs had been here, on and off, for the last week. Including yesterday, the day he died." She

stopped and fixed me with a stony stare, and I wondered what she expected me to say.

I had nothing new to give her. "I'm sorry, I honestly didn't recognize Mr. Scruggs. As president, I've had very little interaction with the construction crew, although I've met Joe Logan, and he was present at our board meeting. If Mr. Scruggs was working here yesterday, I don't recall seeing him. Do you think his death outside the building was anything more than a coincidence?" How I hoped that wouldn't be true!

"Don't know yet. You said the building was cleared out when you left. Any reason why someone would've stayed behind?"

"Not that I know of. Bob's been careful to keep an eye on the workers. They have to sign in when they arrive, and sign out when they leave, so Bob can make sure they've left for the day. If someone wanted to steal something, there's not much here of interest to non-scholars. We don't keep a lot of money around, and most of our computer equipment and the like is out of date. If Mr. Scruggs wanted to steal artifacts or documents, that's a whole different story. Did you find anything unexpected on him?"

"Nothing on him at all, except his wallet. Certainly nothing stuffed in his pockets that

looked like it came from this place."

"Does he have family? Where did he live?"

"He lived alone in a small place a few blocks from here, the other side of Spruce."

"Do you know anything more about him? Had he worked for Joe Logan for long?"

"We've just gotten started with our investigation. You sure you don't know anything about him?"

"I could have seen him in passing in the building, but I haven't overseen the cleanup process, other than to make sure that nothing is damaged or misplaced. Yesterday I did a walk-through with the architect, but otherwise I stay mostly on the third floor." I hesitated a moment before asking, "Did you talk to the staff about when they left?"

"Yeah. The ones who left last all agree — the place was cleared out. Bob says the same thing, and he's a solid guy."

"So," I said slowly, "even though you now know that this man had been inside this building on the day he died, you still have no reason to connect his death to us at the Society?"

"Not yet," Detective Hrivnak said darkly.

"Well, I don't know what more I can tell you. If there's anything you need, just ask." I suppressed a shudder, picturing Hrivnak and her crime scene crew tearing through

71

the building, dusting our fragile collections for fingerprints of the dead man just to check where he might have been. I reminded myself that the construction team would have had no reason to invade the stacks, and I'd made sure that our own staff had handled every move of collections materials. The workers this week had been nowhere near them.

"Has there been an autopsy?" I asked. "I mean, maybe he was reeling from a drug overdose or something, which would explain why he fell backward."

"Sure there's been an autopsy — preliminary only. As far we know there were no obvious drugs in his system, and he wasn't drunk, either. I'm sure you can figure out what kinda shape the body was in, after being hit by a car, so it's hard to tell if there were any other marks on his body, but we're not done yet. You got anything else you want to tell me?"

Why did she always make me feel guilty, even when I hadn't done anything wrong? "Not at this moment. But if anything occurs to me, I'll tell you. And, of course, you can ask us for anything that might help."

"Don't worry, I will." The detective stood up, which I took as a signal that our conversation was over.

"If that's all, I'll see you out." I escorted her back to the lobby and watched her leave, then turned to Bob. "I've forgotten — have we been asking all the construction crew to sign in and out every day?" I'd kind of fudged my answer to the detective, because I really didn't know.

He shook his head. "Yes. Plus we have lists of who was working here from the contractor and the architect, both for payroll and for their insurance purposes — they provided insurance against theft or damage. Like I told the detective, this Scruggs guy wasn't on any of the regular lists. I guess he got a call only when they needed some extra hands. Some of the other guys knew him, though, and he'd worked for Logan before. Sorry."

"That's not your fault, Bob. I just wondered if anybody had seen the victim here, on the job or in some other part of the building. I feel badly that I didn't recognize him." And I was pretty sure that looked suspicious to Detective Hrivnak, but I was usually nowhere near where the work was going on. I leaned closer to Bob and lowered my voice. "As far as we know, Mr. Scruggs died where he was found. There could have been any number of reasons for him to have been on the street that had nothing to do

with us."

Most of the possibilities were not savory — behind our building, screened by the large Dumpster, it would be a quiet corner out of sight, the perfect place for a quick leak or an assignation where money changed hands — but those options were preferable to someone looking for a way to break into the building. Still, he was dead, maybe by somebody's hand, mere yards from our back door. And Detective Hrivnak clearly had suspicions, although she hadn't yet gone so far as to call the death a murder. Was it?

I didn't quite manage to stifle a sigh as I went back upstairs. I had a feeling this problem was not going to go away quietly.

CHAPTER 6

The rest of the day passed without incident.
James offered me a ride home and I accepted happily. It was a luxury to have time
for normal, everyday activities and patterns.
It probably wouldn't last: James was still
being treated with whatever the modern
equivalent of kid gloves was by his office
mates at the FBI, who, after the most recent
crime we'd both been involved in not long
before, respected his abilities but felt a little
guilty about the way they'd downplayed his
concerns. Those concerns had ultimately
been proved correct and had nearly gotten
him killed. Unfortunately, I had little to say.
I'd kept myself busy all day, but now I was
mentally gnawing over what Detective
Hrivnak had told me and what it might
mean — and I couldn't see any way the
outcome could be good. Hrivnak hadn't
come out and called Scruggs's death a
murder, but why else would she have talked

to me and my staff?

James was not a chatty driver, and he gave the rush-hour drive back to Chestnut Hill the attention it deserved. It was only after we'd pulled into the garage at our home that he said, "You've been quiet."

"Detective Hrivnak came back to see me a second time, after I called you," I said, unsure how to go on.

"Can you talk about it?"

"She didn't say I couldn't. But let's wait until we get inside."

We made our way into the back of the house, where a couple of low lights over the stove in the kitchen glowed a welcome. "Am I cooking?" I asked.

"You cooked yesterday. I'll make something. You can keep me company and tell me what's bothering you."

"Deal."

We changed into nonwork clothes and made our way back to the kitchen. James beat me downstairs, and there was a glass of wine waiting for me on the table when I joined him. I sat and sipped and watched him assemble something or other. It was such a treat to have a man who could and would cook — and even occasionally look like he was enjoying it. I had known he liked good food (and liked sharing that enjoy-

ment with me), but consuming and creating didn't always go hand in hand.

After a few minutes of silence, he nudged, "You know, I can listen and cook at the same time."

"Is multitasking part of your FBI training?" I teased. I spun my wineglass. "So, as I said in the car, our favorite detective visited me twice today. It turns out that the victim *had* been in the Society building — he was a construction crew day laborer, and apparently had worked on the cleanup. So I might have seen him there and not noticed, and the same is true for a bunch of other staff. Sad that we treat people like him as invisible, isn't it? But aside from making me feel like a bad person and looking suspicious to the detective for not recognizing the guy, I'm still hoping it's just coincidence. What am I supposed to think? As far as we can tell he didn't steal or damage anything, and there was no sign anyone else tried to get into the building last night."

"Well," James began thoughtfully as he sautéed onions in a skillet, "the first choice is coincidence. Did he live nearby?"

"That's what Detective Hrivnak told me. Walking distance."

"Then it could have been something related to his home life, not his work one."

"True."

"Could it have been an ordinary mugging?"

"Only if he was carrying a wad of cash in his pocket — which he might have been, if it was payday yesterday. Hrivnak said he had his wallet on him — that's how the police ID'd him." I realized I hadn't asked her if he still had any cash, but Hrivnak hadn't said it was gone.

"I assume you've come up with other worst-case scenarios?"

"Of course. That's what I do in my spare time." The wine seemed to be doing its work, and I could feel my tension seeping away. "If we presume that Mr. Scruggs was pushed, which probably means he was having an altercation on the sidewalk with someone, why? Was it a drug deal gone wrong? Was he attempting to mug someone who fought back? Could it have been related to sex — a jilted lover, an angry spouse? Could he have been the victim of a hate crime, bashed because of his sexual orientation or his ethnic background, neither of which I know anything about, or because somebody didn't like the way his face looked?" I realized the wine was hitting me hard and fast.

"An excellent summary, except that you

left out aliens from space and terrorism." James didn't look at me as he said that. Maybe he was trying not to laugh.

"Well, pardon me. Of course, my true worst-case scenario is that he was killed over something that has to do with the Society, except nobody has a clue what that might be, and how the heck do we look for something when we don't even know what we're looking for?"

"I understand, you know," he said gently. He put a lid on whatever he was making, then came and sat across from me, bringing the bottle of wine with him. "We need to clear something up, if we're going to get into this."

That sounded ominous. I held out my glass for a refill. "All right, what?"

He obliged. "You know by now that my jurisdiction as an FBI agent does not extend to Philadelphia police investigations, except under certain unusual circumstances."

"Yes, James, I am well aware of that. And I am aware of the fact that this may be no more than an ordinary suspicious death, being investigated by the city police, and therefore not requiring your special skills."

"Exactly. That having been said, I am more than happy to listen to your thoughts, serve as a sounding board for you, and make

suggestions, so long as you don't bludgeon the detective over the head with them, because she's going to know where they're coming from."

"You think I can't come up with intelligent theories of my own? Seriously, I don't expect you to involve yourself. That said" — I took a sip of wine — "if my victim turned out to have a rare seventeenth-century pen wiper in his pocket, one that had once belonged to William Penn and that still had an accession label from the Society on it, would that make it your problem? Under some form of cultural theft?"

"Possibly. Or not. It depends."

"Well, I am so glad we cleared that up! And you'd better feed me soon before this second glass of wine makes me totally incoherent."

"I'll start the pasta."

I watched as he moved neatly and efficiently around the kitchen. I had to say, even though it was undeniably modern and therefore wildly wrong for a classic Victorian house, I really liked this kitchen — well, except for the humongous refrigerator and the frightening stove with lots and lots of dials, both of which I assumed I'd come to understand eventually — and we were getting to know each other slowly. The room

was well laid out, and it was a pleasure to work in, with plenty of room for both of us to cook at the same time, unlike either of our former homes. Large windows on two sides let in lots of light during the day; there were also plenty of well-placed lights for dark nights.

Dinner. I was still getting used to the idea of cooking regularly. James had proved to be a fair cook — after all, he had survived on his own for years, and from the look of his physique (and I did look!) he hadn't relied on junk food. I was more haphazard, making — or not making — whatever I fancied from night to night. It had always seemed extravagant to get takeout all the time, and I did enough of that for lunches anyway. But whichever one of us ended up cooking, the other could sit with a glass of wine or Scotch or whatever and chat. It was nice, just still kind of new.

As James cooked, I turned over in my mind what he had said. I knew there were things he could not and should not involve himself in, and that included a lot of the crimes that I somehow found myself in the midst of. I didn't want to compromise his job, and at the same time I didn't want him to think he had to step in and throw his weight around and save the little woman,

i.e., me. I could handle my own problems, criminal or other. But he did have a wealth of experience and a good analytical mind, so I would take advantage of whatever insights he was willing to offer.

Ten minutes later he set heaping bowls of steaming pasta and sauce in front of us both, and sat down. We devoted some serious time to eating, and after most of my bowl was empty I realized how much better I felt with some food in me. And my brain seemed to be working better, too.

"Have we mutually rejected the coincidence theory?" I asked.

"Probably. Why? Do you have a front-runner among the other theories?"

"I don't like coincidences. I still think the man was killed just outside our building for a reason, but I don't have enough information to know why."

"Well, you don't have to do anything right now. You watch and wait, and either the information floats to the top and you have more to work with, or no information ever emerges and the crime goes into the unsolved pile. And you go on about your business."

"You make it sound simple. Call me self-centered, but if there's a dead man a few feet away from the Society, I'm inclined to

believe it has something to do with the Society, and therefore probably involves something historical. We know Mr. Scruggs had been working in the building, on a crew he'd worked for in the past. Nothing unusual there. But I know next to nothing about the man. Was he honest? Did he have any interest in history? Was he gullible enough to do a quick job for someone who asked?"

James smiled. "You wouldn't buy that he was merely curious about a grand old building and was hoping to prowl around after hours?"

"You mean, he might have snitched a key or found a way to wedge open a door, and he planned to come back and enjoy the place alone? But as far as we know he never made it inside, and there was no key on him. I'm sure Hrivnak would have asked if she'd found an odd key. But who would have stopped him? And is that enough to explain how he ended up dead? Is there ice cream?"

James looked momentarily startled by my quick segue, but he rose to the occasion. "There is. But before I allow you access to the ice cream, let me say that you need to let the police finish their canvass and collect some more information. That's what they

do, and they do it better than you could. If you're lucky, Detective Hrivnak will share some info with you, and then maybe you can offer her some suggestions — tactfully, of course."

"And you will be free and clear of any involvement whatsoever. That's fine by me. We are in agreement to do nothing right now except eat ice cream. And maybe watch a rerun of *Law & Order.*"

"Wise decision."

We settled in for the evening. We still hadn't sorted out where we "lived" in the house — the parlor was gorgeous, but I felt like an interloper sprawling on a couch watching television in there. There was a nice sunroom at the rear, but it wasn't heated and the old windows weren't double glazed or even airtight (note to self: buy some putty before winter sets in!). If we wanted to spend serious time there, we'd have to make some changes. For that matter, the couch we were using was both ugly and too uncomfortable for two, plus it sullied the majesty of the parlor. But I didn't want to relegate either of us to one of the overstuffed chairs we'd brought along; I liked the physical closeness of sitting next to James.

"James, are we looking at furniture this

weekend?"

"Huh?" he said, half dozing. "Furniture? Sure, I guess. Where? Auction? Department store?"

"I don't know. But we're intelligent people — we should be able to figure that out, right?"

"Okay," he said agreeably. I'm not sure he had heard me.

The next day started normally enough — the new normal, that is — but when I arrived at the Society, Bob nodded toward the corner of the lobby, where once again Detective Hrivnak graced our premises — the second day in a row. She did not look happy.

"Good morning, Detective. Did you want to see me again, or were you just browsing?"

"Ha!" she barked. "I need to talk to you. We've found out some new stuff."

Of course. "My office? We can have coffee." Of course, if I took her upstairs it might be harder to get rid of her again, but on the other hand, she might be more relaxed and forthcoming.

"Sure, sounds good." She followed me to the elevator.

While we waited for it, I said, "This

85

investigation is really moving fast, isn't it?"

She looked around before answering, but there were no staff members in sight. "Yeah, but we only had to look a few blocks in any direction. Not like you — you seem to find trouble spread over a couple of counties."

"And don't forget New Jersey," I added with forced cheerfulness. She was right, but she should be glad, since that put a lot of the Society's issues outside of her jurisdiction, thus saving her work.

Eric had already arrived and looked startled to see my companion. "Eric, could you please get us some coffee? How do you like yours, Detective?"

"Black's good."

Eric raced off toward the staff room, and I escorted Detective Hrivnak into my office. "So, are you asking me questions or telling me something?" I began.

"Both. Like I told you yesterday, we know who the guy was. You still don't remember him?" When I shook my head, she went on, "Okay, so you said everyone had cleared out of this building by, what, six? Nobody saw him go home — he lived over past Spruce — not that that means anything for sure. But say he didn't go straight home after work. The guy didn't look like the fancy-restaurant type, and he was still wear-

ing his work clothes, so where did he go? Had to be either a cheap restaurant or a bar — no shortage of either within a coupla blocks. So that's where I had my people look first, talking to people, seeing if anybody remembered our vic."

"Okay," I said cautiously. "And?"

"Found him. Bar over on Chestnut, the opposite direction from his house, and apparently his favorite, because the bartender knew him. Scruggs sat at the bar and had a burger and fries. Alone, which was normal for him. Or at least alone at first."

Was she actually spinning out the story? I didn't think she had it in her. "And?" I prompted again.

"Okay, so he spent an hour, maybe even two hours there. Kept nursing his beer, then ordered a second one. He wasn't drunk. After a while, when he was paying for one or the other of his drinks, he pulled a handful of change and bills out of his pocket and dumped 'em on the bar, see? And mixed in with the wadded-up bills and coins was this dirty thing, maybe two, three inches long, says the bartender. It was a slow night, so the guys talked, and our guy Scruggs said he found it in a trash heap where he was working and wondered if it was old. So the bartender took a rag and cleaned it up a

bit, and said it looked like it's a thing that goes on a drawer or something. It was brass. Our vic looked disappointed — maybe he was hoping it was gold."

"Did he say where he got it? Which trash heap? The Society's trash heap?

"Nah, just that he'd just picked it up, and it was pretty dirty, so it couldn't have been in his pocket for long. Bartender said it polished up real pretty, and it might have been old. I mean, not something you pick up at Home Depot."

This was all very interesting, but where was she leading? "Detective, what's your point?"

Detective Hrivnak grinned kind of wolfishly at me. "Thought you might be wondering."

At that point Eric appeared with two cups of coffee, which he set down carefully on my desk, making sure there was a coaster under each. I waited as patiently as I could, then said, "Thank you, Eric. Can you shut the door on the way out?"

He retreated silently, shutting the door behind him. I turned back to the detective. "Yes, of course I am. You're here, so I assume you need me for something. What is it?"

She sipped some coffee before answering.

"Okay, so the vic and the bartender were poking at this brass thing, whatever it was, and this *other* guy came over and looked at it, and he went, 'Where'd you find that?' And the vic said something like, 'What's it to you?' And the guy went, 'Looks like it's eighteenth century. Was it just lying around somewhere, or were there more bits like it?' And the vic shrugged, so the new guy sat down and cozied up to him. Then a bunch of people came in and the bartender got busy, and the next thing he knew, he saw the vic and the other guy headed out the door together. And that's the last he saw of them."

"Was the bartender able to describe the second man? Was he a regular?"

Hrivnak shook her head. "Nope, the bartender didn't remember seeing the guy before. White male, maybe in his thirties, average height, average weight, blah-colored hair, blue eyes, dressed in chinos with a Windbreaker. No outstanding physical features at all. There's a tape, but it's not worth much — not enough for any good ID."

I sat back in my chair and thought a moment. "So the good news is, you have a suspect — if Scruggs met with foul play. The bad news is, the description fits about

a quarter of the population of the city." Another question occurred to me then, and I thought I already knew the answer. "Detective, did the police find the curly metal thing on Mr. Scruggs's body?"

"Nope. Not anywhere near it, either."

"But his wallet was in his pocket, right?"

"Yup."

"So you're guessing that somebody took that thing away with him?"

"Exactly. And we'd like to know why."

I was getting frustrated. "Detective, I appreciate your sharing this information with me, but what is it you want me to do?"

She grinned. "I want you to find a bunch of old brass things about two inches long, to show to the bartender so maybe he can identify what he saw."

"Oh, sure, no problem," I said, not bothering to hide my sarcasm. "You have anything more to go on?"

"It was flat and kind of curly around the edges."

That didn't help much, either. But I had to ask the big question. "Detective, do you believe that this shiny, flat, curly brass whatever-it-is came from the Society?"

"Yup. Don't you?"

Unfortunately, I did. "And you think it

had something to do with Mr. Scruggs's death?"

Detective Hrivnak didn't answer directly, but looked at me steadily for several seconds. "Let me know if you find anything that matches the bartender's description."

"Of course."

Chapter 7

Having dumped her problem in my lap, Detective Hrivnak departed for her office, escorted downstairs by Eric, who still looked scared to death of her. He'd had some minor run-ins with the law before he came to work at the Society, so I could understand why he was spooked. He returned quickly. "Anything I need to know about, Nell?" he asked.

"No. And don't worry — it's not anything bad. She actually asked for my help on something."

"It have to do with that poor guy who died?"

"I think so, but I'm not sure yet. I'm going to have to think about it. Could you close the door again?"

When he was gone, I sat sipping my tepid coffee and thinking, as I had told Eric. All right, the dead man had had in his pocket a grubby metal object that appeared to be

brass when polished. The bartender said he and Scruggs thought it looked old, but they weren't exactly experts. Then a stranger had walked in and agreed with them, and the stranger and Scruggs had gone off into the night. The bartender hadn't recognized the stranger, and didn't have a clue about what qualifications he had to judge random pieces of metal. Not much later, Scruggs had ended up dead in a rather peculiar accident.

I tried to work out a path for poor Carnell Scruggs. He had left the Society at the end of the workday and had apparently gone straight to a pub on Chestnut — only about three blocks away from the Society, toward the north. He had eaten a meal, had a couple of beers, and been befriended by a someone who left the bar with him. It was not clear whether they had stayed together outside the bar, or gone their separate ways. Then the plot got murky: Detective Hrivnak had told me that Scruggs lived a few blocks to the south of the Society, so it was somewhat logical that he might have walked by there on his way home from the bar. Regardless of why he was there, it was when he was near the Society that he had fallen or been pushed in front of an oncoming car and died. The metal object, whatever it was,

had not been found on the body, or anywhere around it, although his wallet had remained intact. Was that important or incidental? Maybe he'd given or sold the metal thing to the stranger, maybe his new friend had stolen it, or maybe he'd dropped it somewhere or tossed it away after losing interest in it. I trusted Detective Hrivnak enough to believe that if her crew hadn't been thorough in their first search earlier, they were going to scour the route Carnell Scruggs had followed now, looking for "an old, flat, curly metal thing."

Much as I hated to admit it, now that we knew the man had been at the Society on the day he died, the odds were pretty good that he had found this object *in* the building. From the vague description it certainly didn't sound like something a man like Scruggs would ordinarily carry around with him. The problem was, the Society had plenty of old, flat, curly things, and they were scattered all over the building. And Carnell Scruggs *could* have gone more or less anywhere, once he'd signed in, although I had no reason to believe he left the area where he was working. As Hrivnak had reported it, it seemed as though he hadn't known what it was he'd found. It sounded like something he had just picked up and

absently stuck in his pocket. He might not even have looked at that as theft. So where had it come from?

Duh. Scruggs had been part of the crew in the basement. That was the only work going on the day Carnell Scruggs had died. I needed to talk with Joe Logan, the head of the construction crew. I called down to Bob at the desk. "Has the construction crew come in yet?"

"Sure, they were here at seven thirty," he told me.

"Where are they now?"

"In the basement."

"Thanks, Bob." I sat for a moment, trying to frame what questions I wanted to ask without sounding like I was accusing anyone of petty theft. Then I stood up and walked out to the hall. "Eric, I'm going to go downstairs and talk to the construction guys. I'm not expecting anyone, am I?"

"No, ma'am, you're clear."

"Okay. I don't know how long I'll be, but I won't leave the building without telling you."

I took the poky elevator down to the basement. It was easy to tell where the crew was working, because they were making a lot of noise. That wouldn't make the patrons above them in the reading room happy

when they arrived, but they'd been warned about the construction more than once, and there was nothing to be done about it. I followed the noise and recognized Joe Logan, but not any of the workers. I approached Joe and said loudly, "Can I talk to you?"

"Yeah, sure. Let's take this outside." He nodded toward the door I'd entered through.

We moved out into the hall, where the noise level was much lower. "This about the noise?" he asked.

"No, I expected that." I moved a little farther down the hall, so no one could overhear. "What can you tell me about Carnell Scruggs?"

"Carnell? Poor guy — never could catch a break. He wasn't part of the regular crew, but he was usually available on short notice for pickup jobs — I've hired him before, short-term, because I wanted to help him out. Terrible thing, what happened. The guy was a little short of a full deck, if you know what I mean, but he was willing and dependable, if you told him what to do. Why you want to know?"

I wanted to say, *Because he's dead, you dope,* but I didn't. "Was he a good worker?"

"Yeah, sure. Not the fastest guy, but he was careful, and he cleaned up after. I had

no complaints about him, hired him when I could, like I said."

"He was working down here the day he died?"

"Yeah. He helped clear out that hole we found."

Lightbulb moment: What if the curly thing had come from The Pit?

"Where did the stuff you pulled out of it go?"

"You asked us to keep it, so we dumped it in a box, or maybe two — it's around here somewhere. Wasn't much down there, mostly trash. *Old* trash, though. A couple of bottles, broken stuff. Nothing modern, like no plastics. We figured the hole had been covered up a while ago, and then people had put stuff like cabinets on top of it and forgotten about it."

"Any sign that it had been opened before you found it?"

"Nope, not for a long time. Lots of dust and stuff."

"Who else was working on clearing it out?"

"I dunno — two, three guys? We didn't get around to clearing it out until the end of the day, and everybody wanted to get home. I didn't check to see who did what by then, but I know it got done."

"How'd you get the stuff out? Was it big enough for someone to fit down there?"

"Just. Carnell was the smallest guy, so we sent him down."

Bingo! I said to myself.

Joe went on, "Even he could barely bend down to reach his feet. Then he passed whatever he could reach out to the guys at the top. Good thing there wasn't a lot more, because he wasn't too happy about it. Didn't like feeling all closed in."

I wondered briefly if Hrivnak would send a forensic team to do a proper excavation and analysis of the pit, then almost laughed out loud. The construction foreman was telling me that our dead man had been in the hole on his last day, but we knew that the man had been killed outside. If — still an if — whatever he had carried away had come from the hole, how was I supposed to convince the Philadelphia Police Department that spending time and money on examining the pit would be of any use? I'd have to settle for seeing whatever else had been pulled up at the time.

Joe Logan was getting twitchy. "We about done here? Because we've got a lot to do if you want this project to stay on schedule."

I turned my attention back to him. "Oh, sorry, yes. Thanks for answering my ques-

tions. Are you going to be heading up this project until it's finished?"

"Yeah, for the construction part. The shelving and HVAC stuff, that gets contracted out." He led me back to the room where we had started and pointed toward a couple of covered Bankers Boxes shoved in a corner. "There, that's the stuff from the hole."

"Would you mind having someone bring it up to my office? That would be a big help." I wasn't sure I wanted the mess in my more-or-less-pristine office, but I was worried that the boxes would somehow disappear if I didn't keep my eye on them. After all, they might contain evidence of a murder. If they didn't, I promised myself that I would get rid of them.

Joe assigned one of his men to pick up the boxes — which he did as though they weighed no more than his lunch — and he followed me to the elevator, rode up, and then trailed behind me to my office.

I thought I recognized him from my first visit to the basement. "I'm sorry — I never learned your name."

"I'm Frank. Ritter. Nice place you've got here."

"Thank you, Frank. You can put the boxes anywhere. Were you there when Carnell was

clearing out that pit?"

"Yeah, I was there. Awful thing, that. He was an okay guy. He wasn't real happy about getting more dirt on him, but he did what he was asked."

"Do you guys get paid daily? Like, at the end of the day?"

"Mostly. Scruggs got paid that day because there wasn't any more work for him. Was he robbed?"

"I don't know. He still had his wallet, anyway. Well, thanks for carrying the boxes for me. Was there anything interesting down there, do you know?"

The man shrugged. "Can't really say. Mostly dirt and broken stuff, as far as I could see. But you wanted it, so here it is. That all?"

I wondered if he was surly or just naturally brusque. "Did you know Scruggs well? Outside of work, maybe?"

He shrugged. "Carnell? Worked with him now and then. Can't say we were friends — didn't hang out after work or anything like that. I'm sorry he got killed."

"What was he like?"

The man scrunched up his face as if it was hard to picture a man he'd seen only two days earlier. "Quiet, like. Kept to

himself. Showed up on time, worked hard, left."

"So you didn't all get a drink on the way home?"

"Nah, nothing like that. He was kind of a loner. Look, I gotta get back downstairs." He shifted from foot to foot.

"Go ahead. Thanks for helping me with this."

"No problem." He turned to leave, and I motioned to Eric to see him out. That left me sitting in my office staring at a pair of dirty boxes making dents in my nice carpet.

What now? Call Hrivnak and tell her she should look at the contents? She'd laugh at me. Dig into it myself? But I wasn't even sure what I was looking for, and I was afraid if there was anything fragile in there, I might do more harm than good. I stalked around the boxes like I was circling my prey, and that's when Eric returned.

"What're you doing?" he asked, looking bewildered.

"I'm not sure. This is the stuff that came out of the hole in the basement. I'm wondering if maybe the man who died outside the building might have found something in the pit and taken it away with him, and that's what got him killed. But now I'm afraid to look."

Eric still looked confused. "Sorry, but you're going to have to back up a few steps. I don't know what you're talking about. I mean, I know about that poor man, but why would he find anything in the building here?"

I realized that I hadn't told him about the conversation I'd had with Hrivnak. I didn't recall her saying that I couldn't talk to people about what we'd discussed. Did that mean I could ask my colleagues to help? I didn't feel I had to explain to all the staff, but Shelby would want to know because she was a friend and as development director she had access to a lot of the older records for the Society, and Lissa had already heard my suspicions and was looking into the history of privies. Marty marched to her own drummer and would no doubt show up and know more than I did, but I could talk to her later. I made my decision. "Eric, could you call Shelby and Lissa, if she's in the building, and ask them to join me here?"

"Yes, ma'am." He hurried to his desk.

I hoped I was doing the right thing. This wouldn't count as interfering with a police investigation, would it? If we found anything that might have a bearing on the man's death, of course I'd tell the police ASAP. But other than that, all we were doing was

going through a heap of old trash from the basement. Did that make it a de facto part of the Society's collections? I briefly considered adding Latoya to the group, to represent the collections side of things, but rejected it on the grounds that trash, no matter how historic, was definitely not her kind of thing. If we found anything that needed analysis or identification, I could bring her in then, I reasoned.

"They're both on their way, Nell," Eric reported a minute later.

"Great. Look, I want you to come in, too — saves me repeating everything. You can hear the phones from here anyway."

Shelby had only to walk down a short hall, so she arrived promptly; Lissa appeared a minute later. "Haven't seen much of you this week, lady," Shelby said to me.

"I know — sorry. But in case you haven't noticed, we've had a few small crises." Like a body on the street, and multiple visits from Detective Hrivnak. I knew I could count on Shelby to understand — we'd puzzled through a couple of earlier "crises" together.

"I hear you. I assume you need our help? What's up?" Shelby asked. "And what's that all about?" she added, pointing to the boxes in the middle of the floor.

"Ooh, is that what they pulled from the privy?" Lissa said, looking eager.

Shelby turned to her and made a face. "Privy? Is that what it sounds like?"

"Sure is. Don't worry, it's clean," Lissa told her.

"Okay, gang, listen up," I said. "Detective Hrivnak told me this morning that Carnell Scruggs, the man who died, apparently left here after work and went to a bar a couple of blocks away on Chestnut Street, where he showed the bartender something small and made of brass that he pulled out of his pocket. It may be a stretch, but I'm guessing that it was something he found here. The construction foreman Joe Logan tells me that Mr. Scruggs was working on the basement cleanout before he died, specifically in the pit — he was the one they sent down to clean it out. These boxes here contain whatever stuff they found down there. I asked the crew to save it, in the interest of preserving our history." Smart move, in hindsight, although not for the reasons I had expected.

"Is that all of it?" Lissa said, sounding disappointed.

"That's what I was told."

"And we care about this why?" Shelby asked, still looking confused.

"While the late Mr. Scruggs was showing this object he found to the bartender, someone else started talking to him about it, and they left together. I'm wondering if the second guy had reason to think that object meant something important. Whatever it was, Carnell Scruggs didn't have it on him when he died, so either he lost it on his way home, which could have taken him down Thirteenth Street outside, gave or sold it to this mysterious stranger, or that the stranger took it from him. That's why I want to know what's in that box of stuff. If we find something similar and it's nothing important, we can go back to business as usual. If there *is* something, we turn it over to the police as a clue. Everyone okay with that?"

Shelby gave me a searching look. "What're you thinking? You're guessing that this has something to do with why the man ended up dead?"

Well, yes, but that was a can of worms I didn't want to open. I chose my words carefully. "The police are treating this publicly as a tragic accident, but since Detective Hrivnak is on the case, they must think there's more to it. They have no evidence to suggest anything else. However, the object that Carnell Scruggs had in his pocket is a

wild card here, so if it came from the Society, I want to know what it is."

Nods all around. "What're we looking for?" Eric asked.

"I don't really know," I said. "Something that survived being down in that pit for who knows how long — the foreman said everything that they pulled out was from a pre-plastic era, and Lissa can tell us when that hole in the ground would have been closed up. Hrivnak said the bartender described it as a few inches long, metal, maybe brass, flat, and curly."

Shelby grinned. "So we're looking through old trash for something flat and curly. Beats writing begging letters any day."

"From 1907 or earlier," Lissa said. "That's when construction was finished here, that time around."

"Let me get something to cover the floor," Eric volunteered, "so then you can spread everything out."

"Thanks, Eric." He disappeared down the hall, and I turned to Shelby and Lissa. "Who said working here was dull?"

"Do you seriously think that this trash has anything to do with the man's death?" Lissa asked.

"You know, Nell," Shelby said, her tone skeptical, "traffic accidents happen all the

time in the city."

"I know that, Shelby, but I don't believe it was just a random traffic accident. I swear I'm not looking for trouble. But you all know that it seems to find me."

"Does that detective think there's something suspicious about Mr. Scruggs's death?" Lissa asked.

"She hasn't said so, not in so many words, but I think she has doubts about the accident theory, too. She made sure to tell me that the man fell *backward* into the street, in front of that car."

"Oh," Shelby said, quick to grasp the significance of that. "She thinks he was pushed?"

"Officially this is still an accident. But if we brought her some new information, I think she'd listen. All I'm trying to do now is eliminate one possibility and make sure that the Society is in the clear."

"What does Mr. Agent Man think?" Shelby asked.

"He thinks this is not his problem, and he has faith that I can handle this all by myself. He doesn't know all the details."

Eric returned with an aged drop cloth that was already dirty — perfect. He knelt and spread it out on the floor, then looked at me. "Should I hunt down some gloves?"

"Ladies?"

The women both shook their heads.

I waved a magnanimous hand. "Then dig in. Just try not to break anything — if there's anything breakable in there. And watch out for splinters and broken glass, please."

"What about spiders?" Shelby asked with a wicked grin.

"Don't even go there!" We all knelt around the battered boxes, as if worshiping at some obscure shrine. I figured I had first rights, so I reached in and pulled out . . . a broken fountain pen. I laid it carefully on the drop cloth. "Next?"

We went round and round the group a few times. The boxes emptied, and the pile of detritus on the floor grew. We'd nearly reached the bottom when Lissa stopped and pointed. "There. It's metal, flat, and curly."

We all peered into the depth of the box, and I reached in and pulled out . . . a flat, curly piece of metal. I laid it on a clear patch of the drop cloth and we all stared at it.

CHAPTER 8

It was flat. It was curly. It was the right size to fit into a pocket. Eric handed me a tissue without even being asked, and I rubbed the piece gingerly. To my eye it appeared to be brass. And I was going to guess that it dated from a long time before 1907.

"What is it?" Lissa finally said.

"It's got to be from a piece of furniture," Shelby said. "It's got two screw holes, to attach it to the wood."

Like the bartender said, according to Detective Hrivnak, it looked like a drawer. "I think they call it an escutcheon," I said tentatively. "It goes behind a handle on a drawer, maybe to protect the wood. Anybody have a guess how old it is?"

"Eighteenth, early nineteenth century?" Shelby suggested.

"I'd agree, although I'm no expert," I told her. "Let's see if there's anything that goes with it in the bottom of the box?"

With renewed energy we started sifting through the remaining bits and pieces and came up with a handle, a single hinge, a few brass screws, and some large splinters of wood. We lined up the wood pieces and the metal bits together on the drop cloth and studied them.

"Well," I said intelligently, then stopped because I couldn't think of anything to add.

"You got that right, Nell," Shelby said. "Looks like we've got pieces of something made of wood with brass fittings. And that biggest metal thingy is definitely the right size and shape to match the thing that bartender described, so maybe we can guess there was a pair of 'em? And the dead guy pocketed the other one? He must've missed this one."

"Works for me," I said. "It would have been easy to miss. It was dark in that hole, and there wasn't much room to move down there — I bet he just grabbed a handful at a time and passed it up. Not that it looks particularly interesting or important. I wonder why this thing, whatever it was, ended up in the hole."

"Looks to me like it was broken a long time ago, but who knows if it was already broken when it was pitched into the hole, or the fall broke it up," Lissa added.

I considered that comment. "Let's assume no one carried it into the privy with him. Unless it's like one of those television shows where somebody's traveling with a briefcase chained to his wrist. It doesn't look like it ever got wet, so maybe it went in after it was no longer a privy?"

"Hey, could somebody explain this whole privy thing to me? Is that really what it was?" Shelby said plaintively.

"Lissa, you want to take that?" I said.

"Sure. Shelby, there's a long rich history of the archeology of privies in Philadelphia, even some that were known to have been used by Ben Franklin and his peers. A surprising array of stuff fell in or got tossed in over time."

"Such as?" Shelby appeared honestly interested.

"Broken china, glassware, pipes, buttons, coins, dice, even the odd doll or toy. They offer amazing insight into ordinary life at various points in time, before the widespread use of indoor plumbing. For the most part, privies were located outside and behind a residence, but not too far, of course. When one would get . . . um, exhausted —"

Shelby interrupted her. "You mean, filled up?"

Lissa nodded. "Yes. Then the homeowner would often just close it up and dig another one, near the first."

"This may be off topic, but what did they use for, uh, paper?" Shelby asked.

"Whatever they had," Lissa said. "Out in the country, that would be grass, leaves, corncobs, maybe scraps of sheep's wool. In the city, maybe newspapers or, if you had money, cloth. Standards were a bit different in those days."

"I'm glad I live now," Eric said.

"And we think this pit was a privy, why?" Shelby asked.

"Because it lay just outside the foundation of the original building on this site, which was built over just after 1900," Lissa told her.

"I don't see any paper or cloth here," I commented. "Would they have survived? Some of the wood did."

"Maybe?" Lissa replied. "That's not really my area of expertise."

"What? There aren't graduate courses in sanitary management of the eighteenth century?" Shelby joked.

"Let's stay focused here," I said, trying to keep this discussion on track. Despite its absurdity, we were dealing with the death of a man. "With the old mansion, the privy

would have been outside, but when the new building was built, the addition would have extended past its location. Ergo, we can deduce that the wooden item with the brass thingies went into the pit around the same time as the new building was built, because there wasn't a whole lot of stuff down there."

"Nell, you want me to call that detective for you, so you can tell her about this metal thing?" Eric volunteered.

I thought for a moment. "Let's hold off on that just a bit. I do think we should share the hardware with her — she'll want to show it to the bartender and see if he recognizes the escutcheon — but first I want to take some pictures and measurements and all that important stuff, because once we turn it over to her, we may not see it again." Was I on shaky legal ground here? I wasn't concealing anything, and I did plan to turn over the escutcheon to the police. "It's not like she's going to get any finger-prints from it, not after this long," I rational-ized.

"Will she want the wooden pieces, too?" Lissa asked.

How was I supposed to know? I was concerned that if the dead man had walked out of the Society with a twin to this

escutcheon, and someone had seen it at the bar and killed him because of it, then what we had here could be important, although the downside was, if the pieces matched, that pointed straight to the Society. But I wasn't sure if Hrivnak would see how a bunch of splinters could help. Maybe there was a compromise: what we needed was someone who specialized in antique furniture, or things with handles. There should be a record of one or more members who did somewhere in the Society's files . . .

"What's going on?" Marty was standing in the doorway, staring at the four of us all still kneeling on the floor, around the array of century-old trash.

Maybe the solution had just walked into the room. "We're trying to figure out what it was that Carnell Scruggs showed the bartender." When Marty looked blank, I realized I hadn't told her about Hrivnak's latest crumb of information.

"The good detective told me this morning that the police had found where Scruggs had dinner after he left the Society. He showed the bartender a metal thing, which attracted the attention of a stranger, who then left with Scruggs. The bartender gave kind of a weird description of it — it was metal, curly and flat, and possibly old —

114

and I figured that since Scruggs had been sent down the pit in the basement to clean it out, maybe he found something there that he pocketed, figuring it wasn't important. I asked Joe Logan to let me have the other stuff that they'd hauled out of the pit, and that's what we're looking at here."

"Let me get this straight," Marty said. "You're trying to figure out why this man died by sifting through trash from our basement?"

"Exactly."

Maybe her question had been facetious, but Marty being Marty, she immediately zeroed in on the critical piece among the scattered objects. "That came from the pit?" She pointed to the escutcheon.

"It did," I said. "You know what it is?"

"Hardware from a piece of eighteenth-century furniture, I'd guess. Why was it in the pit?"

"That is an excellent question, to which we have no answer. You have any idea what kind of item it came from?"

Marty shook her head. "I'd have to do some digging." She realized that Lissa and Shelby were looking at her with curiosity. "Terwilligers know furniture," she said bluntly. "Nell, you think this matches the thing that Hrivnak told you Scruggs showed

the bartender?"

"I think it may," I answered. "First we need to record what we have here, and then I need to call the police and tell them what we've found. I was hoping you might know someone who could analyze these pieces — the wood and the metal and the finish and anything else — and tell us what they used to be."

"Sure, I know a guy. Let me make a call." Even as she spoke, Marty kept her eyes on the pieces of metal. What was so fascinating about them to her?

Then she shook herself. "I'll go call him now." And with that she walked out of the room.

The rest of us looked at each other. "Was that odd even for Marty?" I asked.

"Maybe," Shelby said, getting back to her feet. "Do you need me for anything else? Because I've got a whole pile of . . . privy deposits on my desk that need my attention."

"Go," I told her. "Just don't spread this around, okay? This could be part of a murder investigation, kinda sorta."

"We hear you. Right, Lissa?" Shelby looked at Lissa, who nodded. I knew Eric would be discreet. It wasn't that I didn't trust them, but the knowledge we had just

uncovered might have led to someone's death, and I didn't want to put anyone else at risk, remote though that possibility might be.

Lissa and Shelby went out the door just as Marty returned; Eric was already back at his desk. "What the heck is really going on?" Marty demanded, dropping into a chair in front of my desk.

"I told you, I had yet another chat with the charming Detective Hrivnak," I began, and quickly explained what I had deduced based on what the detective had told me, and what had led to our own mini–archeological dig. "So my best guess is that Mr. Scruggs found the mate to this escutcheon here when he was in the pit, and he showed it to somebody who recognized it for what it was, and might have known or guessed where it came from and how Scruggs came to have it, and the next thing we know Scruggs ended up dead, and the escutcheon was not on his person. Does that about cover it?"

"Close enough," Marty said. "And that's all the stuff that came out of our basement here?"

"That's what the construction foreman told me. You have doubts?"

"No, of course not. People find privy holes

all over the city, every time they dig. I'm surprised nobody noticed it here — you'd think it would have been filled in years ago, when they built the new building on top of the old one."

"That would be the logical thing to do, but we know it didn't happen, and we'll probably never know why. Maybe the construction workers back then were in a hurry, or they didn't feel like trucking a lot of fill down to the basement, so they just slapped a cover on it. In any case, the question is: What is there about that piece of metal that is so important?"

"You really think that's what's behind all this?"

I shrugged. "I don't know, but I don't have any better ideas. Are you comfortable labeling this death a 'random city crime'?" I made air quotes. "I'm not saying it wasn't. Luckily for us, the police have labeled it an accident, so the press hasn't gotten hold of it — we've had enough bad publicity. But I'm not sold yet on the accident theory, and I'm betting Hrivnak isn't, either."

"This isn't going to hold up the renovation project, is it?" Marty asked. The Society was always at the top of her priority list.

"I don't think so. As far as I know, the only connection to the Society Detective

Hrivnak has found is that the victim was briefly a worker on the crew here, and had been in the building on the day he died. There's no suggestion that he died here. The police can't shut us down just in case, can they? So far there's no indication that they want to."

"What about once you show them this stuff?" Marty waved her hand at the little pile of brass and splinters.

"It might change their minds, but maybe not. The detective may think I'm making a lot out of nothing. Which would probably be better for us. But I'll give it to her anyway."

"My furniture guy said he could see us this afternoon. Can you wait until after that to tell the cops?"

Given the feeble connection between our find and the dead man, I didn't have a problem with that. It wasn't that we were concealing evidence, because we weren't sure it *was* evidence, merely a string of guesses. Whether or not we found out anything more from Marty's guy, I would talk to Hrivnak before the end of the day. "Works for me."

CHAPTER 9

"Lunch?" Marty asked before she got up.

"Shoot, is it that time already?" It had been a busy day, and now it was half-gone. And everything I'd done so far had been unscheduled, which meant the scheduled stuff was falling way behind. Solving mysteries seemed to eat up a lot of time. "Sure, fine. I get cranky when I don't eat. Where?"

"Someplace on Chestnut Street, maybe?"

Hmm. Chestnut Street was where Carnell Scruggs had stopped for his last meal at a bar. I'd like to check what the walking distance actually was. "Sounds good. I don't know if I should clear up this mess . . ." I waved at the junk scattered all over the floor.

"Get Eric to do it — that's why you have an assistant," Marty said firmly.

She was right, although I hated to ask other people to do my dirty work. Especially in this case, when the work was actually dirty. I gathered up my bag and jacket and

went out into the hall. "Eric, Marty and I are going to go find some lunch. Would you mind putting all that junk on the floor back into the box? Except for the brass fittings and bits of wood — see if you can find a small box for those. We're going to show them to someone this afternoon. You mind?"

"Not at all. I'll leave the small box in your office."

I turned to leave, then remembered to add, "Oh, please keep the other stuff somewhere — don't just toss it. You never know — there might be something else important in there that we missed."

"Got it. Have a nice lunch."

Marty and I walked out of the building — after a short detour to wash our hands — and turned right, then left at the corner, heading for Chestnut Street. I didn't get as many opportunities to walk in the city as I would like, and things changed quickly. Plus, as an amateur historian I carried around in my head images of buildings that were long gone — according to old photographs and maps, the parking lot there had once been a school, and the pet food store on the next block had once sold tack for horses.

As we walked I started mentally counting how long it took to reach Chestnut Street.

Not long. Marty and I found a nondescript restaurant and settled at a table. I wondered if she had an agenda — Marty usually did — or if she simply wanted to have lunch with me again. After we ordered, I decided to take the lead. "Do you think I'm making too much of this killing? Should I be doing my best to ignore it and pretend it's just an ordinary crime in the neighborhood?"

Marty raised one eyebrow at me. "You just gave yourself away when you said *pretend.* You know, your instincts are usually right. What does James think?"

"He says he's staying out of this. Not his jurisdiction. He will provide an opinion only if asked by me, and then only officially, and he will not perform any special favors."

"You sound peeved about that."

"Peeved? No, not really. I don't have any right to be, because he's right. I can't ask for help and drag him in every time I have a problem, even if it's a potentially criminal one. We have to keep some boundaries."

"Maybe," Marty said. She did not sound convinced.

Our sandwiches appeared and we dug in. Sorting through trash was apparently harder work than I had thought, and I was hungry. While I ate, I thought about Marty's *maybe* response. Was I being too cautious? My only

significant prior relationship was decades behind me now, and yet I had been surprised to find how much I didn't want to repeat past mistakes with James.

When at least half of our sandwiches were gone, I responded, "You think I'm setting up walls between James and me? Or he is?"

"Not walls, necessarily. Maybe fences. Picket fences, with slats so the wind blows through. Ah, forget metaphors. Look, I know you're both feeling your way into this, and I think you're doing fine, both of you. But I also know it's tricky when your professional lives overlap in unexpected ways."

It struck me that Marty seemed to be trying to say something without coming out and saying it. "What's this really about?" I asked.

Marty picked at the tomato on her plate. Finally she said, "I'm saying it might be happening again — you and the police butting heads over some kind of crime, with James hovering in the background, whether or not he wants to be."

My senses went on high alert. "What? How?"

Marty didn't meet my eyes. "You think this Carnell Scruggs picked up something from the privy trash and took it with him, and you think you've found something that

fits the description — a second one. The police think it may be murder. So that links the Society to it. You're its president, and Jimmy is your whatever. Like I said, it's happening again."

"And I'm going to keep him out of it," I said.

"Good luck with that. Anyway, now I'm taking you to see my furniture expert pal because I may know something about that brass piece you found today, so you can take it to your detective."

I was surprised, yet not surprised. "Hold on — are you going to tell me what it is you know or think you know?"

Marty shook her head. "No, not yet, because I'm not sure."

That hesitation was very unlike Marty. "I've never known you to hold back when you have an opinion. What's different about this?"

"If what I suspect is right, it's complicated. It goes far beyond that poor guy's murder. And back in time. And may bring James right back into it."

"But you aren't going to tell me about it?" I protested.

"Not until I'm sure. Let's wait until we've talked with Henry Phinney."

"That's your furniture guy?"

"He is. And he's a relative, too, but not close. Point is, he knows everything there is to know about Philadelphia furniture. It's not just his stylistic opinion — he's pretty sharp on the science side, too."

"Like a forensic analyst for furniture?" I asked.

Marty nodded, her mouth full of sandwich. I took the opportunity to finish my own. It was not surprising that Marty knew someone useful like this Henry Phinney, nor that she was related to him, because she knew everybody in the greater Philadelphia region and was related to half of them. Including James. What was more interesting was that she thought a more rigorous scientific analysis was desirable in this case. When our mouths were both empty, I asked, "What time are we seeing him?"

"Three."

"Is he nearby?" I hoped he wasn't out in the burbs.

"He has a shop just off Market Street, close to the Delaware River — we can walk over together."

"And that's all you're going to tell me?"

"Yup. For now."

I couldn't get anything more out of her, and after lunch, Marty headed off for the stacks to do . . . whatever the heck she did.

She didn't have an office or a real role at the Society, apart from her seat on the board, but she spent a lot of time in the stacks somewhere. I went to my office to find that Eric had tidied up as promised, and there was a plastic shoe box sitting on the blotter on my desk, carefully lined with bubble wrap. I pulled off the top to find the brass bits nestled safely inside, along with the larger shards of wood. Sitting on my desk, which was mahogany, the old wood looked a lot like mahogany to me, but I was no expert. Could someone extract DNA from wood? Were there DNA profiles of different kinds of wood?

"Lissa came back and took some pictures of all the pieces," Eric told me.

I'd forgotten about doing that, and was glad she hadn't. I didn't know if the mysterious Henry would need to keep what we'd found, including our flat, curly thing, aka The Escutcheon. So at least we'd have a record — and something to give Detective Hrivnak, if Henry for some reason held on to the brasses. If after talking to Henry we still thought there was something to tell.

Marty reappeared in my office at two thirty, looking unhappy. When I raised an eyebrow at her expression, she shook her head. Still not ready to share, it seemed.

"Here's what Eric assembled for us." I held up the box.

"Everything?" she asked.

"I think so. We're walking?"

"Yeah. I could use the air."

We set off again, heading for the river, past the back end of Independence Hall. I always enjoyed envisioning the city as it once was, when the blocks closest to the Delaware had been home to the grand houses of the city's elite in the later eighteenth century. Those glory days hadn't lasted long, and shops and factories and warehouses had taken over quickly in the early nineteenth century. Henry Phinney's place of work occupied a narrow brick building that looked as though it had been there for a couple of hundred years itself. There was no shop front, merely a shabby paneled door embellished with a handsome brass knocker. Antique or reproduction? I couldn't tell. Seemed like a furniture expert would have an original, but then again I wondered if a real one would long since have been ripped off. Either way, Marty rapped it smartly, and the door opened quickly.

Marty's relatives were a mixed bunch. I'd been half picturing a gnomelike character sprinkled with wood shavings, but Henry Phinney was a thirtysomething young man

with close-cropped hair, and his arms, revealed by his ratty T-shirt, sported a variety of tattoos. He looked more like a biker than an expert on antique furniture.

"Hey, Auntie M! Good to see you! This is your pal?" He looked at me.

I stepped forward and offered my hand. "I'm Nell Pratt, president of the Pennsylvania Antiquarian Society." Wow, I sounded pompous even to my own ears.

The younger man recoiled in mock horror. "Oh my God, the president herself! Please enter my humble abode." He stepped back and made a sweeping gesture.

"Henry, behave yourself," Marty said mildly. "We need your help, fast."

Henry grinned, unfazed by the reprimand. "You wouldn't say much over the phone. What's the story?"

"I didn't say much because I didn't want to prejudice you. We have some items that we want you to look at. They may come from an old piece of furniture."

"Yeah? You probably know more about styles and makers and all that stuff than I do."

"Maybe," Marty said, "but we want your special expertise. We need to know if the remains really are old, and if so, how old."

"Why the rush?"

Marty and I exchanged a glance, and I let her decide whether she could trust her nephew. Apparently she could. "It's connected to a police investigation," she said.

"Whoa!" Henry's face went serious quickly. "Would I have to, like, testify or anything?"

"I don't think so, but I won't say no. Right now it's just to satisfy my — our — own curiosity. That's all I'll say for now. Will you take a look?"

"Sure, no problem. But if I have to go to court, you'll have to buy me a suit. Come on back."

We followed him farther inside. The building was typical of early Philadelphia row houses, with a narrow hallway next to equally narrow stairs on one side; closed doors presumably led to adjoining rooms. Henry kept going toward the back, where what had once been a kitchen had been converted into a workroom-slash-laboratory, ringed with large windows that let in a lot of light. It was surprisingly neat, given that Henry must deal with a lot of wood, and it smelled of pungent solvents mixed with lemon oil. Odd dismembered pieces of furniture were scattered around the room — a leg here, an arm there.

That much I had expected. What I hadn't

foreseen was his array of high-tech machines I couldn't begin to identify. I spied what I thought was a binocular microscope in a corner, protected by a clear plastic cover, but that was where my expertise ended. It was as though the eighteenth and the twenty-first century had collided head-on in this room.

Henry was watching me with an amused expression. "Go on — you can ask."

"Okay. What the heck is all this stuff, and what do you do with it?"

"How much has Aunt Marty told you?"

"Next to nothing. Plus my scientific expertise is limited, so keep it simple, please."

"No problem. I analyze and restore furniture, okay? A buyer or seller can bring a piece to me and ask if it's authentic, or if it's been repaired and when. If a piece gets damaged, I can fix it, well enough that ninety-nine percent of people could never even tell. It's both a skill and an art. The fancy equipment allows me to analyze woods so I can tell you where they came from, and what I'd need to use to patch a piece. I can also analyze finishes — and then replicate them. And it's not as simple as whittling a new piece of wood or slapping on some replacement hardware. I have to make sure it matches visually."

"Wow," I said, impressed. "I didn't know people like you existed. Of course, I don't have anything that needs your kind of high-end attention. In fact, I don't have much of anything at all in the way of furniture. Not to be rude, but can I assume you make a good living at this?"

"Good enough. I'm a contract consultant for a couple of the museums in town as well of some others, and I live pretty simply. A lot of what I make goes into the high-tech stuff, but they're my toys and I love to play with them. So, Auntie M, what is it you want me to check out?" Henry asked.

Marty handed him the box. "Tell me what we're looking at."

He took the box and opened it, then removed the contents one piece at a time, and spread them out on a clean worktable. He shuffled them around until he was satisfied with the arrangement. Given what he'd said about the nature of his work, I was almost surprised that he didn't slip on gloves. The ensemble now looked a bit like a reassembled skeleton, and I guessed that he was trying to reconstruct what the original piece might have been, with a lot of missing bits. He perched on a stool and studied the arrangement, then began picking up individual pieces, starting with the

escutcheon. Then he turned his attention to the screws, which surprised me, since they didn't seem that special, and finally the wood shards. For the last he pulled over a magnifier mounted on an arm and studied the grain of the wood carefully. Then he looked at Marty. "Where'd these come from?"

I answered him. "We pulled the pieces out of what we think was an old privy beneath the Society. As you can no doubt tell, the original object was broken when we found it."

"Noted. How old's that building?"

"The current building opened in 1910, but the construction stopped in 1907. There was an earlier mansion there before it. We figure the privy hole is from the mansion's era."

"This stuff's definitely older than 1910. You two want the quick and dirty version?"

Marty and I both nodded, so Henry went on. "Looks like brass hardware from the later eighteenth century, and the screws are original and match, so to me that implies the hardware was attached to the original wooden object. You're assuming the chunks of wood were all part of that piece?"

"Yeah, seems logical, since they were found together," Marty said. "What was it?"

"Imported mahogany. As if you couldn't tell, Auntie M."

"You know I hate that name," Marty growled. "Yeah, that's what I figured. Any other analyses we should be thinking about?"

"If this stuff was in a privy, the privy already hadn't been used for a long time when it went in. No signs of, uh, liquid damage. Also, it looks like the old wood was brittle enough to shatter in the fall. How'd you find it, anyway?" He looked at me.

"We're renovating parts of the building," I answered. "The privy was in the basement, under a lot of other stuff."

Henry nodded. "So it's old furniture, but dumped sometime before 1907. Looks like it might have been a box, rather than something larger, if this is all you found. You've got the one handle here — were there more?"

Marty and I exchanged glances. "There might have been one more," I said cautiously.

Henry nodded but didn't comment. Then he turned to Marty. "Do you have another question, Aunt Martha?" He looked steadily at her, his expression serious.

"You think it is?" Marty asked him, without answering his question.

"I do," he answered, holding her gaze. Marty nodded once.

They'd lost me. "Is what? Will you two explain what you're talking about, please?"

Marty gave Henry a warning nod. "I want to check one more thing. Nell, let's go catch a cab. Henry, you hang on to this stuff — we'll collect it later."

"You want me to run other tests?"

"Sure, fine," Marty said. "See what you can find."

"Am I getting paid for this?" Henry grinned.

"Maybe. At least in undying gratitude and a couple of free meals."

"Just checking. Give me a day or two to crank up my machines."

"Sounds good, Henry. Nice to see you. You've got my number," Marty said.

"Nice to meet you, Henry, and thanks," I called out, as Marty all but dragged me out the front door and flagged down a cab. "All right, Marty, where are we going now?"

"The Art Museum."

That made no sense to me, but Marty usually had a reason for whatever she did, so I shut up and watched the city roll by. When we climbed out of the cab at the museum, Marty just said, "Come on." I followed.

134

She stopped long enough to throw some bills at the admissions desk, then set off for the second floor, and I trailed behind. She looped around to one of the side wings without looking at anything else, and half-way toward the back, she stopped abruptly, and I nearly ran into her.

"Look," she said. She pointed to a display of furniture and related items arrayed along one wall.

I paused long enough to read one of the labels and realized she'd brought me to the Terwilliger collection of antique furniture and paintings. I followed her finger and looked at a handsome table with drawers. And the drawers had pulls with escutcheons. And to my eye, they all looked a heck of a lot like the one we'd pulled out of the privy.

I looked at Marty. "They're the same?"

She nodded. "I think so."

That made no sense, yet it made perfect sense. And opened up a whole new can of worms.

CHAPTER 10

It was easy to see that Marty was troubled, although it wasn't clear to me why. "Marty, you think that the escutcheon we found in the pit, and most likely the one that Carnell Scruggs found, came from a piece of furniture from the Terwilliger family?" I recalled then that James had mentioned something about a murky family history with that furniture, but I didn't see where our splinters fit in the picture.

Marty gave me a one-word reply. "Yes."

"And Henry can do tests that will confirm that?" I was reminded that Henry had held on to our "evidence" and Detective Hrivnak probably wouldn't be happy about that. But she wouldn't know unless and until I told her, which I wanted to delay until I had gotten more out of Marty.

"Probably."

Since it was still before the rush hour, we had no trouble finding a cab back to the

Society. It was a silent ride. We went into the Society and took the elevator up, still without speaking. Outside my office I greeted Eric. "Any messages? Or anything else I need to deal with?" I was afraid to ask if there had been anything new from Detective Hrivnak.

"No, ma'am," Eric said, smiling. "Nice and quiet. Of course, it's Friday, so maybe people don't want to start something right now."

Would a murder investigation wait until Monday? But then, Hrivnak didn't know we might have a clue. Or not. I still didn't know what Marty was thinking. "Thanks, Eric."

I led Marty into my office, closing the door, and she flopped into a chair while I went around the desk and sat down. "Okay, Marty — talk to me."

She stared at me for several seconds, her expression bleak. "Like I said, I'm pretty sure the brass pieces came from a piece of Terwilliger furniture."

"I kind of guessed that, when I saw those pieces of furniture at the museum. So?"

"I think they're related to my family. My grandfather, probably."

Well, that didn't exactly clear things up for me. "What makes you say that?"

"I don't know yet."

I studied her. I had known Martha Terwilliger for a while now, under some pretty intense circumstances. I knew she was honest, often to the point of bluntness. And I knew she cared about the whole Terwilliger family, past and present, and valued their long association with the Society. If the brass escutcheon was what she thought it was, it could possibly link her family to a modern-day death, which might even be a murder. I could see why she would be upset — but I needed more information to make sense of it. "What can you tell me? And why do you think the brass bits are connected to the Terwilligers?"

Marty avoided my eyes. "I don't really *know* anything. If I had to guess, I'd say it has something to do with the Terwilliger Collection at the Society."

I was beginning to feel an urge to shake Marty, rather than trying to pull information from her bit by bit. "But we don't have any Terwilliger furniture here, you know."

"Not now." She stood up abruptly and headed for the door. "Look, I have to think this through on my own."

I stood up as well. "Marty, wait! There's a police investigation involved. You can't just walk away now, not if you think you know

something."

She stopped and turned to face me. "How about if I promise you that I don't *know* anything that has anything to do with the death of that man?"

I was troubled by her repeated emphasis on what she did or didn't "know'; her word choice kind of hinted at evasion. But Marty was also deeply committed to her family connections. I wondered where those intersected. But I could play the same game. "Marty, can you say that *not* telling me what you guess right now will *not* affect finding the killer, nor will it put anyone or anything at risk?" Wow, I'd just strung together a very awkward sentence. But Marty knew what I meant.

"I will say that this may be an issue that goes back many years, and I'm not sure what that means for the present. Give me one night, Nell. Let me get my head on straight about this, and I'll fill you in tomorrow, as much as I can."

"What about James? You said he might get sucked in." Although I still had no clue how or why, other than his own family connection to the Terwilligers. This whole discussion was making me increasingly uncomfortable.

Marty shrugged. "I can't stop you from

talking to him."

"Marty!" I protested. "That's not an answer."

"I'm not going to tell you to hide anything from James. But I'm not asking for his help. I'm going home."

Without waiting for my reply, she turned on her heel and left. I was bewildered and confused and a bit pissed off that she was dragging me around investigating whatever it was that she wouldn't tell me about. It put me in a very awkward position, both with the Society and with James, not to mention the police, who still didn't know about the second escutcheon. If this problem had to do with the Society's collections, I had some legal responsibility to look into it — although I wasn't sure what the statute of limitations might be for a long-past event, but that's why we kept a law firm on retainer. If it somehow had to do with the extended Terwilliger family, they were inextricably intertwined with the Society, so I couldn't just dismiss the issue. And James was a part of that family, and close to Marty. And now close to me. If I had to draw a diagram of the current situation, everything would intersect with James and me. How could I not tell him?

While I was still trying to work things out

in my head, the phone on Eric's desk rang, and after picking it up he put a hand over the receiver and said, "Agent Morrison for you."

Great, now James is reading minds over a distance of several city blocks. I picked up. "Hey, what's up?"

"You want a ride home?"

I looked at my watch. How could it possibly be after five already? "Sure. I'm ready to go."

"Be there in ten." He hung up.

So I had ten minutes to figure out how to explain to him what I didn't understand myself.

I met him outside of the building when he pulled up, and slid into the passenger seat. "You know, I'm getting spoiled by all this door-to-door service."

"My pleasure. Besides, it probably won't last — something always comes up and our schedules will get crazy."

"Are there crime seasons in the FBI? Like more in summer, fewer in winter?" I asked as he threaded the car through the city streets.

"With street crime, maybe, but white-collar crime? Not so much. By the way, I got a rather cryptic message from Marty, just before I left. She said, 'Tell Nell it's

okay to talk to you about it.' Does that make sense to you?"

"Unfortunately, yes. It can wait until we get home. Can we get takeout?"

"Sure. What flavor?"

We bickered cheerfully about what kind of food to get. We were still learning about our new neighborhood, which offered a range of options, most of them very good. We settled on a Thai place and even found parking nearby. I ran in and ordered while James sat in the car, and I emerged ten minutes later with a couple of bags of food that smelled heavenly. "Home, James!" I said brightly when I got into the car, then asked rhetorically, "Where the heck does that phrase come from, anyway?"

"To the best of my knowledge, it was the title of an old silent film — a romantic comedy where the guy masquerades as a chauffeur."

I gave him a look. "Why on earth do you know that?"

"It's not exactly the first time I've heard the phrase, you know."

We arrived home in mutually happy moods, changed into grubby clothes with lightning speed, and settled ourselves at the kitchen table and dove into the Thai food. Our pace of consumption had finally slowed

when James asked, "So tell me, what was Marty's message all about?"

I took a breath before beginning. "Marty thinks she may know something that may be somehow distantly connected to the death of that man outside the Society. But she isn't sure, and she doesn't think she has enough to share with the police, or even with me. It may be clearer to you if I tell you what we did today, and when Marty called you she was giving me permission to share. But you and I also talked about setting boundaries between us."

"You mean, keeping the personal and the professional separate?"

"Kind of. I don't want to be the type of woman who goes running to a big strong man every time she has a problem."

His mouth twitched with amusement. "However, your problems do seem to involve major crimes rather often. That's not something the average citizen *should* be able to handle, and in fact, I am an official crime solver."

I burst out laughing. "Okay, okay! But I'm not asking for your help, unless it's to keep me on track or tell me if I'm missing something. Does that work for you?"

"It does. On a case-by-case basis, maybe."

"Fair enough. So here's what's going on."

I launched into a summary of the day's events, starting with Hrivnak's visit and the information she had imparted, then the sorting through the trash from the pit with my staff, to the discovery of the brass fittings and pieces of fractured mahogany, to the visits to Henry Phinney and the Art Museum, ending with Marty's reluctance to voice whatever it was she seemed to suspect. James listened silently until I was finished. "Well?" I asked.

"When most people ask, 'How was your day?' they don't expect anything like this," he said wryly. "Where do you want me to start?"

"Well, after thinking about it for a couple of hours, and then telling the story out loud, I'm guessing that there's some deep, dark, shameful secret that involves the furniture of some departed Terwilligers. Does that ring any bells with you?"

"I'll have to think about it. You know I'm not exactly tight with the extended family, right?"

"I've gotten that impression. Do you have a problem with them, singly or collectively?"

"No, not exactly. A number of them, including my parents, were rather surprised when I chose to work for the FBI, but they're polite about it. I simply don't see

much of any of them, other than Marty."

"You told me earlier that the Terwilliger furniture was valuable."

"It is, when it comes up for public sale, which is pretty rare."

"But it wouldn't have been valuable around 1900, right?"

"No, nowhere near the current value, which these days can run into the millions — if you can find any Terwilliger pieces at all. So if what was found in that pit in the basement of the Society was in fact a piece that belonged to the Terwilliger family, nobody would have thought it was a treasure back then — it was just a box."

I gave a start. "A box. Of course! That's what Henry said, and now it makes sense. Handles, hinges, but not a lot of wood. It would have fit easily into the pit — not like a chair or a dresser, say. And a box could have had something in it. But what?"

"You didn't find anything else interesting among the trash?" James asked.

"Not really. Bits of glass, china. I won't say we reached the level of an archeological dig, but we looked at what little there was."

"Maybe there was nothing in the box," James said slowly. "If it was a box. Maybe that was the point — there was something removed from the box, and whoever re-

145

moved it didn't want people to know it was gone, so he — or she — pitched it in that convenient hole."

I considered what James had said. "That would mean that we now have to look for something that's missing, but we don't know what. It's smaller than a bread box, anyway. So now we're looking for something that maybe was in the box, which was small enough to fit into the pit, which means that whatever was in it was smaller still. It may have been there before 1907 and been removed. It may still have been there this week, when Carnell Scruggs or somebody else removed it. Or it's still lying at the bottom of the pit. And it may connect somehow to the Terwilliger family. And somebody may have thought it was worth killing Scruggs to keep it secret. Does that about cover it?"

"More or less. I'm going to hazard a guess that Marty has some ideas about that."

"I think you're right. She was acting awfully odd today." I stood up and started clearing our plates from the table. "Well, it's useless to speculate without additional evidence. Thinking of furniture, are we going looking for some tomorrow?" I was beginning to sound like a nag, but we really needed some more pieces.

"Sure. Where?" James replied amiably.

"I have no idea. I've never actually gone furniture shopping in my life, except for a bed or two. All the rest I inherited, or picked up here and there, or someone dumped it on me. Do we go to a furniture store? Flea markets? I'm clueless."

"What about Lambertville, in New Jersey?"

"I've heard the name. Why? What's in Lambertville?"

"They have a lot of antique shops there, and even an auction house. Kind of one-stop shopping. It would be a good place to start, and it's a nice excursion."

"Oh, goodie — a road trip. Sounds perfect."

James and I were still experimenting with weekends. Recently I'd been reminded of that song from *Camelot*, "What Do the Simple Folk Do?" While we weren't exactly King Arthur and Guinevere, we were kind of at a loss when it came to doing ordinary things together to fill our weekends. Neither of us was obsessed by housework, so we sort of did what we had to and then closed the blinds so we wouldn't notice the rest. Nor was either of us much of a tinkerer, so we didn't take on DIY repair projects or pursue elaborate hobbies. James did not tie flies; I

did not knit. And though our careers were important, we weren't serious workaholics, either.

The net result was that we were free to take off on excursions at the drop of a hat, and I was already compiling a list of future possibilities. An impromptu excursion to Lambertville fit nicely. Just over the river in New Jersey, it was in easy reach, and when we arrived there the next morning I realized how well it suited our needs. We wandered through store after store, from junky to high-end, and pointed out what we did and didn't like. We didn't make any serious decisions, just filled in the broad outlines. It was fun, especially once we discovered that our tastes were more or less in tune. Although I loved Victorian styles, even I was willing to admit some of them were kind of overblown, so we both gravitated toward plainer designs. Still, with so much space to fill, we had a long way to go. We rambled, and tried sitting on various pieces, which either creaked ominously or felt like concrete (usually the ones with the original horsehair stuffing, which was as prickly as James had said). We picked up and put down a few dozen items, and even bought a few small odds and ends, then simultaneously fell in love with a small, simple end table that

probably dated to around 1800, and would even fit in the car. We managed to haggle down the price — or rather James did. Clearly his agent training paid off, because he had only to fix the vendor with a silent glare and the price miraculously dropped. We found a lunch place and talked piffle over coffee and sandwiches. It all felt good, and right. We had fun. I'd almost forgotten what that was like.

At the end of the day we meandered our way home via country lanes, and pulled into our driveway in the gathering dusk. There was a car parked in our driveway, and Marty was sitting on the front steps waiting for us. When we were within earshot she said, "We need to talk."

CHAPTER 11

James and I exchanged a look, then he went up the steps and unlocked the front door. He held it open for Marty, and I followed her in. She'd been inside the house once or twice before, but never for more than a few minutes since we'd moved in. That made her our first official guest, not that we'd invited her or anything.

"Love what you've done with the place," she muttered, as she strode toward the back. James shut the door and we followed.

In the kitchen she turned to face us, almost belligerently. "You got anything to drink?"

I assumed she wasn't talking about iced tea. "Wine? Or the harder stuff?"

"Scotch, if you've got it. I don't care how many malts or whatever."

I located a glass in a cupboard — after opening only two wrong ones — and half filled it with Scotch. I looked at James, and

he nodded. What the heck — Scotch all around. Now I knew where the glasses were, so I filled another two and set the bottle, seriously depleted, in the middle of the kitchen table.

Marty sat; we sat. She addressed me first. "You told him?"

"Yes, last night."

When James started to speak, Marty held up a hand. "Let me tell this in my own way, okay? You can ask all the questions you want at the end."

Marty took a healthy swig of her Scotch before starting. "You know that the Terwilliger family has been involved with the Society for a long time, starting back when the place was more like a gentlemen's club than a serious collecting institution and there were only a couple of actual employees. Terwilliger family members sat on the board, raised money, solicited donations of family papers — the whole nine yards." She glanced briefly at James before resuming.

"My father married late, so he seemed old when I was young. He's been gone almost twenty years now." She took another drink. "I never knew my grandfather, but he donated a large portion of the family papers, going back to the first Terwilliger to set foot

in this country, when he was on the board. My father donated another portion years later, while *he* was on the board. That's pretty much all the historical documents the family had, except for bits and pieces scattered around among different relatives. If you recall the official catalog description, there's something like a hundred thousand items in the Terwilliger Collection, housed in five hundred boxes. I've been working for almost two years on organizing all the stuff into a detailed catalog."

Another swallow finished her drink, and then she helped herself to the open bottle. "After a while I realized I wouldn't finish until I was a hundred and seven at the rate I was going, so we hired Rich to help, and he's been great. He's pulled stuff from all over the building and brought it together, and even this recent shuffling for the renovation, inconvenient though it is, turned up a few more bits and pieces. Bottom line, there's a lot of stuff from a lot of Terwilligers, and we're still not finished sorting through it, and I don't know when we will be."

I interrupted gently. "Marty, if you're going to keep drinking, you'd better eat."

"I'm not hungry," she muttered like a sulky child.

"I can make us all eggs or something," I coaxed. "I already know a lot of this story, so I'll listen with one ear while you tell James the rest. Okay?"

"Yeah, sure, fine." She waved me away. I got up and went to explore the contents of the refrigerator as Marty resumed talking. James, bless him, let her set her own pace. He was a good interrogator, and that meant he knew when to keep his mouth shut.

Marty continued, "So Grandfather had a seat on the board, and if you think *I'm* a busybody around the place, he was worse, from all I've heard. When he got too old to get around, he kind of handed the role off to my father. Not that my father minded — he'd more or less grown up at the Society and he loved it, too, though maybe that was because there were so many good hiding places in the stacks and nobody bothered him. Anyway, he passed the crown on to me before he died. And here I am."

As I broke eggs into a bowl, found leftover ham in the freezer and onions in a basket, chopped, and mixed, I was trying to figure out when Marty would get to the meat of the matter. She hadn't yet said anything that I hadn't heard before.

She drank some more, her glass near empty again. "So after Rich and I dug into

the Terwilliger collection of documents and had created some kind of order — my relatives may have been nice people, but they had no concept of organization — we started from the beginning chronologically. As you might guess, there's not much from the real early years, but by the mid-eighteenth century there are boxes and boxes of records, as the Terwilligers settled in and started making money. And those guys did keep good records. Then the war came along and John Terwilliger signed up early and ultimately became a general. Washington really respected him, and there's lots of correspondence between the two of them, as you know, Nell."

For Marty, "the war" was always the Revolutionary War. "Yes," I answered from across the room, where I was heating butter in a pan. "I've enjoyed looking at some of the originals."

She twirled her half-empty glass between her hands, watching the liquid slosh around. "Grandfather made an inventory of the family furniture, back before it got split up among the relatives — I'm sure you know that story, James." He nodded silently. "Anyway, when I left you today I went home and looked at his list, and I noticed something I hadn't paid attention to before — a

description of a wooden writing desk General John bought. Which could have been anything, but given when he bought it, it might have been a lap desk, something that he could have taken along on his military campaigns. So I dug around some more among the family papers and found more short references that pointed in that direction." She looked up at me then. "It was a small mahogany box, with brass fittings, made by one of the joiners who'd made several other pieces of Terwilliger furniture."

Was Marty telling us in a roundabout way that she thought we'd held whatever had been left of that box earlier that day? It seemed possible.

I was struggling to wrap my head around that piece of information when I realized the toast was burning, and I jumped into action before all the smoke alarms went off. Marty fell silent, staring glumly at the bottom of her glass. James looked . . . perplexed, but he seemed to be waiting for me to take the next step.

I dished up eggs, threw some toast on the plates, and slapped them onto the table before sitting down. James wordlessly got up, found forks and napkins, and sat down again.

I picked up the thread again. "All right,

I'll go ahead and say what we're all thinking: what we pulled out of the pit in the
basement is what's left of General John
Terwilliger's campaign writing desk.
Whether it held anything when it went into
the pit and broke is anyone's guess."

"I think so," Marty said, and began poking at the food in front of her.

That still didn't explain why she was so
upset. "Was that part of your family's gift to
the Society?" I asked.

Marty started eating, avoiding my eyes.
"It's not on the accessions list," she mum-
bled between bites.

I took the opportunity to eat a few bites
of my own dinner, which gave me time to
think. My guess was that Marty was trying
to tell me something she didn't want to put
into words. Her ancestor had had a fine
writing desk. His descendants had given
much of the family treasures and documents they had held to the Society, over
time. Had they included the lap desk? If it
had been in the donated collections, Marty
would have recognized it immediately, even
in pieces, because she'd combed through
the Society's Terwilliger collections many
times. She hadn't been sure, so she'd looked
at the items at the Art Museum and then
checked with Henry Phinney. Which

meant . . .

"So that particular lap desk shouldn't be at the Society at all?" I asked. Another nod from Marty. "And you think that somebody really doesn't want anyone to know that it *was* there a century ago?"

"You got it," Marty said and drained her glass again.

We all sat in silence for a minute or so, digesting what we'd heard. "Just to be clear," I said slowly, "that unrecorded Terwilliger lap desk was hidden in the pit, and you believe that Carnell Scruggs's finding it was what led to his death?"

"I think so," Marty said.

I swept the last of food on my plate into my mouth, chewed, swallowed, and demanded, "Okay, what now?"

James looked pained. "You know you don't have evidence of anything, just a lot of guesses and leaps of logic. And some bits of wood and brass."

"That's the way we work best," Marty said.

James turned to her. "Yes, Martha, I realize that, but what kind of action are you suggesting? You go to the police and say, 'I think somebody did something a hundred years ago and that's why the construction worker was run down this week'? I assume

you can guess just how the police will react to that."

"James, don't be unkind," I said. "We've only just heard this for the first time. It's not like we have a plan. Just more questions."

"Nell, I can fight my own battles," Marty said sharply. "Jimmy, I'm only suggesting this as a possibility, but I think it hangs together."

"So what've we got?" I asked. "This lap desk belonged to your family but was not part of any of your family's gifts to the Society. But we may have found it smashed in the bottom of a privy under the Society building, and we have no idea why. Are there any sale records for it?"

Marty shrugged. "Not that I know of, but I haven't looked for them yet. You know, it was around 1900 that a lot of the furniture changed hands, and some family members were really ticked off. Not that it was worth a lot then, or at least, it didn't bring real high prices. Maybe somebody smashed it as revenge because it turned out to be worth less than he thought. Or something."

"Then why dump it in a pit in the basement?" I demanded. "That makes no sense. How about this? Maybe it was stolen, and the thief thought someone was close to find-

ing out, so he ditched it. Although wouldn't the statute of limitations have run out for theft? James?"

"Probably," he agreed tentatively. "But you both sound crazy."

"Maybe," I replied. "But remember, a man is dead, and we're pretty sure he was last seen alive showing off a piece of this presumed lap desk. Which piece is now missing."

"Which could also be lying in a Philadelphia gutter or storm drain and have nothing to do with his death," James countered quickly. "You're getting ahead of yourselves."

Marty blew him a raspberry, and I realized she was rapidly getting drunk. "You're no fun, Jimmy," she said.

"What, you two enjoy wallowing in crime?" he responded quickly. "As you pointed out, a man is dead. This isn't a joke."

I knew he was right, but I didn't know what any of us was supposed to do now. "James, of course it's not a joke. It's just a very fragile link between his death and something he may have found while at the Society — something that was not supposed to be at the Society at all. It could be a coincidence. Or there could be something else

going on."

James regarded me with what must be his professional stare: calm, level, and giving nothing away. "So you're saying that you think Carnell Scruggs may have died because of what he found at the Society? Then tell me this: Who knew about the box? Who recognized that brass piece for what it was? Most important, who cared?"

That silenced Marty and me.

But not for long. "It's going to sound petty and/or pompous if I say it out loud, but the Terwilliger family has had a long and important history in Philadelphia and the area. We may have petered out, and God knows we've spent most of the family fortune, but we still have our good name. The same is true at the Society: we're proud that the Terwilligers have nurtured it and kept it strong all these years. So if there's something fishy about this, and it led to that man dying, then it's a nasty blot on our record, and as for the Society, either Grandfather or my father may have been personally involved."

"Fair enough," I told her. "James, what do you think?"

He sighed. "Martha, a century is a long time. How do you intend to prove that anything happened back then, and then

160

figure out who might have done it, and *then* figure out who might have a motive now that led to the murder of an innocent stranger?"

"Jimmy, we've done it before — right, Nell?"

"Uh —" I began.

Marty ignored my clear lack of enthusiasm. "Look, I know the Terwilliger family tree inside and out. I'll start there. Who in the family back then knew about the lap desk? Who had the last known possession of it, and where did it go? Who had the means, motive, and opportunity to toss it in the pit?"

James couldn't suppress a smile. "Martha, you are a piece of work." But his smile faded when he added, "I cannot see the police swallowing your absurd story — they're already stretched thin. And I cannot involve the FBI. You — and presumably Nell, and your intern, Rich, and any other innocent bystanders you can dragoon — are on your own. But, absurd or not, be careful. If your wild assumptions turn out to be correct, there could be a modern-day killer out there."

"Thank you for your concern, Jimmy," Marty said sweetly. "We'll be careful. Won't we, Nell?"

Great — now I was stuck between the two of them.

CHAPTER 12

Marty bounced to her feet. "I'd better get going."

James rose more slowly to his six-foot-something height. "Martha, you've had, by my count, at least three straight Scotches. You're not going anywhere."

Marty cocked her head and studied his expression, then caved with some dignity. "Oh, goodie — a sleepover!"

I had a moment of panic. Much as I supported James's suggestion, I couldn't remember if we had any clean sheets for the guest beds, or where I'd last seen them since we moved in. And then there was the bathroom issue: there was only one on the second floor. Oh, it was a palatial bathroom, about as big as my former living room, with a magisterial claw-foot tub that I adored — but there was still only one. And the spare towels were probably hiding along with the sheets . . .

But Marty's safety came first. "James is right, Marty — you shouldn't drive. Please stay."

"You guys are the best. Which way are the stairs?"

Marty was definitely acting un-Marty-like, so I thought we'd made the right decision, however inconvenient. "Right behind you," I said, pointing to the back stairs that led up from the kitchen. I gently pushed her in that direction and followed so she wouldn't fall backward, although she seemed steady enough. "James, we'll meet you upstairs posthaste." *Posthaste?* I remembered that I'd had my own share of Scotch, which seemed to have affected my vocabulary. In any case, by the time Marty and I made it to the top, we were met by James (who'd taken the front stairs), bearing towels. No wonder he was such an asset to the FBI.

"The bathroom's that way, Martha," he said, handing her the stack of neatly folded towels. She took them and disappeared into the room, closing the door behind her.

"I don't suppose you found the sheets, too?" I asked hopefully.

"I did. Let's go make the bed."

"Have I told you lately that I love you?"

"Not often enough. But let's save that until we get Martha tucked in."

"Gotcha."

By the time we had assembled the bed, complete with blankets, a duvet, and pillows, Marty emerged from the bathroom. "Aw, you guys . . ."

"Good night, Marty. We can talk in the morning." I all but grabbed James and we made a swift exit toward our room at the other end of the hall. But once there we kind of lost momentum.

"Did you know what Marty was so worried about?" James asked.

"No. Marty's been very closemouthed about all of this, and now I can see why. She's very protective of her family — all of it, past and present. Does it matter? What she told us, I mean?"

He shook his head, but I wasn't sure whether he was responding to my question or merely to the mess of the situation. "I can't say that it does. And I meant what I said — there's nothing you can take to the police. They'd laugh in your face, and I can't say that I'd blame them."

"Hrivnak asked me to find the curly thing, which I think we have."

"All right, give that to her. Don't spin out your wild stories. If she asks, tell her what you've guessed. But don't be surprised if she doesn't swallow it."

I'd have to retrieve the remnants of the box from Henry tomorrow. "Agreed. So what do we do?"

"What do you mean *we,* kemosabe?"

"Oh, right, you're keeping your nose out of our business." I wondered how long that would actually last, but I wasn't about to challenge him on it at the moment. I was tired. We'd had a long and pleasant day, and then Marty had showed up and dropped her bomb on us, and all this emotional seesawing was really exhausting. "Can we pick this up again in the morning? Because I must perform my ablutions." All right, I was definitely a bit tipsy.

"Of course. I'm sure if all this started more than a century ago, it's not going to disappear overnight."

With that, we went to bed, although I won't say we went to sleep right away.

Sunday morning I stumbled down the stairs to find Marty already sitting at the kitchen table, looking disgustingly chipper.

"I made coffee," she said, "although it took me about ten minutes to find all the stuff I needed. How long have you been in the house now?"

"A month. Yes, I know it's a mess. We're still trying to figure out where to put things,

except there's either too much — like books — or not enough — like furniture. Come back in, oh, a year or two, and we might be settled."

I helped myself to a cup of coffee and dropped into a chair at the table. The coffee was strong enough to make my hair stand on end, but it worked quickly. "Marty, about all that stuff you told us last night . . ."

"Yes, I remember telling you, and yes, I feel a lot better getting it off my chest and sharing. Question is, what now?"

"That's what I was going to ask. Is this kind of murky family history typical for the Terwilligers? Stories that are hinted at but never explained? Did your father ever let anything slip?"

"No details, if that's what you're asking. Like I told you, he loved the Society all his life. But he was never comfortable serving on the board. I just pegged it as shyness — he was a private person, and he never liked ordering people around, so being board chair was difficult for him. He was always honest, extremely loyal to his friends, and took his responsibilities very seriously. But sometimes I wondered if there was something more — things he wasn't telling us. I don't know. I didn't ask questions back then. Now I wonder, if he hated being on

the board so much, why did he stick to it for decades? Maybe he thought he was guarding secrets. But nobody ever came out and said anything."

"Did he recruit you? For the board, I mean?"

"Not in so many words. I mean, like him, I kinda grew up in the place, and we had more bits of history scattered all over our house. So it seemed natural. If you're asking very indirectly, did he give me any hints or warnings, the answer is no. He never sat me down and said anything weird, like, 'We the mighty Terwilligers have committed a great sin and it falls upon our shoulders to pay the price.' "

I tried and failed to imagine that. "So he never told you directly that he had been party to or had knowledge of a theft committed by somebody somehow connected to the family."

Marty studied the grounds in her coffee cup as if looking to read them. "I'm going to have to go back and reexamine a lot of things now, based on what I'm guessing. And look through a bunch of stuff. That's the problem with history — you have to keep reinterpreting it."

James came down the back stairs, freshly shaved but wearing grubby sweats. "I smell

coffee. Is there more?"

I waved toward the counter by the stove. "Be warned, Marty made it."

"Ah. Thank you for the warning."

"Jimmy, you're a wimp. If you ordered that in a restaurant you'd pay extra and it would come with a fancy Italian name."

"Understood. Breakfast?"

"Feel free to forage," I said. He did.

After we'd eaten something, Marty said, "Thanks for looking out for me last night, Jimmy. I hadn't realized how bent out of shape this whole mess has made me. But the big question is, what do we do now?"

"Marty," James said with what I thought was admirable if annoying patience, "as I've told Nell repeatedly, there is no *we*. I cannot involve myself in this . . . I won't even call it an investigation. I will not undertake any research into what may be wild conjecture. Certainly not on FBI time or with FBI resources — not that I think they'd be relevant anyway. You may recall I have a full-time job, and I've recently returned from sick leave, and you wouldn't believe the backlog of stuff on my desk. I don't mean to be rude, but I don't have time to get into your problem."

"It's your family, too," I reminded him, "but I do understand about your time com-

mitments." I turned to Marty. "So it's you and me? What about Rich?"

"Rich is a good kid and he works hard, but he doesn't know all the family details."

"He's been working with you and the collection for going on two years now — he must have picked up something. And he does bring a fresh eye," I countered.

"True. But what do I tell him to look for?"

I shrugged. "Got me. What was your father like? I never met him, remember. Why would he have created or maintained any mystery about this lap desk? I mean, anybody who loves history, and who recognizes how much we've lost and how hard we have to fight to preserve what has survived, would probably feel a responsibility to leave some kind of record. Don't you agree? Maybe he was conflicted because he knew it was a family member who trashed the piece, and family came first. Maybe he did write down a clear account saying Cousin X stole it to buy his mistress a town house with the proceeds, and then had a change of heart. Or maybe he was torn for another reason, like Cousin X stole it to sell because he needed the money to pay for lifesaving surgery for his mother, but she passed away before it could happen." By now both Marty and James were staring at me as if I'd gone

nuts. "What?"

"You've gone from zero to about seventy in no time flat," Marty said. "I'm impressed. Except none of your stories explain why it got smashed and why it's in the pit. Neither my grandfather nor my father would have done that."

"But you agree with me that there are other possibilities?" I knew Marty was sometimes touchy about comments about her family, and I wasn't sure if I'd stepped over a line. It had happened before.

"I do, much as I hate to think my father hid things from me. I reserve the right to believe that if he did, he had a good reason, like you pointed out. He really did care about history, family or not."

James spoke up for the first time in a while. "Aren't you two losing sight of the main issue here? Carnell Scruggs, the man who died? It's all well and good to speculate about what your father or grandfather might have thought a century ago, but a man was killed last week. If you believe the two are related, you've got a lot of work to do."

Marty answered quickly. "Jimmy, you think we don't know that? We're trying to figure out *why* that poor guy ended up dead, and what little we've got points to the Terwilligers. So I feel an obligation to get to

the bottom of it. Nell here can help, but only if she wants to. And don't forget you're a Terwilliger too, Jimmy."

"My mother never bought into all that society stuff, if you recall."

"Blood will out!" Marty declared dramatically. "Nell, you in?"

"It involves the Society, therefore I am involved. I can't play ostrich and pretend it's not happening. We know about it now." *Or think we do,* I added to myself. I had nothing better to suggest.

Marty slapped her palms on the table, startling both James and me. "So let's move forward. Look, I've got some digging to do at home. Nell, how about I come by the Society tomorrow morning and we can go over what I find, or don't find? This may take a little time."

"Construction is going on tomorrow, so things are going to be unsettled," I reminded her.

"When aren't they?" she retorted. "You're okay if I bring Rich into this? We can use his help."

I wondered if it was wise to drag someone else into this growing mess, but I agreed that we could use the help of another trained researcher. "Go ahead, Marty. He should know the Terwilliger Collection

pretty well by now."

"Will do." Marty stood up. "Thanks for your hospitality, you two. We'll have to work on your furniture problem once we get this other thing cleared up. Bye." With that, she picked up her bag by the front door and left before James and I could muster a protest.

We were left staring at the closed door. "What just happened here?" I asked James.

"Martha Terwilliger wants to play detective. I must say I have mixed feelings about it. I'll concede that she has a point, and that solving this crime may hinge on information that she has unique access to. Or it may be a wild-goose chase. Either way, I know I can't stop her. But I worry about what she's dragging you into. There's already been one death."

How sweet: he was worried about me. I couldn't remember the last time someone had looked out for me, before James. "Thank you, James. I'll certainly try to be careful. But as I said to Marty, since this does seem to involve the Society and its collections, I have a responsibility here."

He reached out and took my hand. "Of course. You know I've got your back."

CHAPTER 13

James and I spent what was left of the morning doing not much of anything. I made another pot of coffee, and we read the Sunday paper (I checked the obituaries to see if any of the Society's current or former members had passed away and if I should send condolences the next day, a morbid but not infrequent task). He went out to the car and retrieved our new old table, and we wandered around the house trying it out here and there. It looked lonely. I tried to visualize pieces of furniture that we didn't have in spaces that we had too many of. I looked at the tall, handsome windows with their opulent moldings and shuddered to think of the yardage of fine damask that would be required to adorn them in the manner they deserved. I couldn't just go pick something off the rack at the local department store. Good thing I liked lots of light — and that there were no

neighbors near enough to peer through our windows. Although I made a mental note to revisit that conclusion come winter, when the leaves had fallen.

When we discovered we had done all that and it was still only midafternoon, I asked James, "Are we workaholics?"

"Why do you ask?"

"Because I have no idea what to do with free time, and as far as I can tell, you don't, either. We're supposed to be spending quality time together now, but doing what?"

He took my question seriously. "You're saying you aren't happy just sitting with me and smelling the roses?"

"I guess. Sad, isn't it?"

"I do know what you mean, Nell. All right, it's a beautiful fall day, and we have about three hours of daylight left. What fits into that? A museum? An historic site? Bowling?"

I gave an involuntary snort at that last suggestion. "Do you bowl?"

"The last time I tried, I think I was twelve. Do you want to think about getting Eagles tickets for some future game?"

I'd never once considered that. "Maybe. Let's keep that on the list. Do you even like art museums?"

"In small doses. Too much art and my

brain short-circuits."

Much as I hated to admit it — I mean, I work at a museum, for heaven's sake — mine did, too. What can I say? My imagination was fired more by history than by paintings. "Theater?"

"Maybe. What about movies?"

"You like weepies or ones where things go boom?" I tossed back.

"We could alternate," he offered.

"Which do you think I prefer?" I hated to admit a secret affection for the ones with lots of explosions, but there it was.

"I'll pass, thanks. Realistically, we should probably continue hunting for furniture at the moment. We tried the antique side yesterday — how about some nice contemporary stuff today?"

"Okay, I guess. If ever we get to the point of deciding on carpets and drapes and paint colors, are you going to run screaming or find an important case that has to be solved?"

"Wait and see."

So we went to high-end department stores and looked at nice, large, stuffed things, and then we found a pleasant restaurant and ate an early dinner, and then we came home and watched television — just like an old settled couple. Had it really been only a

month since we'd moved in?

Marty did not call. The FBI did not call. It was all very peaceful.

I do not trust peaceful anymore.

Monday morning began uneventfully. Detective Hrivnak hadn't put in an appearance yet. I hoped that was a good sign, and that the police had resolved Carnell Scruggs's death or decided it really was an accident. I was braced for a few weeks of chaos now that construction had begun. At least my office was as far from the banging and clanging of renovation as possible, but since the building was constructed of metal and concrete, there were bound to be reverberations.

Eric had arrived early today. "Mornin', Nell. Coffee's ready. Nice weekend?"

"Very nice, thank you." *Except for Marty's intrusion,* I thought, but Eric didn't need to know about that. "I take it the crew is already hard at work?" Silly question — I could feel their presence through the soles of my feet.

"That they are. Your architect left you a list of where they expected to be working over the next few weeks, so you can warn the staff and the patrons. It's on your desk."

"Good for him! I'm glad we hired some-

one who's worked with museums before. I'll get some coffee, then hide out in my office, unless somebody really needs me." I dumped my bag and coat in the office and went down the hall to the coffee machine, where I helped myself to a cup. Once back in my office I sipped appreciatively and riffled through the papers Eric had left for me on my desk. Mostly business as usual: reports on grants, lists from Shelby on prospective donors, collections status updates from Latoya, a mockup of the next newsletter, which should go out sooner rather than later, now that construction had begun. I dug in with my red or blue pen, as appropriate, and the next time I looked up, Marty was standing in my doorway.

"Got a minute?" she asked.

"I think so, unless you've got a crisis, in which case I'd like to schedule that for a week from tomorrow." Seeing her expression, I added, "Joke! I thought you'd be busy until tomorrow?"

"Yeah, well . . ." Marty flopped into a chair. "I think I've got a working plan. I'll be the first to admit that what we talked about relies on a whole string of assumptions, aided by some decent Scotch, and if any one of those is false, the whole blinking thing falls apart. I wrote them all down, so

we could take them one at a time. And decide if and when we need to bring in more help."

"Help like Henry Phinney, you mean? Or in-house help, like Rich or Shelby?"

"Whichever. You want to hear the list?"

"Do I have a choice?"

"No." Marty proceeded to read from a piece of lined paper. "Assumption number one is the biggie: the death of Carnell Scruggs is somehow connected to the brass fittings that were found in the pit in the basement."

"Okay," I said cautiously, "pending confirmation from the bartender that what he saw was one of those fittings. Which reminds me: I have to collect the one we have from Henry to take it to Detective Hrivnak so she can show it to the bartender."

"Don't interrupt," Marty said. "Assumption number two: those brass fittings came from a piece of Terwilliger furniture. Three: those fittings were part of the lap desk that belonged to General John Terwilliger. Four: that writing desk once contained something — we don't know what, but we think it wasn't the logical thing, which would be papers, but something else instead. Or maybe nothing at all, but I didn't give that a number on the list. Five: somebody

179

dumped the box in the pit sometime in the past, but before 1907, thinking no one would ever find it, which was pretty close to true. You with me so far?" Marty fixed me with an eagle eye.

"Yes, with some reservations. Like where was the desk between the time it left General John's possession and when it ended up in the pit? Who had it?"

"An excellent question, and I'm getting to that. That's one of the things I wanted to check after I left your place yesterday. I told you about my grandfather's inventory?"

"The one he made before the family split up the furniture? Yes, you mentioned that."

"Good. That box described on it pretty much has to be the lap desk. You okay with that?"

"I think so. And?"

"That means we know it was in the family at that time, and that he had it. The thing is, it doesn't appear on the inventory of his gift to the Society, which we have right here in this building. Yet we found what was left of it in pieces here at the Society."

"So how'd it get here?" I asked.

"Don't interrupt — we'll get to that. Suffice it to say, my grandfather had it. Assumption Six: my father might have known something about it. And finally, Assumption

Seven: someone now does not want any or all of this information to come out, and that's why that poor man died." She sat back triumphantly and challenged me with a look.

"Interesting," I said, stalling. It was a surprisingly methodical analysis, especially from someone who should have been hungover yesterday, and I couldn't disagree with any of Marty's points. But neither could I prove them, apart from Grandfather Terwilliger's inventory. The only tangible evidence we had was some brass pieces and some chunks of old mahogany, and an approximate terminal date for when they went into the pit: 1907. "You're minimizing that last and most important point: Why would anyone care enough today to kill someone to keep all this quiet? It's been more than a hundred years since whatever it was happened. The central question is, who feels threatened by this discovery?"

"That's what we have to find out," Marty said firmly.

"Great," I said glumly. "What do you suggest we do next?"

"Take a look at the things we can find out about. Check out the furniture — who made it, where the brass came from, and whether there's any record of anyone other

181

than John Terwilliger buying a lap desk from the same Philadelphia furniture maker. There could be a bill of sale."

"Okay, that sounds good, and you're in the best position to look for that. Go on."

She nodded. "Then we go after whatever was in the desk."

I sat back in my chair. "Marty, how the heck are we supposed to do that? We don't know if there was anything in there, and it's not there now, nor is it in the pit. What do *you* think was in there?"

"I'm not ready to rule out papers altogether, because if it was pulp-based paper it could have disintegrated, but there might still be traces. Maybe. If it was rag paper it would have survived longer, so I'd expect you to see at least fragments."

"Are you missing any Terwilliger papers that you know of?"

"No, but I haven't memorized the whole inventory. We can go back and look at what we've inventoried and see if there is a hole in the middle of it. I can ask Rich to do that — he knows the collection."

"Oh, this just gets better and better." The Society had already suffered through one disastrous theft of important documents, and I refused to contemplate the fallout if we had to admit it had happened again.

Even if the theft had occurred generations ago, my staff and I would look incompetent by association. "Somebody destroys a nice antique lap desk in order to steal whatever was in it, except we don't know who stole it or what was in the box or why anybody would steal the contents between whenever your grandfather made that inventory of his and 1907. And then poor Carnell Scruggs comes along and finds the bit of hardware and carries it off in his pocket, but whatever that was, it was *not* found with his body on the street. Having personally sifted through the trash, I'm inclined to think it was *not* papers, but I haven't any idea what it might have been. So if he did take something, then somebody had to have taken it from him. Which implies that it was valuable, either for its cash value or because it meant something to someone."

"At least we're on the same page," Marty said, slightly less enthusiastically.

We stared at each other. "Marty, what are we doing?" I finally asked. "We've got a busted-up box and a dead man, and we're jumping through hoops to try to connect them. But so far we have no evidence of any crime."

Marty shrugged. "We're flailing around in the dark, is what. But why did the guy fall

backward in front of that car?"

"Maybe he was a klutz?" I volunteered.

"Right. Go ahead, blame the victim," Marty muttered.

"But no one can prove he was pushed, either," I protested. "Or if so, that it was on purpose. Maybe some drunk bumped into him and he stumbled onto the street." I was now officially grasping at straws. "How about this? We check who was working here in the early twentieth century. I can go through the Society's old records, and it's not going to be a big number. You know, anybody who had access to the building while it was still under construction, and therefore to the pit."

Marty considered for a few moments. "That's not a bad idea. Come at it from the other side, sort of. We know the box was there, and somebody put it there on purpose and never mentioned it."

"Did your grandfather figure out that it was missing? Or did he give it to someone or sell it, before he made the gift to the Society?" I tried to phrase my next question delicately. "Marty, you're the only person who can look at your grandfather's history and see where he might fit. I'm not saying for a minute that he was involved, if there even was a theft or an incident of vandal-

ism. But if there was, why did he look the other way and do nothing?"

"You're right — that's my responsibility, and I can't ask anyone else to do it. I'll deal with it. That all?"

"Who else should or shouldn't we involve? Lissa either already knows or guesses that we're looking into it. Have you talked to Rich?"

"I'll see him today — I wanted to check my personal papers before I set him to hunting."

"Since it's collections-related, we should probably include Latoya." I didn't relish the idea, because we had a slightly rocky working relationship, and I didn't think she'd approve of this use of Society staff time.

"What about Hrivnak?" Marty asked slyly.

Yes, I still needed to get back to her — after I retrieved the escutcheon. Today, or I'd lose whatever points I'd scored with her. "What the heck is there to tell?" I protested. "We think somebody might have stolen something a century ago, but we don't know who or what? She'd laugh us right out of her office. James agrees about that."

"But we do need her to confirm the point about the brasses, just to dot the *i*s and cross the *t*s, and I'm betting she will," Marty retorted. "So you reach out to her and tell

her you have something to show her. Take the lead on this so you can maintain control of the information. Tell her the bare facts: the brasses came out of the Society pit, where Scruggs was working on the day he died — that, we can pretty much prove. That's all you *know,* and it's the truth. Can she prove that one of those brasses is the thing Carnell Scruggs showed the bartender?"

"But if the answer's yes, she's going to want to know more."

Marty was not about to be silenced, now that she was on a roll. "Volunteer to do some research for her. Then she'll owe you."

"And why are we not telling her our thoughts up front?"

"Because we don't really know anything," Marty tossed back at me. "And I want to figure out how deep into this my family was before it all goes public. Maybe that's selfish of me, but I just want to buy time to find out all that I can. Can you understand that?"

I certainly knew about Marty's feelings for her family history. "I think so. Why don't you call Henry and tell him that I'll swing by this afternoon to pick up the pieces, and then I'll take them straight over to police headquarters from there?"

"Sounds like a plan. I'll go call him now."

Before I could protest, she leaped up and left my office. I stared after her, afraid to wonder where all this would lead.

CHAPTER 14

Marty poked her head back in long enough to confirm that Henry would be in his workshop all afternoon and was expecting me. Then she disappeared again. Afraid I'd have more uncomfortable questions for her?

I thought I understood where she was coming from. Marty was proud of her family history, and this murky mess looked as though it could besmirch it. Stupid word, that, but there was something almost Victorian about this scenario, with its potential for close-held secrets and family honor intertwined. I had to keep reminding myself that there was a very real, very modern murder involved, whether or not it had anything to do with the Terwilligers. I sighed. Damn that pit: I'd been the one to request that it be cleaned out and the contents saved, at least until someone could take a look at them. I should have let the construction crew fill it in and build over it.

Then maybe Carnell Scruggs would still be alive.

But it was too late for that, and now I thought the responsible thing to do was to retrieve the escutcheon and convey it to Detective Hrivnak and let her follow up. If the bartender told her the thing looked totally wrong, the whole issue would go away. If he really couldn't tell, we weren't any further along. If he jumped up and down and cried, "Eureka!" then we were in the soup.

Of course, that metal piece might have been available at the eighteenth-century equivalent of the corner hardware store and appeared on eighty-seven percent of colonial furniture made in Philadelphia. I could ask Henry about that, as soon as I got myself over there.

Shelby popped by not long after. "Lunch? Noonish?" she asked.

"Okay."

She disappeared again as quickly as she had arrived. I checked my watch: only eleven, so I had an hour to kill. I decided to go find the construction foreman, Joe Logan, again and see how things were going. I stopped by Eric's desk to update him on my plan. "Eric, in case I don't get back to my desk, I'm going to go check on the

construction progress, and then I'm having lunch with Shelby, and then I have an errand to do, but I should be back before the end of the day. Anything critical on my calendar?"

"Nope — just ordinary business."

"Good." I wandered off toward the second floor, where the loudest noises seemed to be coming from.

The Society's building had been declared structurally sound, thank goodness. Mitchell Wakeman's generous contribution was going to pay for a thorough overhaul of our antiquated heating, ventilation, and cooling systems, and the installation of modern compact shelving wherever feasible. Compact shelving optimized the use of storage space, because the shelves actually moved, rolling silently on tracks, either electrically or by hand-cranking a large wheel, so that only one or two aisles had to remain open at any time. Of course, we'd had to verify that the floors could sustain the weight of the additional shelves — they were heavy! — plus the collections they housed, and there were limits on how much we could add. And since we were also upgrading our fire systems, now to be sprinkler-based, we'd had to factor in the weight of *wet* books and papers, which would be heavier

than normal. How ironic it would be if the collections were saved from fire but the floors collapsed around them!

Joe Logan was where I expected him to be. "How's it going?" I called out, as men in hard hats disassembled the century-old metal shelves. I wondered if they were recyclable and whether we would get anything back if they were sold as scrap.

"Good, good," Joe said, his gaze not leaving the workers.

"No more surprises?" I asked, half joking.

Now he turned to me. "You mean, like that pit? Nope. Nowhere to hide up here. You know, the police said to leave the pit alone for now, since that's where Carnell was working. Luckily we'd planned to start up here anyway. You need something?"

"No, I just wanted to keep tabs on the progress so I can report to the board and our members. We're on track?"

"Yup, all good. But it's only day one, remember."

"I promise I won't hover over you for hourly updates. You've worked in places like this before, haven't you?"

"Sure have." He rattled off a list of local libraries whose names I recognized.

"Scott Warren and his company brought you on, didn't he?"

"Yeah. We've worked together before. You've got a top crew working here. Must be nice to have the funding to do it right. I can't tell you the number of times we've had to scale back a project because of lack of money."

"I hear you," I told him. "We're very lucky, and we plan to use the space wisely."

I could tell he was itching to get back to work, and I didn't have anything more to add, so I left. I wandered down the hall to the processing room, which now looked like utter chaos. Normally it was a large, open room with big tables where items could be spread out. Now the perimeter was lined with (acid-free) boxes, stacked three deep, and there were more tucked under the tables wherever possible. Still, Rich and Ben seemed to have found a way to ignore the noise from the adjacent stacks and the confusion in their work space and appeared absorbed in their own work. I envied them their focus.

"Hey, guys!" I called out. "Everything going okay? Where's Alice?" Alice was one of our newest employees, a delightful twenty-something young woman whom we'd hired to please her donor uncle, but who was more than proving her worth.

"She had a family thing — a vacation in

Europe with her uncle or something," Rich said. "Did you need her?"

I'd forgotten that Alice would be out for a bit, on a trip funded by her generous uncle. Since the Society benefited from his generosity as well, I couldn't exactly say no to her, although such absences were not standard Society policy. And in truth there wasn't a lot for Alice to do at the moment, with the collections shifting frequently. "No, I was just checking in. This place just keeps getting more and more crowded, doesn't it?"

"Sure does," Ben said. I realized that of course he'd be the person most aware of that, because it was hard to maneuver his wheelchair around all the added boxes. "We haven't seen much of you here recently, Nell."

"Well, there's been a lot going on, here and at home — James and I just moved into a new place. What're you guys working on?" As collections researchers they both reported to Latoya, head of collections, but I didn't always know what projects she assigned, and I wanted to hear it from them.

"Marty Terwilliger asked Rich to do something or other with the Terwilliger Collection," Ben said, "so I'm looking into the history of the waterfront for him and plod-

ding through those FBI acquisitions the rest of the time. Oh, and working on the next newsletter with Shelby, since Alice is out this week." Ben was our newest addition, as registrar, but his background was in database management rather than historic collections, so I was glad to hear that he was getting up to speed.

"That sounds good. I'll let you all get back to it — I'm just making the Monday-morning rounds. Carry on!" At that out-of-character comment they both stared at me as though I were daft, so I left.

Since by now it was almost noon I wandered down to Shelby's office, where she was ready and waiting. "Where do you want to go?" she asked.

"Can we head toward Independence Hall? I have an errand that direction after lunch."

"The Bourse work for you?" Shelby asked.

"Sounds great." The Bourse had started life as a commodities exchange center in the 1890s. Now it housed a rich assortment of shops and eateries. It was an impressive space, and fun, too. It was also a good day to walk, so Shelby and I chatted amiably as we made our way toward what had once been the heart of Philadelphia.

Once inside and provisioned, Shelby said

bluntly, "You and Marty are hatching something."

It was hard to hide anything at our place, I'd long since discovered. "Yes. Marty has a theory."

Shelby grinned. "Ooh, tell me! Does this have to do with the body?"

"What, are we playing Twenty Questions now?"

"You didn't answer the question, so I'll take that as a yes. Is Mr. Agent Man involved?"

"No."

"But Marty is?"

"Yes."

"Is it bigger than a bread box?"

I stared at Shelby for a moment, then burst out laughing, since I'd said the same thing to myself. "About that size."

"Is it valuable?"

"No." Not now, not in its present condition. But what it had held might have been. If only we could prove what it was!

"Does it have to do with Marty's endless family?"

"We aren't sure, but maybe."

"You really aren't going to tell me, are you?" Shelby asked.

I sighed. "Shelby, once again there is a suspicious death involved. Much as I'd like

to believe it has nothing to do with the Society, I'm afraid it may. I'm responsible for the Society, and that includes all its employees, and I can't let people go poking around in matters that involve the police. Believe me, it's not that I don't trust your discretion, and I do value your insights. Do you understand?"

Shelby's expression had turned serious. "I think so. But you will let me know if I can help?"

"Of course. I'm just trying to keep you and everyone else safe." And for a brief flash I realized this was how James must look upon my involvement in things that often put me at risk.

"Okay. Shall we talk about your hunky guy now? How's living together working out?"

I was relieved that Shelby had changed the subject, even though the new one she'd chosen was also touchy, in a different way. "Good, I think. It's only been a month. So now it's just the two of us rattling around a lot of gorgeous Victorian space and wondering what we're going to do for furniture. It appears that we have both lived rather minimalist lives hitherto."

"Hitherto?" And Shelby and I were off, talking about interior design. A nice, safe topic.

The next time I checked my watch, it was well past one. Once more the day was slipping away from me, and I still had to visit Henry, the Furniture Guy, and My Favorite Detective. "Shoot, I've got to run. This has been fun."

"Glad to hear it. Nell . . ." Shelby hesitated, turning serious again. "You do know I'm serious when I say that you can ask, if you need help?"

"I do, Shelby, and I really appreciate it. Who knows — this may turn out to be nothing, or I may have to muster the troops and involve everybody. I'll let you know, I promise."

"Deal," she replied.

We parted ways at the front door, she to head back to the Society, me in the opposite direction, looking for Henry's place. I was pleased with myself for actually finding it, since I'd been there only once before, and it wasn't marked. I rapped on the door. And rapped again. *Maybe I haven't found the right place . . . ?* I thought I heard a few crashes and curses, and spent about twelve seconds picturing Henry being attacked by the same Person Unknown who had caused the death of Carnell Scruggs — but why would anyone *else* know that Henry had the matching hardware? I shook myself, trying to quiet

my overactive imagination.

Henry finally pulled the door open, looking undamaged. "Hey, Nell. Aunt Marty said you'd be stopping by. Come on in."

I followed him down the hall, savoring the scent of sawdust and varnish. I spotted our plastic box in the middle of Henry's worktable. "Have you found anything new?"

"Marty told you she thought the escutcheon you found might match some of those on the Terwilliger furniture, like the ones she showed you at the museum, right?"

"She did. So, do they match?"

Henry nodded. "These are identical. Probably all came from the same shipment to Philadelphia."

"They aren't locally made?"

"Nope. The furniture is — nobody was supposed to import anything from England back then, but there were plenty of talented furniture makers in the city here. But metalwork is something else. Of course, somebody could have laid in a supply before the war, but that would have been a pretty big investment — those babies weren't cheap."

"Did Marty share her theory with you?" I asked.

"That the fragments came from a Terwilliger piece? Or that it was a lap desk? Yeah,

we both arrived at that conclusion pretty quickly. I think she's right, at least in terms of style and size. She can dig into the history side of that — you've got all those records."

"You haven't talked about this to anyone else, have you?" I asked.

"Nah. Marty said not to, and I don't see a lot of people anyway, so who would I tell?"

"Just be careful — please. I don't want anyone else to get hurt." The list of possible targets was growing daily, which made me anxious.

"You sound like Aunt Marty. Don't worry, I can take care of myself. And I've got a lot of weapons handy." He waved around his workroom, and I could see plenty of gleaming chisels with nice sharp edges. And lots more things I didn't recognize, but all with wicked points or evil blades. I relaxed just a bit.

"Good. Well, I'd better get over to the police station and hand the stuff over."

Henry slid the plastic box with the fragments into a padded envelope and handed the envelope to me. "Will you get them back?"

"I hope so. They're not exactly evidence, although if they find the matching escutcheon, the one we have might be. I'm not go-

ing to worry about it now. I just plan to give them to the detective."

"Oh, hey, I kept some of the smaller wooden bits," Henry said before I could leave. "The brasses were pretty much standard issue, but I'd like to run a few more tests on the wood, see if anything pops up."

"Sure. Since the police are only interested in the metal, no one will miss them You run whatever you think is best and let me know if you find anything useful. Thanks, Henry!"

"No problem." Henry escorted me out again, and I turned toward the Roundhouse, aka police headquarters.

CHAPTER 15

The Roundhouse, which houses the Philadelphia Police Department (although possibly not for much longer, if the city's movers and shakers have their way), is a rather odd building built in the 1960s, and, yes, parts of it are round, or at least curved. I'd been inside it before, and not under the happiest of circumstances. I found it hard to believe that I was entering it voluntarily now, but I was fulfilling a police request, hoping to score a few points against any future issues. Besides, it was my civic duty to present potential evidence in a major crime, even if the police weren't officially calling it a crime. What Detective Hrivnak would make of what I gave her, I couldn't guess.

Clutching my plastic box in its bag, I entered by the front door and stated my business. Someone called upstairs and ascertained that Detective Hrivnak was busy

in a meeting and asked, would I wait? I thought waiting was preferable to leaving and coming back again, so I sat in a hard chair and stared into space while I tried to construct my story.

All Hrivnak knew was that the bartender had seen a small, flat, curly metal object in the dead man's hand, as she had told me. So had someone else, who had buddied up with Carnell Scruggs, and who had left with him. A short time later Scruggs was struck by a car, and there was no metal object found on his body. It was a rather fragile link between that man and what I held in my hand, but it was still a possible one.

Twenty minutes later, Detective Hrivnak finally appeared. "So it really is you. What do you want?"

"I may have some evidence in that death next to our place. Can we take this somewhere private?"

"Yeah, whatever." She turned and went around the screening devices. I went through the screening, though, of course, my "evidence," being metal, set things off, so we had to sort that out. Hrivnak was not happy, but she didn't say a word until we reached her small, messy office. "So, what you got?"

"We found something in the basement of

the Society when we were cleaning it out." I was careful not to specify *when* we found it, since we'd been holding on to it for a few days now. "Since that's where the victim was working on the day he died, we wondered if it might be connected." I opened the plastic box and withdrew the escutcheon. "I thought this might be a match to that 'flat, curly metal thing' that the victim showed to the bartender."

"What is it?" Hrivnak asked, her eyes not leaving the piece.

"It's called an escutcheon — it's a plate that goes behind a drawer handle on a lot of eighteenth-century furniture."

"Where's the furniture?"

I pulled the rest of the items out of my box. "This is all we found: a couple of hinges, some screws, and some chunks of wood." I didn't mention that we'd held back some of them.

"Where did you say it was found?"

"In a pit beneath the basement floor. That was the last part of the building to be cleared out for our construction project. That's where Scruggs was working. I'm sure the construction foreman will confirm that."

"Huh," Hrivnak said, then stopped. I resisted my impulse to start babbling about the theories my friends and I had come up

with. Let her draw her own conclusions.

She didn't appear impressed by my fabulous find, and gave me no credit for bringing it to her, even though she'd been the one to ask for it. But at the same time I was relieved: if she didn't think it was important, then she wouldn't push it any further, and the Society wouldn't be officially involved. I knew full well that Marty wasn't going to give up her search for more information, but I wasn't about to tell the detective that.

I got tired of waiting. "Well, I'm sorry I bothered you, then." I stood up and reached for the items, but she stopped me.

"Leave 'em here. I'll see if that bartender recognizes the es-thing."

"Will I get them back?"

"What do you care?"

"They came from the Society. We collect and keep things. This is a piece from our history."

"Fine. Talk to me after we've wrapped up this thing with Scruggs's death."

Since I had her attention, I thought it was worth asking, "You have any leads?"

"That's police business. Where's your FBI buddy?"

"What's he got to do with this?" *Why was she asking?*

"Just wondering — thought you two were

204

a team." She hesitated for a moment. "There is one thing . . ."

"Yes?" I prompted.

"We figure that driver got it right — the man was moving backward when she hit him, based on the accident reconstruction. Lot of scratches and bruises on him, but it's hard to say if that was because of the car or something else. Like someone pushing him."

"But he was still okay not long before, in the bar, right? No fight there?"

"Yeah," she replied reluctantly. "And it's a pretty tight timeline. He left with that other guy, who we're still looking for, but the street cams don't show them and we don't know how long they stayed together. Anyway, whatever happened, happened pretty quick after they left that bar."

"Was he on his way home, do you know?"

"Maybe — he was headed that direction, toward Spruce. He'd gotten paid for the work he'd done, so he could have been going to another bar to celebrate."

One of his coworkers had mentioned that he'd been paid in cash. "You told me he'd had a couple of beers at the first bar?"

"Yeah, but he wasn't drunk enough to stumble, if that's what you're thinking. Not without help."

Detective Hrivnak was being very chatty,

for her. After all, if the Society wasn't involved, she had no reason to share anything with me.

She stood up, signaling that our chat was over. "Let me take you downstairs."

She escorted me back to the first floor, and I left the building feeling kind of deflated. All right, I'd done my duty. No one could say I was hiding anything. Of course, she hadn't asked any of the right questions, but I didn't feel I had to volunteer information. And it wasn't information I had kept quiet about, really — more like educated guesses, and, I'd be willing to admit, a lot of wishful thinking. I wasn't looking to make trouble. I didn't have to — it kept finding me.

It was now past three. I contemplated briefly stopping by James's office, which was only a block away, but I'd see him soon enough. I should go back to work for a couple of hours, and hope that Marty didn't spring any more surprises on me.

She didn't. The only surprise was a call from Hrivnak about an hour later. "The guy at the bar recognizes that whatchamacallit," she said without preamble. "It worth much?"

"Not without the piece of furniture it belonged to. Nobody would want to steal it,

206

if that's what you mean."

"You aren't missing any, over at your place?"

"We don't have room for furniture in the collections here." Which was sort of true. Of course, now would be the moment to elaborate on some of our suspicions, starting with the likelihood that both of those brass pieces had been in the pit for a hundred years. That sure wouldn't make the detective any happier, so I kept my mouth shut.

"Huh. Well, I'll hang on to it for now, see if anything pops up. Thanks for stopping by." She hung up. At least she'd thanked me.

Then Marty showed up, either because she'd been eavesdropping or because she had some weird kind of radar. "What's the news?" she asked.

"Hrivnak says the bartender ID'd the escutcheon. Definitely, not maybe. She's going to keep it for now."

I couldn't read Marty's expression. On the one hand, it was the first validation of our convoluted theory: the escutcheons were a pair, they had both come out of the pit, and Scruggs had carried one away with him. On the other hand, I wasn't sure Marty or I were looking forward to following that

theory to the conclusion we'd sketched in for it. It was troubling that we wouldn't have known about any of it, save for the death of a stranger, and it was all too possible he'd died only because he'd picked up something he thought looked pretty.

"What'd you tell her?" Marty asked.

"As little as possible, I guess. She didn't ask much — I think she wanted to talk to the bartender first. I don't think she believed it was important, but now she does. What do we do now?"

"Look at the list," Marty said. "I'm checking out the history of portable writing desks. There aren't a lot of 'em, or maybe they weren't important enough to talk about. I don't know how they were carried around. Slung over a horse? In a backpack? So I need to do some homework. Maybe it was where they kept the good silver, for all I know — more than just letters, anyway."

"Was Henry any help with that?"

"Henry's a good kid, but he's more into the fixing than the history. He can tell you how old a piece is, and what it's made of, but who made it? Not so much. He usually calls me. He give you anything new?"

"Only that our escutcheon was a clear match to the Terwilliger ones, which we'd already guessed. But there must be other

local experts on colonial furniture, if you're stuck on the lap desk part."

"Yeah. Let me think about it and see who I can ask. Maybe someone at Sommerhof." Trust Marty to know people at that renowned institution, even though it was in Delaware. She stood up abruptly. "I'm going back to the files." She disappeared before I had time to say good-bye.

James called minutes later to say he was headed home, and did I need a ride? I told him I did, and gathered up my things. I was waiting on the curb when he arrived, and climbed into the car quickly. "Hey," I said as I buckled my seat belt.

"Hey to you. Hard day?" James said, pulling away smoothly.

"Mentally if not physically, although I did do my share of walking. I almost stopped by to say hello this afternoon, but I thought that would be complicated. Don't I need security clearance or something to get into your offices?"

"We're not that bad — just give me a call if you want to come in. Why were you in the neighborhood?"

"I stopped by the Roundhouse to turn over the brass bits and splinters to Detective Hrivnak."

"I see," James said neutrally. "What did

she say?"

"Nothing at the time. But she called back later to say that the bartender said the escutcheon matched the one Scruggs showed him."

"Ah."

I turned in my seat to face him. "Ah, what? 'Ah, I'm making random sounds because I don't know what to say but I think I have to say something'? Or, 'Ah, that's what I expected'? Or maybe, 'Ah, now you've stepped in it, Nell'? Which is it?"

"Don't bite my head off, Nell. I was just acknowledging that I'd heard you. And I was trying to think about what that might mean, as I navigated this two-ton hunk of metal through streets that were laid out over three hundred years ago for much smaller vehicles."

I must still be on edge, I realized. "I'm sorry I snapped at you. Look, without going into details, Marty came by with a — well, I guess you'd call it a matrix of suppositions and what we would need to confirm or eliminate any of them. Determining that the two escutcheons matched was the first item on that list. We guessed right, at least so far. I just don't like where we go from here. Maybe I don't want us to be right. Maybe I'd like this to be an overblown fantasy that

will simply collapse from its own idiocy."

"Why? I'm not just making conversation, you know. I know you, and I know you don't back off easily. Why with this?"

"Because it involves so much — my friends, your family, the place I work for and am responsible for. Somebody is going to come out of this unhappy, and that's probably Marty, because she'll never view her grandfather and maybe her father in the same way, if we're right."

"She already knows that, but it's not stopping her."

"I know! That's why I can't just tell her to drop it. If she can face the truth, I don't have a choice except to back her up and follow her lead. Sorry, that phrasing makes no sense, but you know what I mean."

"I do. I understand."

I struggled to get a grip on myself. Where had that little tempest come from? "I know you do. I'm just venting."

"Feel better?"

"A little. But I'd feel even better after a good meal."

"That part I can handle."

We found a nice restaurant in Chestnut Hill, one we hadn't tried before, and after a couple of glasses of wine and some good food, the world looked much brighter to

me. When we got home, before I could even hang up my coat, James turned me around and wrapped his arms around me and held on, and I leaned into him. I was not alone in this battle, whether or not the FBI was involved. I was working hard to get used to having someone to depend on. It felt good.

"Thank you," I said into his coat.

"I'm here, Nell. We'll figure this out."

I believed him.

CHAPTER 16

Poor Carnell Scruggs had been dead for nearly a week, and we were no closer to knowing why, save for our discovery of one small piece of metal that might have had nothing to do with his death. I'd watched enough cop shows on television to know that if a murder wasn't solved quickly, it might never be. On the other hand, I also knew that history didn't move quickly. If this was a crime that was related to another crime that had taken place a century earlier, we were sort of on track, or at least not *off* track. Heck, we'd solved older crimes than that.

James dropped me off at work, and his parting comment was that he had an all-hands meeting after work he had to attend, so I'd have to make my own way home and I'd be on my own for dinner. I assured him I'd be fine with both. I could take the train home, though I enjoyed our shared

commute.

When I walked into the Society, I found it a beehive of activity. The reading room doors would remain closed to give whatever determined researchers came in a little more peace and quiet, but the big main room beyond the lobby had somehow become a staging area, with boxes both of files and of incoming shelving and tools and whatever. At least the crew had had the foresight to cover the floor with sheets of plywood, because replacing it was not in the budget at the moment.

Felicity Soames, our head librarian, was standing in front of the reading room doors, arms folded, looking disgruntled. I went over to say hello.

"How long will this go on?" she all but yelled in my ear. "Our researchers are going to pitch a fit!"

"The contractor promised only a couple of weeks, but you know how that goes," I yelled back. "There are almost always surprises with construction."

I could see Felicity's sigh, even if I couldn't hear it. "Tell me it will be wonderful when it's finished?"

"Fingers crossed!" I shouted, then pointed toward myself, the elevator, then up. Felicity nodded, then returned to the relative quiet

of the reading room, ready to soothe patrons when and if they arrived after we opened for the day.

Upstairs I was surprised to find Latoya waiting for me by Eric's desk, looking impatient. "Were we supposed to meet?" I asked her.

"No, we had nothing scheduled. I thought I should touch base, though. With all the collections shuffling around the building, I'm concerned that some things may be . . . misplaced."

As if we hadn't already reviewed the plans for temporary relocation of records more than once, with the entire staff. I suppressed a sigh. "Come on into my office," I said, leading the way. "You want coffee?"

When she nodded, Eric jumped up and went down the hall.

Once we were settled in the office, I decided to take the bull by the horns. "Are your concerns specific or general?"

"You mean, am I just worrying about the total chaos under my purview, or do I have reason to believe that specific items are being — how shall I put this — systematically misplaced?"

"Are you talking about theft?"

"Not yet, but you have to admit the possibility is there."

"You mean the construction crew?"

"I do."

That was not something I wanted to hear, especially now.

Eric appeared with two coffee mugs, and Latoya stopped speaking until he had gone. Didn't she trust him? Or did she not trust anyone?

After Eric had shut the door, I pressed, "Can you be more specific?" I'd worked with Latoya for several years now, and I knew that in general she was unflappable. She might also be a bit stiff and arrogant, but she knew our collections and she was diligent in managing them. If she was worried enough to come talk to me, I should be worried, too. It came with the job.

"Nothing specific," she admitted, "but I'm always troubled when there are a lot of strangers coming and going in the building. The construction crew has more or less unrestricted access, and there's little oversight. Before you say it, I know they're bonded and all that, and that we're insured against loss, but that's not really the point. If items from our collections go missing, they're irreplaceable, no matter what their financial value."

She had a point, of course. "I won't argue with your concerns, Latoya, but I'm not

sure what more we can do. Bob is keeping an eye on things in front. The construction workers sign in and out each day — they'd do that anyway, because they're paid by the hour. If they wandered into the public spaces they'd be pretty obvious, but there's no way we can watch all the stacks at once, and I'll admit they can easily gain access to them. I suppose we could ask the contractor to hire extra people to check every bag that's going out the door, which we can't afford to do, but I'm not sure how we can trust the watchers, either. Do you have any ideas?"

"Not really. I just wanted to go on record as having said it may be a problem. I hope it's not."

Yes, Latoya, your derriere is covered, should anything disappear in the course of renovation, thank you very much. "Is Ben providing much help?"

She nodded. "He is, despite having been here only a short time. He has created an excellent matrix and has been scrupulous about tracking what items have been shifted and where they have gone. He's also been proactive about evaluating the capacity of the new shelving and assigning priorities to collections that have seen the most use over the past few years — as long as we've been

tracking them electronically. He was a good choice for the position."

Coming from Latoya, that was high praise indeed, especially since Ben had more or less been presented as a *fait accompli* when we brought him in — he was an old friend of James, and he had really needed the job.

"I'm glad to hear you say that. So his management and data skills are making up for his lack of historic collections experience?"

"So it would appear." She stood up. "That's all I wanted to say. Unless you want to add anything?"

It was only then that I realized there *was* something more I could do. "This may seem a bit late in the game, but could you pull together the records for earlier renovations? I don't mean the architectural plans — I think the architect has all those. What I was thinking of were things like budgets, or board discussions during the planning stages. Would that be hard?"

"Those records might be distributed in several places — for example, the board minutes would be in one place, while the collections records would be in another. But the records are not extensive, and Ben and I have already begun assembling them. I'll make another pass at the collections files, in

case I missed anything, and then I'll make copies of everything for you. When do you want them?"

"It's not urgent. Mostly it's to satisfy my own curiosity. Maybe we can get an article out of it, for our website. You know, a 'then and now' kind of thing."

She nodded. "That might be entertaining. I can have most of it together in a couple of days."

"Thank you, Latoya. And I'm glad you came to me with your other worries." To my surprise, I meant it.

Having heard Latoya's side of the situation, it occurred to me that I ought to talk with Ben. I hadn't had much contact with him since he'd been hired, and I was happy that I could pass on Latoya's compliment to him. I wandered downstairs and into the processing room, where Ben was dug into his corner with the specially altered desk that accommodated his wheelchair. I came up behind him, trying not to startle him. "Hey, Ben, how's it going?"

He swiveled in his chair. "Hi, Nell. As well as can be expected. You need something?"

"Nothing specific. I'm trying to keep an eye on a lot of things at once." I pulled up a chair and leaned toward him, though there was no one to overhear. "I also wanted to

let you know that Latoya thinks you're doing a great job with managing the movements of our collections during the renovation process."

His eyes lit up. "That's good to hear. The challenge is to keep track of the stuff — it doesn't matter whether they're priceless antiques or boxes of rubber bands. You know, where they started, where they're supposed to go when this is all finished, and where they wander to in between, so we know where everything is at all times. Of course, there are other specific variables here, like frequency of accession, fragility, storage requirements, but those can all be factored in."

He really did sound in command of the situation. "Sounds good to me. I know I wouldn't want to try to do it. By the way, I asked Latoya to find records from our past renovation campaigns, and that would include the construction of this new building on top of the old. Lissa may have told you the chronology — this building opened to the public in 1910, although it was finished in 1907, and I imagine there was a lot of sorting out of the collections in those three years. Obviously the collections were much smaller then, but so was the staff. I was curious about how they kept track of

things. She said you two had already started looking at those?"

"Sure have. I needed to know what was where before it went somewhere else. I'll keep my eyes open for anything more historical. How's everything else?"

"Like, how is the great experiment of living with James going?" Since Ben knew James, his curiosity didn't trouble me, although as a rule I didn't share the details with the rest of the staff. "Fine so far, but it's early days yet."

"I'm glad. He's always been kind of a loner."

"So have I, I guess. What do you get when you put two loners together? You know, that sounds like the start of a bad joke, but I don't have a punch line for it. If we ever get things settled, we'll have to have a house-warming party." Even as I said it, I wondered how that would work: FBI agents plus historic researchers? It would be an odd mix — if any of them came. But no doubt we'd have plenty of Terwilligers. I stood up. "Thanks, Ben. You'll let me know if you see any red flags with the construction or with stuff migrating around the building?" I wasn't about to tell him about Latoya's concerns — I'd let her handle that.

"Of course. Maybe next time we do this

we could get GPS trackers for each box and a computer program to follow them all over time."

"Interesting idea, but probably expensive. And I hope there won't be a next time, at least not on my watch!"

Since I seemed to be on a roll, I decided to stop by Shelby's office and add one more piece to the puzzle. I stuck my head in the door to find her desk covered with stacks of paper. "You look busy," I said.

She looked up. "Good, because I am busy. You need something?"

"I was wondering if you could find fund-raising records for earlier building campaigns — you know, begging letters and what they claim about what the Society was doing and what was planned? Contribution records? I'd love to go back to the construction of this building, but's that more than a century, and I have no idea if there are records that old, or where to find them."

"Oh, sure, give me the easy jobs." Shelby softened her comment with a grin. "You want this yesterday?"

"No rush — end of the week is fine. I've asked Latoya and Ben to look out for the same kind of thing for their areas of responsibility. When I put it all together, I'll see

what we've got and what we can do with it."

"Sounds good. Now go away and let me get something finished."

"Yes, ma'am!" I left and went back to my office, and was about to dig into my daily paperwork pile when I realized there was one more detail I wanted to follow up on. I walked out to stand in front of Eric's desk.

"Eric, you know where the board records are, right?"

"Sure do. You need them?"

"It occurs to me that I don't know much about the early board members, particularly the ones who oversaw the construction of this building. I've asked Latoya and Ben to go through collections records for that time, and Shelby to find contribution records, but I don't know the people involved. Can you hunt those down those old ones for me?"

"I can do that. When would you like them?"

"Friday would be okay."

"I'll find them. Anything else?"

"Nope, not now. I see you left me a pile of goodies on my desk, so I'll get right on them."

Back in my office again, I mentally patted myself on the back for having figured out what details I might be able to contribute

to this investigation. Of course, the records might be missing, or they might have nothing useful in them (board minutes in particular tended to be dry as dust, and for all I knew, when there were only a few people involved back in the day, maybe they'd skipped taking minutes at all). But at least I would have checked. I set to work reading what Eric had left for me.

The day passed quickly; Eric brought me a takeout sandwich so I could stay focused on my own work. Everything was peaceful until Marty showed up about four, looking unhappy.

I sat back in my chair and stretched. "What's up?" I asked, although I probably didn't want to know.

"I've been doing research on lap desks," she said.

"You mean like the one we think was in the pit?"

"The very same. How much do you want to know?"

"What do I need to know?"

"They were mostly an English phenomenon, often used for military expeditions, but they also showed up in libraries and drawing rooms. They usually had a slanted front for the writing part, when they were open, and often, inside, there were wells to hold

containers for ink and sand for blotting the ink. And sometimes there would be one or two side drawers to hold letters and so forth."

"And drawers mean drawer pulls, right?"

"Yup. Some of the lap desks even had secret drawers, although I have no clue where you could hide one of those in a smallish box. There was a particular military style, also called a campaign box. You want details?"

"Sure, why not?" I thought Marty must be leading up to some point, and I was in no rush.

"They were often made from mahogany, with reinforced brass corners. Early ones had drop-down handles — I guess later they kind of streamlined them with inset handles, which makes sense if you're traveling with them. Bottom line, these weren't necessarily pretty parlor pieces — these were mostly made for business. Think of them as the briefcases of their day."

"Okay, that's nice," I said.

"Ah, but there's more. Thomas Jefferson had one he said he designed himself before the Continental Congress in 1776. A little presumptuous, since we know there were plenty in England, but maybe he wanted a colonial product, or wanted to control the

design. His had a folding top and a drawer on one end."

"You're not going to tell me that's the one the Society had, I hope?"

"Nah, it's safely tucked away at the Smithsonian. Impeccable provenance — he made a gift of it to his granddaughter, and her descendants gave it to the nation in 1880. Anyway, what's more important for our purposes is that Jefferson asked a Philadelphia cabinetmaker to execute his plan for his so-called writing box. A man named Benjamin Randolph, who set up shop here in Philadelphia in 1764 and did well enough that he moved to a bigger place on Chestnut Street."

I was about to ask why Marty was telling me this, but I realized I could guess. "Don't tell me: this Randolph made furniture for John Terwilliger."

She gave me a thumbs-up sign. "He did. Plus he left good records of the Terwilliger sales, which we've got right here at the Society. He closed up shop and retired in 1778." Marty paused, and when she finally spoke she enunciated very clearly. "Randolph made a lap desk or campaign chest or whatever the heck you want to call it for General John Terwilliger, along with a lot of other furniture." She waited one beat, two.

226

"There is no record that any such item was ever in the Society's collections. Nor any record that a member of the Terwilliger family sold it, at least not publicly. It appears in the general's will, when he dies, and in a couple of heirs' later wills. Unfortunately some of the family stopped making detailed inventories in the later nineteenth century."

She lapsed into silence, which gave me time to work through what she had just told me. Marty had confirmed that lap desks were in general use in the later 1700s, and that was the date we had tentatively assigned to the hypothetical box we had found in the pit. Some of those lap desks did have drawers with handles. That was good. We could point to a link between such a box and a Philadelphia craftsman who had made pieces for the Terwilliger family, at the right time and the right place, and there was proof that he'd sold one to General John. Also good. And Terwilliger family records showed that Marty's grandfather had included a lap desk in his personal inventory. Odds were good that it was the same one. But it had never appeared in the Society's acquisition records, although all the other items the family had donated were well documented.

I looked Marty squarely in the eye.

"You're not going to try to tell me there were two boxes, are you?"

"Nope. The broken bits we found must have come from the original lap desk. But that doesn't tell us squat about why it ended up in that pit in pieces," Marty said reluctantly.

"So what do we do now?"

"I have no idea."

CHAPTER 17

"So do we back up and start over?" I suggested. "Reverse ourselves and say that the brass *didn't* come from that particular lap desk but could have come from something else altogether? Or that we're barking up the wrong tree and the desk didn't contain something important? It was there — in pieces — because some workman probably broke it sometime in 1907 and dumped the pieces into the convenient hole and hoped no one would notice, and nobody did."

"So why is that man dead?" Marty said.

"He drank too much on payday, then got into a brawl with a stranger, who led him into a dark alley and beat him up and then shoved him in front of a car?"

"You think the police haven't thought of that? Besides, nothing was taken, except maybe that escutcheon," Marty snapped back.

"Of course they have — that's what they

do. Of course that's the answer they'd like — it's simple. I'm surprised that the detective even went to the trouble of asking the bartender if he recognized that piece of brass. And I bet she was surprised when he did. But she did, which tells me that she still has some suspicions about the death. It still might have had nothing to do with Carnell Scruggs's death. And I'm sure she and her people have looked for the other guy at the bar, but there's not a lot to work with there."

"What about street cameras?" Marty asked, sitting up straighter.

"She said the coverage between the bar and here was lousy. What are you thinking?" I countered.

Marty leaned forward, elbows on her knees. "I see two possibilities. One, this was a chance encounter at the bar — guy wanders in, sees the other guy with something interesting, goes out with him, and whacks him for reasons related or not to the brass thing — maybe Carnell was flashing his pay for the day. The second one is that the guy in the bar knew about whatever Carnell had found in the pit and staged the accidental meeting at the bar, then killed him and took it. All we really know is that Carnell had the

thing, he died, and then he didn't have the thing."

Marty had raised a troubling idea. "Wait — back up," I said. "Why would mystery guy know Carnell had it? Or care?"

"Maybe you should be asking, who else knew about it at all?"

I didn't like the direction this was going. "You mean, like the rest of the construction crew?"

"Yeah. Maybe Carnell was the first to claim it, but maybe somebody else saw him pick it up and knew what it was."

Was this getting a bit too far-fetched? "But that would mean that one of the construction crew could recognize a piece of antique brass hardware *and* had some reason to care."

"That's just one scenario. I didn't say it was a good one." Marty didn't seem miffed by my criticism. "Or it could have been someone else. The contractor. The architect — he must have checked in with the crew to make sure everything was ready to begin the new work. Or someone on the staff here."

That last one hit me like a punch in the gut. "I can't imagine who would be interested — except maybe you, Marty. I wouldn't have known what I was looking at,

at least until it was cleaned up."

"I'm not about to point any fingers," Marty said. "All I'm saying is that if Hrivnak looked at street cam footage for that night, between here and that bar, she might see *someone* following our dead guy from this end, even if she couldn't tell who it was."

That was not a reassuring thought. "There are always people on the street. And I'm not exactly in a position to ask her, you know. She's already given me more information than she had to."

"You told her what we suspect, when you gave her the brass bits?"

"No, I didn't. I didn't think she'd be very interested in our rather fragile string of hypotheses."

"But she did follow up with the bartender, which tells us something."

"True. But I can't see her making the leaps of logic that we did."

"You've got a point there." Marty thought for a moment. "There is another option," she finally said, leveling her gaze on me.

It took me a moment to work out what she meant. "No! I will not ask James to do any favors, legally or otherwise. Besides, what could he do?"

"Get a better look at the street cam footage, or enhance it, or whatever those people

do. I can ask him, leave you out of it."

"No. Marty, that makes no difference. You're a relative and a friend and a member of the Society — your asking him is only marginally different than my asking him. You can't just treat him as a handy free pass to any kind of restricted information. It's not fair to him." My voice kept going up, in pitch and in volume. I felt really strongly about this. I was not going to put my relationship with James at risk merely to make our crime-solving a little easier. No way. And I wouldn't let Martha Terwilliger do it, either. Unfortunately Marty usually did what Marty wanted to do.

I softened my tone. "Please, Marty — there's no need to involve him. You and I are working with the police, as we should. The FBI does not belong in this mix."

Marty looked at me for a long moment, then her shoulders slumped. "All right, I hear you. I can see your point, even if I don't like it. So without James's help, what do we do next?"

"Go back to that first list you made. If we assume that the brass, whatever it belonged to, was why the man was killed, we know that he had the escutcheon when he went to the bar, and we have an eyewitness — the bartender. You've looked into lap desks,

233

and that kind of piece fits what little we know. You're found a connection with the Terwilliger furniture through the brass. You know that the same cabinetmaker made lap desks for others and made other furniture for the Terwilligers. But then we hit a brick wall. We could make an effort to find out what other pieces the furniture maker made using the same brass fittings, and who he sold them to. Henry told us they were commonly used in Philadelphia at that time. Maybe the Terwilliger connection is just a coincidence."

"Yeah, right. You don't really believe that, do you, Nell?" Marty said.

"No, I guess I don't. Where does that leave us?"

"What about what we guess was *in* the box?"

"We're still not sure anything *was* in the box. It could have been empty. Could Henry tell if it was broken before it went into the pit, and how much earlier? All we do know is that whatever it once held — papers or objects — was not in the pit. Or it might have been in the pit but Carnell pocketed it the same way he did the escutcheon. Though, again, if it exists, whoever pushed him took it. It couldn't have been too big, because there were other people

watching when he came out of the pit. So he had to be able to hide it under what he was wearing. Assuming he thought it was worth taking." I was talking more to myself than to Marty. If there *was* something missing, what could it be?

"You have a plan?" Marty asked.

"Maybe I do, kind of through the back door. I want to look at this from the Society's perspective, and I've already started that process — I've asked Ben, Latoya, Shelby, and Eric to look at our in-house records for any Society documents about that particular time period, just before we know the pit was closed up. One" — I started ticking off points on one hand — "how the collections were managed during the building construction. I've already asked Latoya and Ben to pull those records. Two, I've got Shelby looking into bequests and begging letters from the same period, to see if there's any reference to specific collections items in those and who they came from. Three, I've asked Eric to track down the board minutes and correspondence, to see if there was any discussion of collections. Surely if the Society owned a Terwilliger lap desk, somebody would have mentioned it somewhere?"

"Of course they would. My family kept

good records, before and after they were part of the Society. You know that. The lap desk is not in the Terwilliger inventory for the gift to the Society. Look, we know that my grandfather had the lap desk at one time. We have his own inventory from when he made the first donation to the Society, and several later ones. They're in his own handwriting — I recognize it — and the lap desk is *not* included. My father followed the same path, and obviously I know his hand-writing, too. I've been through his papers, and there is no mention of a lap desk. If you believe the documents, the desk was never here."

"Marty, of course I respect your expertise here, but things happen. Maybe it was a late addition. Maybe your grandfather forgot or slipped up. And maybe this whole thing is a wild-goose chase. But it's easy enough to bring together all the documents we have relating to the construction in the early twentieth century and see if there's anything we haven't seen before, or that we misinter-preted the first time we looked at it. We've got a real asset in Ben in that regard, because he has no preconceptions."

Marty shook her head. "I want you to be wrong, since I've been living with this stuff all my life and I'd argue I knew it inside

out. But at the same time, unless we find something real, this whole thing goes away, and I don't want that, either, not until we know what really happened, if that's even remotely possible. So prove me wrong, if you can. And we'll do it the old-fashioned way, with hands-on research. And without James's help. Good enough for you?"

"Yes. Thank you."

"Don't thank me. I've got a very personal stake in all this. It's my family."

And the Society was my institution, but I didn't need to tell Marty that — and I didn't feel quite the emotional and psychological attachment to this building and what we held within it that Marty did to her multiple generations of Terwilligers.

"I understand, Marty, and I know what it means to you. Look, once everybody has collected all the bits and pieces from all over the building, let's set up somewhere central where we can spread it out and cross-reference everything. I don't know that anybody's looked at the whole picture, at least since this building opened."

"How about at my place?" Marty asked.

I considered that. Since Marty lived alone, she had some room to spare, and it was close by. I was reluctant to let our documents out of the building, but on the other

hand, it seemed like a good idea to keep what we had collected away from prying eyes. "No offense, Marty, but I'd rather keep them here. We can find a safe place for the documents."

Marty looked frustrated, but she gave in. "I understand. Besides, who's to say they'll take up more than one lousy folder?" She looked at her watch and leaped from her chair. "Jeez, look at the time! I'm meeting Eliot in fifteen minutes."

"Wait just a second, Marty," I interrupted. "If we believe your second scenario, there could be someone at the Society who knows something about what's going on. We can't afford to spread this around any more than we already have."

"You said you talked to Latoya and Ben and Shelby. That going to be a problem?"

"When I asked them to look for the records, I specifically did *not* tell them we were looking into the murder. It was an appropriate request coming from me, and we can use the information. I can't stop them from making inferences, but I do trust those people."

Marty gave me a searching look before responding. "So we're talking about collections management, period. Got it. I've got to run, but we'll pick this up tomorrow, and

by then maybe we'll have more to work with, if people come through. Bye!"

And she was gone before I could open my mouth. Just as well: I needed to sort through what I thought and what I guessed — again. It was a moving target. I reached for my bag and pulled out a train schedule. After ten years living in Bryn Mawr I'd memorized those trains, but I hadn't yet had the chance to work out the best way to get to Chestnut Hill. The next train left in fifteen minutes, so I could just make it if I hurried.

Eric stuck his head in. "You leaving now?"

"Unless you give me a reason not to," I replied.

"No, ma'am! Just checking to see if it was okay if I left, too."

"You go right ahead."

"Thanks. And I'll get onto that, uh, project you asked about first thing in the morning."

"See you tomorrow, then. Hey, I'll walk down with you."

The halls were empty as we went down to the first floor. I nodded at Bob, still at the desk, and Eric and I went outside. Eric turned toward the river, and I angled my way toward City Hall and Suburban Station. I caught my train with two minutes to spare, and let my mind drift for the half-

239

hour ride.

When I reached Chestnut Hill it was beginning to grow dark. I wasn't sure what this neighborhood would be like at night, later in the year. It was lovely — residential, with large old houses and broad, well-maintained sidewalks and plenty of streetlights, but it was still within city limits. *Don't borrow trouble, Nell.*

I made the ten-minute walk home with no problems, taking the front steps quickly and letting myself in. James and I had talked briefly about the existing alarm system, but I was ambivalent about them. My former home in Bryn Mawr hadn't had one, but I'd had nothing worth stealing there. Of course, I had the same lack of valuable stuff here, but the house looked as though there *should* be good pickings, whatever the reality.

Once inside, the door locked behind me, I wondered if I'd ever be able to live up to the house's standards — or if I even wanted to. I changed into something comfortable, and since James had said he would be late, I rummaged in the refrigerator for something to eat, eventually heating up some leftovers and helping myself to a glass of wine.

While I ate I thought about the problem

of "stuff." I was the president of a collecting institution, with literally millions of items under my care, but I had never been infected by the collecting bug. I acquired things that meant something to me, and I had inherited a few, but I had never felt the desire to surround myself with material objects, no matter what their commercial worth. What I did want was furniture that matched the general style of the house combined with comfort and convenience — a set of furniture where James and I could sprawl without worrying about spilling anything, which luckily eliminated any valuable antiques. Did such a thing exist? I hadn't yet seen anything that fit that description. But we needed *something:* I didn't plan to live surrounded by cardboard packing boxes indefinitely.

James returned around eight. When I heard his key in the door, I had a fleeting image of greeting him wrapped in plastic wrap with a chilled martini in my hand, but I decided that was too much work, and besides, I didn't have either plastic wrap or gin. He'd have to settle for just me.

He didn't seem to mind.

CHAPTER 18

The next morning James and I were running late — no time to talk over coffee and muffins. We drove in together, although James had to pay attention to crazy drivers, and I didn't want to distract him with conversation.

"How'd your meeting go yesterday?" I finally ventured when the cars on the highway started moving more smoothly.

"About what you'd expect. Before you ask, nothing I can talk about. What did you do yesterday?"

"Nothing I can talk about," I replied, only a bit facetiously.

"Which I assume means you saw Marty."

"Yes. Also Latoya, Shelby, and Ben. Busy day. Didn't even get out for lunch."

"How's Ben working out? If you can talk about that?"

"Latoya actually said nice things about him, which is huge for her. He's been a big

help with this planning for the shuffling of collections all over the building. And, yes, I passed Latoya's comments on to him — I figured he should hear it, in case she doesn't tell him herself."

"I'm glad he can handle things." Back to silence.

After a few more miles, I said, "You know, maybe we should draw up a chart of what we *can* talk about safely."

"Anything, as long as it doesn't involve crime," James said.

"Even if it's a long-ago crime?"

"Probably safer to steer away from that, too. You've already seen how they bleed into the present."

"What if we uncovered evidence of a foiled plot to assassinate George Washington?"

"Have you?"

"No. But it's possible, isn't it?"

He smiled at my persistence, without turning his head. "With you, anything is possible. My first guess would be that the crime or conspiracy or whatever would not fall under the purview of the modern FBI, given that the parties are long since deceased. They are, aren't they? No zombies?"

"Not that I know of. Who should I call if I encounter a zombie crime?"

"Not me, please. We don't handle half-dead perpetrators. Or do I mean undead?"

We piffled along those lines the rest of the way into the city. I told James to park where he normally would, near his office, because I figured I could use the exercise of walking to mine while weather permitted. "Will you be late again?" I asked as we climbed out of the car.

"Not that I know of, but I'll call you later if things change."

We set off in our separate directions. It took me less than ten minutes to reach the Society, where I found Marty waiting for me on the front steps. That was unusual, since I knew she had keys to every door in the place, not to mention all the security codes.

"Good morning," I greeted her. "What are you doing waiting out here?"

Up close, I could see she looked uneasy. "I wanted to talk with you outside the building. I'm not sure who to trust anymore. Coffee?"

"Sure," I replied, mystified. I followed her around the corner to a small coffee shop, where neither of us saw anyone we recognized. When we were seated with thick mugs of bad coffee in front of us, I said, "What's wrong?"

"How many employees do you have at the Society?" Marty asked.

I had to stop and think. "Maybe forty? Of course, they're not all there at the same time. Some are part-timers. Some are cleaning staff, and they usually come in after hours. And don't forget the construction crew that Carnell worked with. Why do you want to know?"

"Because what if there was a second thing that came out of the pit? If it's related to Scruggs's death, we need to know who might have known about it. There are a lot of people who have pretty much free access to go anywhere in the Society building — and who can lurk in dark corners eavesdropping on private conversations. And whilst in hiding could have seen Carnell pocket whatever it was."

"Marty, you're starting to sound paranoid. Can we have a reality check here? You have just postulated that someone saw what Carnell picked up, after it had sat for over a century in a hole in the ground, and that person, rather than telling me or Latoya or someone appropriate at the Society like any honest person would do, decided to pursue Carnell for some unknown reason and quite possibly caused his death. If you heard this story, would you believe it? And what are

we supposed to do about it?" I didn't point out that Marty was suggesting we might have a killer at the Society.

She didn't answer for a minute. Then she said, "I might have an idea. How about we open this up, instead of trying to keep it all secret?"

"What do you have in mind? And won't that make things worse? Either the person behind this will panic and do more harm, or he — or she — will disappear, once *they* know *we* know there's something going on."

"You've already talked to some staff members and asked them to do something that connects to this problem, but you didn't tell them why you wanted the information, did you? You made up a nice, plausible cover story."

"Yes, one that's more or less true. But they aren't stupid, so some of them may make an educated guess about what we're up to."

"You think they all believed your little fairy tale?" Marty demanded.

I thought about that for a moment. "I'm not sure. Latoya wouldn't question it, I think. Eric I would eliminate up front because he's not from around here and has no history with Philadelphia. Shelby . . . She's sharp, and I'd guess she's already figured it out. Lissa, too."

"About what I figured. I think we have to trust somebody, and we know these people pretty well. Plus we can use their help. What about if we flip it and tell them exactly what we are doing, and what we're looking for? It'd be a heck of a lot faster."

"You mean, there's safety in numbers? Spread the risk around? Do we go outside this circle, and how do we know who to trust?"

"I don't mean send an e-mail to everyone in the building saying, 'We're trying to solve a murder and you can help!' but for those people who know the collections and have expertise that might be useful, it would be a lot more efficient to get them all in one room and start tossing around ideas. And then everybody will know that everybody else knows, which might actually make people safer. Unless you suspect the janitor."

"I see your point, I guess. So that would mean you, me, Latoya, Shelby, and Eric — they're already involved. What about Rich and Ben?"

"I've worked with Rich for a couple of years now, and his expertise with the Terwilliger stuff would be important. And Ben couldn't have done the deed, physically."

I nodded my agreement. "And Eliot?"

Marty looked startled. "Why would he be involved?"

"Because *you're* involved. Unless you're going to tell me he won't notice when you don't talk about how you spent your time on any given day? Or will you distract him with your feminine wiles?"

"Are you speaking from experience?" she shot back — avoiding the question, I noticed.

"Maybe. James has made it clear that he wants no part of this investigation, and I respect that. Or maybe that sounds too harsh. He *can't* involve himself in this investigation — those are the rules of his job, and I'm not going to ask him to bend or break those. I've told you that."

"Ah, who needs the FBI?" Marty said with disgust. "We're probably smarter than they are."

I looked at the clock hanging on the wall. "I'd better get to the office before people start asking questions."

"Do you want me to wait five minutes before following you?"

I took a quick look at her to make sure she was spoofing me. "People are used to seeing you coming and going at all hours, so if we come in together no one is going to care. Shall we call a meeting for all our

coconspirators?"

"I guess. What do you plan to tell them?"

Me? How'd I get that privilege? I'd rather we did it together, but I was, after all, the president of the Society, so I should be the one to do it. "I think I'll stick to the collections management procedures during the renovation as a cover for the e-mail, just to bring them together. It would be a natural thing for this group of people to confer with each other regularly to make sure everything is on track, now that construction has begun, so that wouldn't be suspicious. Then after we lock them in a soundproof room and sweep it for bugs, we can tell them what we're really looking for."

"Bugs?" Marty looked momentarily startled, until she figured out what I meant. "Oh, right. Hey, if the Society can't afford surveillance electronics to protect its collections, I'm going to be mighty annoyed if someone has invested in high-tech spy gear, which is not cheap."

"I think it's highly unlikely," I said wryly. "But we should be discreet anyway."

We walked back to the Society and entered as though it were a normal Wednesday morning. Well, it was, wasn't it? Just the usual construction mayhem and crime-solving. Marty and I parted ways in the

lobby. I went upstairs and typed out a brief e-mail requesting the presence of those people Marty and I had listed, at a meeting in the big room under the stairs on the first floor of the building. It was unquestionably quiet and out of the way, and the walls were seriously thick, so no one was likely to overhear anything. Downstairs it was. I set the time for one o'clock.

Not surprisingly, Eric was the first to respond. He poked his head in my door. "You want me there, too, Nell? What about the phones?"

"Yes, I want you there. Forward the phones to voice mail — this shouldn't take long. If anyone else asks, tell them the same thing."

"Will do," Eric said and retreated, shutting the door behind him.

Alone for at least a few minutes, I pondered what I wanted to say at this meeting. The chain of events leading from the discovery of the pit, to its contents, to the death of the cleanup worker, was clear enough and could be simply stated, although I harbored a fear that if I spoke them out loud to a group of people, the fragile links Marty and I had forged might disintegrate. Well, if the reasoning was that flimsy, it deserved to be shot down. Assuming we all passed that first

test and everyone bought into the theory that Marty and I had concocted, the logic that led from the murder to the shattered box and its theoretical contents was even shakier. And how anybody could come up with a motive that connected the unexpected find in the basement to a murder last week was beyond me — which was exactly why I wanted to hold this meeting. Maybe younger, fresher eyes would see something Marty and I hadn't — or maybe we would be laughed out of the room.

I wolfed down a quick takeout lunch and was downstairs early, as was Marty. The others trickled in, looking a little bewildered. I plastered on a fake smile and avoided answering any questions before the entire group was assembled. When everyone had arrived — Latoya, Shelby, Lissa, Ben, Rich, and Eric — I looked at Marty, and she silently closed the substantial doors to the hallway, then took a place at the far end of the table. I waited until everyone was settled and had stopped rustling papers before I began.

"You're probably wondering why I gathered you here today," I began, then stopped when confronted by uniformly blank stares. "Uh, that's a joke? A catchphrase beaten into the ground in mysteries and on bad

television shows? Think Hercule Poirot and Nero Wolfe?"

"Nell, I don't treat collections management as a joke," Latoya said stiffly.

So much for my attempt to lighten the mood. "All right, then, I'll come right to the point. We're not here to talk about shuffling collections around in the building, we're here —"

"To look at that death from last week," Shelby finished the statement before I could. "Am I right?"

"Uh, yes?" What else could I say?

"Pay up, guys," Shelby ordered, and some bills changed hands.

I gave her a mock glare. "You were betting on what I wanted to talk to you all about?"

"Nope, we were betting on whether you two could stay out of this investigation. I put my money on 'no.' By the way, is Mr. Agent Man going to play?"

"No, he is not," I said. "The FBI has no jurisdiction in this matter, and the Philadelphia Police Department has not requested their assistance. This is a Philadelphia homicide, period."

"So it's officially a homicide now?" Shelby said with some surprise. "The papers have been pretty quiet about it — you know,

tragic death, unavoidable accident, it was dark, et cetera."

"Yes, according to Detective Hrivnak, who many of you have spoken with in the past, it looks like the victim was pushed in front of the car, following some kind of confrontation. But keep quiet about that, please. If the police aren't spreading that around, I certainly won't."

"Do the police know we're on the case?"

That was a bit harder to answer. "They have asked me some questions tangential to the death, but we have not been officially involved — with one exception, and I'll tell you about that now."

I proceeded to outline the events we knew about, and the conjectures Marty and I had put together. Marty threw in a few clarifications, but by and large everyone listened respectfully until I wound down. "Any questions?" I finally said.

I was surprised that Latoya was the first to speak. "Why are you telling us this at all? It seems to me that you and Martha could have carried on quite well without involving us."

I weighed my answer carefully. "Two reasons. One, you all know about different aspects of the collections, and Marty and I are convinced that this has some connec-

tion to the Society's holdings in the early twentieth century. We can use your input and insights and undeniable research skills. Two, this may be dangerous. One man has been killed. If we have stumbled onto something that can inspire murder, I'd rather you all know what you're facing so no one bumbles into this unprepared. You're safer this way. I don't want anyone to get hurt."

"How much do the police know about what you've just told us?" Rich asked.

"As I said, I turned over the brass pieces and the wooden fragments to the detective on Monday, and I know they verified that the bartender recognized the brass escutcheon. I did *not* share our theories. My plan at the moment is to tell them anything they ask, but not to volunteer information, and certainly not to suggest speculative connections. I'm not concealing anything, but the police haven't always been welcoming to outsiders like us, whether or not we come bearing evidence. If that troubles you, feel free to take them anything you find, as long as you let me know. We're all on the same side here." I thought briefly about asking them to minimize any discoveries that could put the Society in a bad light, but I decided that wouldn't be right, either.

"So those requests you made yesterday — you think they apply to this situation?" Latoya asked.

I nodded. "I do, and I'm sure you can see why. We need to assemble all possible information about who ran the Society, how the collections were managed, the details of the construction of this building — all between, say, 1900, when planning for the new building began, and 1910, when the building reopened to the public. To be honest, I don't know what we're looking for. I suggest we collect all the files we find that may be relevant, then regroup here to share our findings and brainstorm. How long do you think that will take?" I swept the room with my gaze.

"How about tomorrow morning? Before the building opens?" Latoya said. "Nine o'clock?"

That seemed fast to me, but nobody complained. Maybe there really wasn't all that much to be found in the way of in-house records. "That works for me," I said. "I know I don't have to tell you not to talk about this to anyone else at the Society, much less with anyone outside these walls, but I want to say again, please be careful. And take good care of the files — they are unique and irreplaceable." I didn't see the

point in mentioning the break-ins — it would only spook them. "We really don't know what we're up against."

"Amen," Marty said. "Thanks, everyone."

The group trickled out, until Marty and I were left alone. "Have we done the right thing?" I asked.

"I hope so. And I can't think of anything else to do."

"Then let's hope this works!"

CHAPTER 19

The peace did not last, because Marty appeared at my door a half an hour later. "I got a text from Henry saying that he needs to talk to us, fast. Is your office bugged?"

It took me a moment to realize she was joking. At least, I thought she was. "Let's hope not. You want to call from here?"

"Yeah, I can put it on speaker." She closed the door. When she was settled again, she pulled out her cell phone and made the call.

"Hey, Aunt Marty! You got my message?" Henry's cheerful voice came through loud and clear.

"Obviously," Marty replied briskly. "I've got you on speaker, and Nell's here, too, but no one else. What've you got?"

"I told you I was going to run some additional tests on the wood? Man, these new machines are something else. They can pick up almost anything."

"I assume you found something with your

fancy toys?" Marty pressed.

"If you saw the price tags, you wouldn't call them toys — and they're real sensitive. Anyway, yes, I found something unexpected and I thought you should know."

He paused again, no doubt relishing the opportunity to yank Marty's chain. "I found gunpowder residue and gun-cleaning oil embedded in the wood."

Whoa. That was something I never expected. A lot of questions came bubbling into my head, but I had no idea where to start.

Fortunately Marty did. "You're saying there was a gun or guns kept in that box at some point?" She sounded as surprised as I felt.

"I can go you one better: it was smokeless powder, which was invented in 1884, so the weapon has to have been made after that. It's a really interesting history —" Henry began with enthusiasm.

Marty cut him off. "What kind of weapon are we looking for?" she demanded.

"Aunt Martha, that's a bit hard to say based on the analysis I've done, with very little physical evidence. You're going to have to do some homework. I can probably dig up a list of weapons available in that time period that used that kind of powder, and

since we know roughly what size the box was, we can eliminate the larger weapons, but after that you're on your own. Not my area of expertise. Look for a handgun that dates from between 1884 and 1907."

"Got it. Thanks, Henry — you've given us something to think about. I'll call you if I have more questions."

"Any time, Auntie M." He hung up.

Marty turned to stare at me. "Well."

"Yes. Didn't see that one coming, did we?"

"No way. So there was at least one weapon kept in there at some point, but we did not find any weapons in the pit. The police did not find any weapons upon Carnell Scruggs's body. Why do I sound like a Doctor Seuss character?" Marty asked.

"Because you're in shock. We're both stunned. You're right. We've been focused on the brass pieces and the possibility of some documents or other valuables in the box, but a firearm puts this in a whole new light — a firearm that we can assign to a fairly precise period. I mean, firearms have significant street value, for ready cash. We don't know if Carnell had any criminal history, but we could find out. Would he know what to do with a gun?"

"He'd sell it, probably. A clean gun — one with no criminal trail — would have some

real value on the street around here, and Carnell would probably have known that. Would the thing still work after sitting in that pit for a century?" Marty asked.

"Maybe, but I wouldn't want to pull the trigger without taking a hard look at it. Heck, we don't even know if it *was* in the pit at all — just because the box once held a gun, doesn't mean the gun was in there at the time the desk got tossed. Maybe the gun was stolen out of the box in 1907 and the thief trashed the box to hide that fact. Did your grandfather have any history with fire-arms?"

"You mean, apart from the pistols that General John Terwilliger used in his infamous duel in 1778?"

I stared at Marty for a moment, until my brain worked out that a weapon dating from 1778 could hardly fit the description of what we now thought we were looking for. "I assume your family still has those?"

Marty nodded. "One of my cousins does, but he doesn't talk about it. It's not like he handed them around for the kids to play with at Thanksgiving. I think they're in a safe-deposit box. But they're too early to have anything to do with this. The short answer is yes, my grandfather did have a few weapons around. He made sure we kids

didn't know where he kept them, although I can't imagine that he'd keep them in the lap desk. What do we do now?"

I thought, and then I looked at my watch. "First we go talk to the construction crew."

"Why?"

"You'll see." I crossed my fingers that they'd still be on-site.

They were. I called Bob at the desk, and he told me they were working on the fourth floor today. I thanked him and headed for the stairs, Marty right behind me, then I went straight to Joe Logan. "Can we talk with you a moment?"

He said quickly, "Sure. You got a problem? Because we can't help the noise . . ."

"No, it's not that, Joe. I want to ask a favor. You know that pit in the basement?"

"Sure, what about it?"

"I know your guys cleared it out and gave me what you found, but is it still open?"

"Yeah. We haven't decided if we need to fill it in now, or how, and then with Carnell's, uh, accident . . ." He left the rest of his thought unspoken. "Why?"

"I want to look for something very small, that they might have missed. I know it's a tight fit, but this is important, or I wouldn't ask."

"Hey, you're the boss." He scanned the

group of men in the room, but to my unskilled eye they all looked too big to fit into the hole and be able to maneuver once they were inside it. "Carnell was our smallest guy — I don't know if there's anyone else . . ."

"I'll do it," Marty said.

We both turned to stare at her. The foreman said, "Ma'am, you wouldn't be covered by our insurance. If you can wait until tomorrow . . ."

"I'll sign whatever waiver you want, but I want this done today. Now."

"You'll mess up your clothes," the foreman protested feebly.

"My problem, not yours. Can we do this?" Marty demanded.

He looked at me in mute appeal, and I nodded. "Okay," Logan said. He looked over at his crew. "Hey, guys?" he called out. "Fifteen-minute break." Then he turned back to Marty. "Let's go."

We all took the elevator down to the basement and headed for the back room where the pit was. I was surprised at how clean everything looked now, swept and ready for whatever came next. The pit was covered by a couple of sturdy planks, but they were easily removed.

"You got a ladder or a rope or something?"

Marty asked.

"Carnell went down by ladder, and then we pulled it up so he could move around," Logan explained. "Let me go get it."

Marty waited until he'd gone off hunting for the right ladder before turning to me. "Okay, what am I looking for?"

"One or more cartridges from the gun. It's a long shot — sorry for the pun — but if there was a gun in the desk, there might also have been some bullets in the box, and they'd be hard to see in the dirt at the bottom. Carnell could easily have missed them."

"Got it. So I get to sift through that lovely dirt with my hands, looking for something dirty that's about an inch long?"

"Right. Hey, you volunteered."

"I'm the smallest one around — you wouldn't fit."

"Gee, thanks."

The foreman returned with a relatively narrow ladder, which he slid into the pit. "I'm going to insist you wear a hard hat, or I'll have state and federal authorities crawling all over me. And here's a flashlight, and a pair of work gloves, and some protective goggles." He handed her the items. "We think we cleared out anything big. If you find something small, you can put it in your

pocket. If it's too big for that, we'll have to work something out."

"Fair enough. I'm going in." Marty turned around and backed down the ladder. I heard a few muttered curses, and then she called out, "Pull the ladder up now." Logan did.

I could hear Marty scrabbling around the detritus at the bottom of the pit, and tried not hard to think about the fact that it had once been a privy. A long time ago. At least a century, right? And she'd volunteered, even knowing its history. How bad could it be?

"Put the ladder back," she called out, after what must have been fifteen minutes. The foreman complied quickly, and Marty clambered out.

"Well?" I said.

She nodded, then turned to the foreman. "Thanks for your help, Joe. I got what I needed."

The poor guy stood there for a few seconds, obviously waiting for an explanation, but Marty didn't volunteer anything else, so in the end he pulled out the ladder, picked it up, and left. We waited until we could no longer hear his footsteps.

"Okay, what've you got?"

"Some nice china shards, and what I think is an old pipe — couldn't be sure." Marty

grinned wickedly. "And these."

She reached into her pocket, then pulled her hand out and opened it to reveal three brass cartridges, tarnished and covered with soil — and I recognized them immediately. "Damn! These cartridges are .45 ACPs. They were invented in 1905. The timing fits."

"What?" Marty said. "Wait? Why do you know this?"

"Long story. The point is, we've just narrowed down what weapon we're looking for."

"Hang on," Marty said, "we've just shown there *was* a weapon, probably when the box went into the pit. Unless some idiot came down here and felt like chucking bullets into a hole in the ground. At least they're whole shells, not just the casings, so they weren't fired here?"

"Right again. Ergo, they must fit the missing weapon."

Marty said. "Why are you assuming the gun was in the box when it was tossed? How do you know that the gun wasn't removed first, and then the box was dumped?"

"Like, how do you prove something *wasn't* there?" I retorted. "I can't, but think about it: Why would anyone kill Carnell over a bunch of old cartridges? There *had* to be a

gun. Carnell would have seen it in the pit and known he could sell it, so he hid it in a pocket or under his belt and didn't tell anyone. But somebody *else* saw him pocketing something — maybe one of his construction buddies — and followed him when he left."

"Maybe." Marty didn't look convinced. "So what is it we're supposed to do with this piece of information?" she demanded.

After my first burst of deductive reasoning, I had run out of steam. We still had no more than some chemical traces and some wild hypotheses — and no gun. Nothing worthy of taking to the police yet. "I . . . really don't know. I need to think. You need to shower and change clothes." When I looked at my watch, I was shocked to see that the workday was barely half-over. "Late lunch? Early supper?"

"I smell that bad? No, don't tell me. I'll go home and clean up. You gonna tell Hrivnak? Or James?"

"Marty, please." I held up one hand to stop her. "I need to get my head around this first. Don't worry, I won't do anything without consulting you. Let's go upstairs."

We took the elevator up to the first floor, where Marty in her present condition evoked a couple of stares, which she ig-

nored. She headed straight out the front door, and I went back to my office, where I sat and stared into space, trying to think.

Henry had said the broken box with the brass fittings that we'd pulled out of the pit in the basement dated to the eighteenth century and probably came from the same furniture maker as the famous Terwilliger furniture. I trusted his opinion.

Henry also said he had found traces of gunshot residue — a kind that hadn't existed until 1884 — and gun oil on the bits of wood we'd given him. I was less sure of that fact, since the box had been sitting in a hole in the floor for over a century. But he was the test-machine wizard, and I'd have to accept what he and his machines told us.

And now Marty and I had found cartridges from an appropriate era in the same hole. And I was guessing that there was a weapon, that it also had been in the pit, along with the cartridges, and that Carnell had pocketed it. Should I tell the police that they should test Carnell's clothing for firearms residue? Would their equipment even be able to detect such small traces, and how quickly could they do it?

Had someone seen Carnell take the weapon out of the building, then taken it

from him and made sure he was dead so he couldn't tell anyone about it?

Where did the Terwilliger family fit in all this?

If I tried to explain this to the police, what would they think? But if I didn't tell them and the gun showed up in a crime now, I'd be liable for something, wouldn't I? Would it be concealing evidence if the concealing took place *before* the crime?

And why had the hypothetical gun hypothetically ended up in the pit at all?

I was getting tired of my own thoughts. I hadn't heard from Marty, who lived a short walk away — maybe she was taking a very long bath. And thinking along the same lines I was, about where her grandfather and her father fit in this puzzle, that now included an old or antique firearm. I stood up, stretched, and meandered out to Eric's desk.

"I collected those board files you asked about, Nell," Eric said.

Great — if I wanted to read them in time to talk about them tomorrow morning, I'd have to take them home. James would love that. "Thank you, Eric — that was fast. Nothing from Latoya?"

Eric shook his head.

"Shelby?"

"I saw her for about a minute earlier, but she said she was still working on what you asked."

There was not a whole lot more I could do before the end of the day. We'd all be hearing the new information cold at the meeting in the morning — assuming there was anything to hear. "Okay, let me take the management files home with me and go over them and see if I learn anything. Do they include budgets, Eric?"

"They do. Don't worry — it's not too big a stack, not from those early days."

That was good news *and* bad news. "Let's hope we find something."

CHAPTER 20

I caught a ride home with James, which was a good thing since I was hauling the batch of files with me. They weren't particularly heavy, but they were irreplaceable — and they might contain evidence crucial to solving a murder. A very slim chance, I knew, but it was nice to have an armed FBI agent protecting them. Even if he didn't know it.

We had a pleasant dinner, and then I announced, "I have some Society stuff I need to review this evening. I thought I'd spread out on the dining room table." We usually ate in the kitchen anyway. The table and its four chairs were the only pieces of furniture in the dining room; luckily there was an overhead chandelier, emerging from an opulent cast-plaster medallion, to provide light, even if it was a challenge to replace the bulbs so far above.

"Okay," James said amiably. "I think there's a game on. I'll wash up, if you've got

work to do."

I wasn't about to turn down that offer, so I grabbed up my files and retreated to the dining room. I set them down, pulled up a chair, and started sorting the files into piles. I had to suppress a sneeze — it was pretty clear that no one had looked at these for a long time, and they were dusty.

As Eric had said, there really wasn't very much. Administration circa 1900 had been a bit casual — a bunch of old — and male — friends getting together now and then because they loved history and/or their families had been part of making that history so they felt some kind of social responsibility. And if meeting schedules had been haphazard then, the notes and reports taken from them had been even more so. This was going to take some digging.

However, as I read, I found myself becoming more and more interested. A lot of this was information I had known in broad terms; I'd used a lot of this background when I was raising money for the Society. As I quickly discovered, the period I was interested in was particularly busy in some rather intriguing ways. I started to make rough notes of my own.

Anyone familiar with the history of Philadelphia — or any other old city, for that

matter — knows that city centers and neighborhoods shift over time (often surprisingly rapidly, in hindsight). It looked as though the decision to build a new City Hall for Philadelphia, on a square in the middle of the city, had been a precipitating factor in shifting the focus away from the waterfront.

It was while construction was under way on that building that the Society had purchased the mansion that had stood on Locust Street. As Lissa had told me, the Society had been renting space before that, but as the collections grew, particularly toward at the end of the nineteenth century, so did the conviction that a dedicated permanent space was the best choice. I noted that as of 1899 there were nearly 1,600 members of the Society, and an endowment that sounded sizable but was mostly restricted to collections acquisitions and maintenance — the reality was, member contributions weren't enough to pay for even basic operating costs. And at that point there were only a handful of paid employees — the head librarian, an assistant librarian, a cataloger added in 1891, and a woman who specialized in manuscript repair. There wasn't even a general secretary until 1907.

Still, the flood of collections donations

demanded action, so in 1901 the Society announced a renovation plan, with an estimated cost of two hundred thousand dollars — but only twenty-two individuals contributed money to that campaign. However, by a great stroke of luck, the president of the Society became governor of the Commonwealth right about then, and — surprise — the Society received a nice state grant for fifty thousand dollars, which made it possible to begin construction. That construction was finished in a year. Fast work! I wondered if the money had been paid up front, or if the disbursement was contingent on completion.

Now we were getting to the interesting stuff. After that first success, the Society decided to go even bigger, helped along by another state grant of a hundred thousand dollars — nothing like having friends in high places! — and that was the renovation that required the demolition of all but the foundations of the old mansion. So that had taken place between 1905, when the first phase was officially dedicated, and 1907, when the second phase was completed. Again, a very quick turnaround, considering that it was far more than a mere remodeling. But not everything went smoothly, because the formal opening didn't take

place until 1910. Had they spent those three years sorting out and installing the burgeoning collections? I sympathized, since I was dealing with the same issues.

I made a few more notes, mostly because I was intrigued: the grand staircase followed the outline of the original mansion staircase; the reading room off the lobby had been the only space open to the public; and the nice space under the stairs, where we were meeting in the morning, had once been the librarian's office, since he was supposed to emerge from his lair and greet visitors in the lobby. *Nice office!* The third floor had held only the offices for the cataloger and for manuscript repair, and the fourth floor had been entirely empty, waiting for future collections. I wondered briefly how long it had taken to fill that, because it was certainly stuffed to the rafters now.

I sat back and ran my fingers through my hair. So, what had I learned? That the window of opportunity to hide the lap desk, intact or otherwise, was very brief, as we had suspected — limited to the years between 1905 and 1907. That there was essentially very little oversight of the collections by official staff. That the public had little access but the members probably could roam at will throughout the building.

Next I turned to the board minutes, a pitifully thin pile. Mostly they recorded the date and time of the meeting, members present, and motions taken and approved (there seemed to be little argument among the board members, or if there was, it had been deliberately omitted from the official record). I wondered if the request for state funding had originated from the governor himself, who was probably all too aware of the pressing needs of the Society, or if some board member could claim the glory for proposing the idea. Either way, the money had materialized and been spent in record time. Things were a lot simpler back then.

Then I looked at the treasurer's reports, an equally slim pile. Balance sheets and cash flow. I didn't see anything recording collections contributions, at least not with any monetary value attached (how ungentlemanly that would be!). Maybe Latoya had found those. The balance sheet showed a long list of restricted endowments, as I expected, and the infusion of the state monies. I made a mental note to check with our architect to see if he had been given not only the building plans but also the costs and expenditures of the second construction project, because I didn't see them in the papers in front of me. Or maybe Shelby

275

had copies of them in her files, since there must have been donor contributions to supplement the government funds. I wondered if the Society's treasurer — another unpaid position, appointed from among the board members — was a financial professional or merely a willing volunteer. So many of the board members appeared to be lawyers or bankers — and all were male. The classic group of good ole boys, Philadelphia style. I bet if I looked up their addresses in those days, most would have lived somewhere along the Main Line.

James came up from behind me and set a mug of tea next to me (on a coaster!). "That looks rather dry," he commented.

"It's part of the history of the Society. It's also part of the quest for That Which We Cannot Talk About."

"Ah," he said.

I couldn't resist going on. "It's interesting objectively because the Society had these wonderful collections, even in 1900, with more coming in, especially as Philadelphians fled to the suburbs and didn't want to take their tatty old stuff with them, but the place was run with only a few paid employees and a board made up of old buddies. Remember the wine cellar? That went in during one of the renovations early in the twentieth cen-

tury. Wonder which line item in the budget that was."

"What are you looking for?" he asked.

I debated making a snarky remark, but since he had asked . . . "I'm not sure, really. Anything that seems out of place. Anything referring to the renovation project, particularly the second phase, when the old mansion was torn down. Any financial anomalies. But all the records here are so sketchy that it's hard to know what went on. And in a way it didn't matter — the Society survived, even with the pathetic level of oversight back then. Of course, we're still fighting the same battles now, particularly in terms of housing and caring for the collections, but we're still here."

James was now kneading my shoulders, which was a bit distracting, even as he leaned over to read the exposed documents. "What it sounds like you're saying is that almost anyone on the board or on this small staff could have done almost anything he wanted, and either no one would have noticed, or the gentlemen would have closed ranks to protect one of their own."

What he said made sense. "Exactly. So if John Doe had an affection for, let's say, a choice portfolio of 1870s erotica and took it home for his own enjoyment, the librarian

and his friends would have looked the other way, and there would have been no paper trail."

"You have erotica in the collections?" James feigned horror.

"Yes, that — or even more valuable items, like silver or portraits. I don't have to tell you that if something had belonged to a family for generations, the current generation might feel it was theirs by right, even if the item in question had been donated and changed hands years earlier, with plenty of documentation. I've seen it many times. 'Great-grandpa's letter should be mine,' says the patron, sticking it in his jacket pocket. And then there's the question of money."

"What about it?" James asked.

"Well, there was an unusual amount of it coming in and going out between 1900 and 1907, when construction was finished. At least a hundred and fifty thousand from the state government, for a start. If the treasurer was an amateur, he might not have caught any irregularities. So if someone on the board was helping himself to funds . . . how would anyone know?"

"I don't suppose you have canceled checks from 1906?" James asked.

I wasn't sure if he was kidding — but

then, I wasn't sure we *didn't* have those items buried somewhere in our files. "We might. But I'm not exactly sure where they'd be stored. I can ask Eric to look for them in the morning. Or maybe the bank has records, although they're probably either in digital format now or archived somewhere off-site."

"You've been using the same bank from the beginning?" James asked, incredulous.

"Yes. It's changed names a few times, but the account has never moved. We've shuffled the investment accounts from time to time, to optimize return on the endowed funds that aren't tapped often, but that's about it."

James sat down next to me, a distant look in his eye. I was torn: we had sworn not to talk about this. I wasn't going to drag him into Society business, particularly when it might include a crime. But on the other hand, he was the one who seemed to be digging himself in here. I kept my mouth shut.

"I know what you're thinking," James said, his eyes on the pages spread out over the table.

"That you wanted to stay out of this," I said.

"Yes. But let us say, for the moment, that this is a matter of purely academic interest.

You have a collection of documents here that gives you insight into the management of a nonprofit organization at the beginning of the twentieth century. It also provides a profile of a particular segment of Philadelphia society at that time — just look at the names on the board and the membership list. And now you're a part of it, or it's a part of what you do. That's something we can discuss."

I was impressed. And touched — he seemed to want to help, even though he believed he shouldn't. "Good. Because I'm stumped. What we're looking for is evidence, or even a hint or a suggestion of a crime. But boards seldom say, 'Let the record show that member John Doe has physically removed Object X from the Society's collection for his own personal use and without permission from this body — and, by the way, we're going to ignore it because John is a friend of ours.' How do I find something that I'm not even sure is there?"

"By doing what you're doing — looking at the small details, across categories, so to speak."

"And you think they can add up to something?"

"Maybe. You don't know unless you look."

"I'm not a professional researcher, or an

accountant."

"But you have people working for you who are. And you've already asked for their help, right?" When I nodded, he said, "You've got plenty of eyes on this. If there is something to be found, odds are someone will see it. And then you can put the pieces together."

"And that will point to who killed poor Mr. Scruggs?"

"I can't tell you that."

Fair enough. We'd reached our invisible line. I'd found out several things I hadn't known before, James had nudged me in some new directions, and I was tired. I stuck the few loose papers back in their folders, and then I shut and stacked the folders. "Is there something mindless on television that we can watch together?"

"We can find out. You're done here?"

"For now." But before I walked away, I made a note on a sticky: *Call bank.*

CHAPTER 21

Before I went to bed I took the time to format and print out a summary of the high points of what I'd learned: lists of the board members at the critical times, chronology of the building campaigns, my quick take on the sources of funding for said campaigns. I wanted to capture my first impressions, but I kept the summary short and sweet so I could share it with the rest of my group in the morning. Somehow James and I never quite made it to watching the game but found equally rewarding things to do with our time.

The next morning I carefully bundled up the records and added my own notes, and we set off for the city. I was getting awfully used to this; in the pleasant fall weather I should be trekking to and from train stations, so I could beg for rides when the weather was lousy, but I couldn't bring

myself to say no to James's offers. I might never catch up with my reading, which I usually did on the train, but right now spending time with James seemed more important than spending it with the *New Yorker.*

We arrived in good time, and I let myself into the building and headed upstairs. Eric was already there — he lived only a few blocks away — and I wondered briefly what he did with the rest of his time outside of work, but I hated to pry.

"Mornin', Nell," he greeted me. "Were those files I gave you what you needed?"

"Yes, Eric, thanks. Was that all of them?"

"All the ones that were filed where they were supposed to be. But I've noticed that record-keeping and filing were kind of sloppy that far back."

"I've noticed the same thing, and I can't say I'm surprised. Among other things, I learned that there was no secretary for this place until 1907, so who knows what went on before that. And there were no copy machines then, either, so it's not like there would be duplicates in six other places. But anyway, thank you — and thanks for finding them so quickly."

"Y'all are meeting at nine today? Should I be there?"

"Yes to the time. But I don't know that you have to sit in — you have no institutional memory, so to speak. And somebody should cover the phones up here. I hope you're not offended if we leave you out?"

"No way. Can I interrupt you if I think something is important?"

"Of course. I trust your judgment." I realized that I hadn't heard from Detective Hrivnak since Monday, but that was probably a good thing. She had no questions for me, and I had no information that I was ready to share with her — just guesses that were about as vague as they had been a week ago. The potential existence of a gun could be important, but I was pretty sure that she would just tell me I was wasting her time if I tried to explain our reasoning behind it. Plus I wasn't exactly convinced those facts were leading us anywhere, but I thought we had to try. I reminded myself that I should know when to quit as well.

Nine o'clock found us sitting around the handsome large oak table in the room I now knew had been intended for the librarian. Even the table itself might date back a hundred years, which seemed appropriate. I surveyed my cast of conspirators: Latoya, Marty, Shelby, Lissa, Rich, and Ben. I waited until everybody had settled down

and pulled out their own ragtag collections of notes and papers before launching our discussion. "Why don't I start?" I said. "I asked Eric to pull all the management records for the early twentieth century — board minutes and the like. It's a surprisingly small batch, and I read through them all last night. I boiled it down to a simple summary" — I handed out the sheets I had printed the night before — "and I think there are a couple of critical points. I apologize if I'm repeating myself, but I want to be sure we're all on the same page. One, the construction of this building took place really fast, and there was a big infusion of money from the state government. Two, it looks like the collections were growing equally fast during that period, and between those two factors, there was probably a *lot* of confusion about what we had and where we put it." I paused long enough to let people skim my handouts. Then I added, "Before you ask, we didn't find much in the way of financial records. I'm hoping Shelby can patch in some of those relating to the building from contribution records. But I'd like to hear Latoya's take on the collections management during that time."

Latoya nodded in acknowledgment. "As you might surmise, the records are in rather

poor shape. We know all too well what it's like dealing with vague, inaccurate, or completely missing records, and coupled with an unprecedented influx of donations and a major building campaign, it was a recipe for disaster. My general impression, I'm sorry to say, is that a lot of people simply said, 'Close enough — we'll sort it out later.' Only there never was a later, and we're still playing catch-up."

I knew that Latoya was not just making excuses — she was a rigorous custodian of the Society's collections. "I'm not surprised," I told her. "Nor can I blame those men, I guess — they weren't professionals, and it must have been overwhelming. Can you tell me anything about the Terwilliger donations?"

Marty and Rich, seated side by side at the other end of the table, all but pricked up their ears, but I wanted to hear the official interpretation from Latoya before Marty stuck her oar in, so I gave her a warning look.

Latoya gave what passed as a smile. "I have to say that the Terwilligers, from the first, were meticulous in their record-keeping, at least by the standards of the day. Not everything was photographed, of course — back then that would have been expen-

sive, and the subsequent storage of the prints would have been challenging. Plus, as you mentioned, Nell, there was a lot going on here at the Society, including the demolition of the former building on the site. Sometimes I'm amazed that we can find anything."

"Would you say that that particular short-term situation would have made it easy to remove some items undetected?" *Or sneak some in? Would that confusion have offered a good opportunity to hide something?*

"Certainly. The only constraint would have been the ethics of the participants. Before you protest, Martha, the Terwilligers did the best they could, but once they'd turned over the collections they donated, it was to some extent out of their hands, despite your family's ongoing involvement with the Society."

A new thought struck me. "That raises an interesting point. Marty, do you know why your grandfather chose that particular time to give his collections to the Society? He must have been aware that the renovations would create a lot of confusion. Why didn't he wait until after they were completed?"

Shelby spoke up for the first time. "If you don't mind, Marty, I think I can answer that, or at least make an educated guess.

Nell, you mentioned that the state chipped in a lot of money for the new building, right? And you know why?"

"I do, but I'll let you fill everybody in." I smiled at her — she'd done her homework.

Shelby nodded. "I apologize in advance if you all have heard this before, but I think it's important to what we're talking about there. The president of the Pennsylvania Antiquarian Society, one Dudley Pemberton, was elected governor during his term here, and held on to the title throughout his tenure. He'd barely taken office when the first grant came through — that one paid for some improvements to the former building. And as soon as those were finished — in record time, I might add — the Society turned around and decided to rebuild the whole thing. They took down the mansion, right down to the foundations. And this time they got *twice* as much money from the state government for the new construction."

"Why does that matter?" Ben asked, more curious than challenging.

Shelby turned to him. "Think about it. Say what you will about the local 'old boys network,' but our man was new to the office, and he didn't have the same support system available to him in Harrisburg that

he would have in the Philadelphia area. So he must have had to present some kind of case to the state government before they'd authorize the expenditure of a big chunk of taxpayer money. Even back then it meant there had to be a formal grant application. We don't have the record of what went on in Harrisburg, but we do have what the Society submitted, and it shows a healthy level of contributions from the board and high-end members."

We all thought about that for a moment. "But I've looked at the budgets," I said, "and I didn't see a lot of that money flowing through. Was there another account?"

"Yes, a dedicated construction fund — that would have been kept separate from the operating budget."

"Of course! I should have realized that. And you have the file for that?"

"Sure do, and a list of donors." Shelby stood up and handed out copies of a single page.

I scanned it quickly. "Okay, Governor Pemberton ponied up his own money at the beginning, which would make sense — that would shame everybody else into doing their bit. Marty, I don't see your grandfather's name on the list."

Marty shrugged. "The family's always

been cash-poor. I'd guess that his contribution took the form of the collection, which was significant and was arguably of national importance. Of course, that wouldn't pay for construction, but he might have used it for leverage."

"And that would explain the timing," I said slowly. "Say the governor put up cash and your grandfather dangled a major collection of documents in front of the board, and then the two of them sat back and waited for the others to step up. And they did, at least enough to convince the state legislature that this was a worthy project and had support from its board and members. And the funding for the project was rushed through before anybody could change their mind, or before Pemberton left office."

"Would it help if we knew more about what kind of man Governor Pemberton was?" Shelby asked. "Honest? Sneaky? Well connected, or a political newcomer?"

"I can look him up," Rich volunteered.

"Good," I said. "Shelby, can you look at his contributions record? Not just around the time of the rebuilding of this place, but before and after? How did he become president here? He must have played some kind of role here before he went to Har-

risburg, even if it was purely for strategic reasons, like building up his résumé before running for office."

Shelby shuffled through some papers. "It says here in one article I found that he became president of the Society in 1900. Looks like he took an honest interest in history and genealogy — he wasn't just a pretty political face. But by 1902 he was running for governor, and even back then that didn't happen overnight. He must have needed connections and money."

"Did he serve one term or two?" I asked.

"Just one. But there's some interesting stuff about what happened during the building of the new State House, which had burned down a few years earlier, before he was elected. After he took office, he made sure that it was finished on time and within budget, so Pemberton knew how to keep a project moving. But after it was done, the state treasurer started looking at the spending and found a lot of overcharges and suspicious methods of calculating costs." Shelby flipped through some more pages from her sheaf of notes, then smiled. "It says here that there were charges for chandeliers by the pound, and for the airspace under the furniture." That brought a laugh from everyone.

"Did the claims of financial misrepresentation stick?" I asked.

"Looks like they nailed the architect, the contractor, the former attorney general, and the former state treasurer, but the governor was never charged with anything, and the public seemed to think he was clean."

"You're right — that is interesting. He had to have been aware that somebody was cooking the books at the state level, so he knew how things worked, but he got away with it. All this at the same time construction was going on at the Society. Of course, I assume the state capitol building cost a lot more than the Society, so maybe our little project slipped by with little attention while everybody was ranting about the bigger project."

"So what are you saying, Nell?" Marty asked. "Was the governor clean or dirty? And where did the Society fit?"

"I think this information about the big picture that Shelby has given us tells us something about how the man got things done. The governor had to have had some clout, so what I'm wondering is whether he leaned on anybody here at the Society to come up with the cash for this building." *Or for his campaign? No, I wasn't going to get into that.* "Heck, maybe he even gave it back

again after the dust settled, but the construction money was in the bank at the right time to make things look good. Shelby, if you can find any more information about the contributions for the building campaign, that would be a big help."

"I'm on it," she said.

Marty still looked troubled. "What is it?" I asked her.

"Maybe I'm being unreasonable, but you know my grandfather was heavily involved in the Society at that particular time, and I don't like the thought of him doing anything underhanded. I know from my father that it really hurt my grandfather to part with the family collections, although he did his best to guarantee that the Society would keep them together and take decent care of them. You already know that. At the time various relatives were still fighting over the furniture, and they probably might have gone after the documents next. So, fine, he turned them over to the Society to keep the collection intact. Now you're suggesting that the donation could have been his pledge for the building campaign, although it would have meant admitting publicly, or at least among his peers, that he didn't have the cash. He was a proud man, so that would have been hard for him. But I don't

want to think he did anything wrong."

"Marty, nobody is suggesting that. It just happens that we know more about him than we do about the other board members and employees at that time. They should all get the same scrutiny. Shelby, you'll be looking for contributions records for both Society operations *and* for the special building campaign, from all board members plus high-dollar members, although I'd guess they pretty much overlap, just like today. Is there anything anyone wants to add?"

I kind of held my breath, because Marty and I hadn't had time to discuss whether we should announce our discovery of the missing gun, if there was a gun at all and if it had gone missing from the Society or sometime far earlier.

"Nothing I'm sure of," Marty said. "I'm trying to go through the family's records for that time frame, but a few of them are scattered among other family members, so I can't always get at them, or at least not quickly."

"Well, keep trying. You never know what private individuals will hand on to their heirs. So, everybody has an assignment?" Everyone nodded with varying degrees of enthusiasm.

Lissa spoke for the first time. "Nell, what

are your thoughts about this and how it might relate to . . . what happened last week?" she asked.

I wasn't sure how to answer. "To be honest, I'm still not sure we aren't chasing phantoms. My gut says that there's a connection to the death of Carnell Scruggs that we still aren't seeing clearly, but so far we haven't found anything tangible to back that up. I can't point to anything that would give someone a motive to do harm to him. I feel a little guilty wasting your time — all of you — on all this research that may lead nowhere, but I feel I have to do it. Does that make sense?"

Latoya thought for a moment. "I would agree for the following reason: if we don't look and there turns out to be a link to the Society, that would be far worse than if we search and fail to find any connection. We can spare the time." No one disagreed.

"Thank you — all of you. Now back to work!"

CHAPTER 22

We all went our separate ways. Eric watched me as I returned to my office. "Anything I need to know?" he asked.

"Come on in for a moment," I told him. He followed me into my office, shutting the door.

I waved him toward a chair, and he perched on the edge. "Your information was very helpful, Eric. I think we've narrowed down the time frame to right around 1907, for a variety of reasons." Including the cartridges we had found the day before, but I wasn't about to say that yet. "And I'm afraid it's likely that someone on the board or among our biggest donor members back then may be implicated. Did you know that the former president here was also the governor of the state for a few years?"

"No, ma'am, I didn't know that. But then, I'm kind of new to Pennsylvania. You have any aspirations in that direction?" Eric

grinned at me.

I laughed. "Good heavens, no! This place is as much as I want to run. I can't imagine dealing with an entire state, although I'd love to see a strong woman candidate run for that job." Not that I was going to hold my breath for that. "Anyway, I'm sure you've been thorough in looking for relevant files, but keep your eyes open, will you? Between the lack of professional administration and the, uh, sensitive nature of some of the information, what we want could have been filed anywhere. Or it could be long gone, or never committed to paper at all. Sorry to be so vague, but now you know as much as I do."

When Eric left, I shut my eyes and allowed myself the luxury of reviewing what I had heard at the meeting. Possible skulduggery extending from our place here all the way to the top of the state hierarchy — oh my. Financial shenanigans and cover-ups, for a possible menu of reasons — oh dear. And, of course, no one had kindly set all this down in writing and placed it in an envelope saying *In case of future unexplained murder, please open.* Even if he had, where would he have filed it?

When I opened my eyes, Marty was standing in front of my desk, and I jumped about

six inches out of my seat. "You scared me! How do you move so quietly?"

"Years of working in libraries, plus rubber soles. We need to talk."

"We *always* need to talk. What I wouldn't give for a single month with nothing but Society administrative business to deal with."

Marty dropped into a chair. "This *is* Society business. It's just not on your regular schedule. What's your take on what you heard at the meeting?"

I took a moment to line up my thoughts. "Too many coincidences for my liking. For one thing, the timing is too specific. We could probably figure out which month that pit was covered, and then we can put together a list of who had access to the building and the collections — and maybe even who was in town, other than at one of their many 'dilatory domiciles,' as the Social Register so quaintly puts it. So we could point fingers at a mere handful of society movers and shakers who were members here and accuse them of . . . I don't know what, retroactively. Of course, they're all dead now, so I'm not sure what good that does us. Unless you'd rather believe it was some poor workman back then who was responsible for the theft, took what we

suspect was in the box, and then dumped it in the pit to conceal his theft?"

"No, I think you're right." She lapsed into silence again.

"Marty," I began slowly, "what we've kind of tiptoed around so far is that somebody hid or destroyed an antique lap desk right around 1907, and it may have had a weapon in it. I don't know all the details about Pennsylvania gun laws, but I'm assuming it wasn't illegal to possess one. For some reason this weapon was either stolen or hidden, in a place someone assumed would be covered over soon and forgotten about permanently. What we don't know, and haven't really asked, is *why* that gun was so important in 1907, and why it's still important enough today for someone to conceal its existence? We're past considering this a string of random and unrelated coincidences, aren't we?"

"Yeah," Marty muttered, avoiding my gaze.

I wasn't going to be deterred, even though I knew my questions must be painful to Marty. "Is there any reason to believe that your grandfather was involved in this somehow? Some sort of cover-up? Did he commit a crime, or know of one?"

Marty was shaking her head, but I didn't

think it was at me or in response to the question. Then she faced me. "How the hell am I supposed to know? The man died before I was born. Even if he was involved in something, he would hardly have left a memo about it. I don't know what he did with the lap desk. I've already said that he didn't have a lot of cash, not the kind to endow a wing or name a hall, like some of his friends did. The Terwilligers had a rich history and some great artifacts and some good parcels of land, in the city and beyond, but they didn't have a lot of liquid assets, if you know what I mean. I think that theory about giving the collection rather than a financial contribution makes sense, in hindsight — and I know how difficult that would have been for him. It's like giving away a piece of your family. And that's probably why he hung on here at the Society for so long — so he could visit those documents. He also managed to pass that attachment on to my father, and in the end to me. But I keep coming back to his inventory for the donation to the Society, and there's no mention of a lap desk. Maybe he sold it without telling anyone. Maybe someone stole it from him."

"Who had the box in 1907 is only one of our questions," I said. "If we assume that

the gun was in the box then, we still don't know where it came from or when it went into the box. Or how and why it ended up in the box. Was your grandfather interested in firearms in general?"

"No. He was a very nonviolent man. He kept General John's papers because they were important to local and national history, not because they were military. He didn't hunt or fish. So, to the best of my knowledge, there is no reason to believe that the weapon belonged to him in 1907 or any time before that." Marty's look dared me to challenge her.

"I'll accept that, Marty. But in that case, where did it come from?"

She slumped just a bit. "I don't know. Look, you seemed to know what kind of gun it was — what does that tell you?"

"I'm making an educated guess, based on the ammunition we found, that it was an early Colt pistol. Back then, each new model of weapon required a new type of cartridge, and the type we found dates very specifically to between 1905 and 1911. These days that weapon would be very collectible, but back then it would have been experimental — not in wide use, to say the least. Did your grandfather hang out with any military friends?"

Marty sighed. "I understand why you're asking, but how am I supposed to know who my grandfather's pals were decades before I was born?"

I had to smile at that. "I know, it's ridiculous. If only he'd kept a social calendar along with all those other papers in his collection. So that brings us back to the people we *can* learn about, who were involved with the Society at that time. Do we have any other collections of militaria at the Society?"

Marty cocked her head. "Actually, I haven't looked at much of anything that wasn't relevant to the Revolution. So I can't help you much there, but I'm sure you can sic Rich or Lissa on looking into it."

I was struck by another thought. "Maybe the gun was given to the Society, in which case there might be accession records. Maybe then it was stuck into the lap desk during the construction phase — we know how sloppy record-keeping was back then — and then the box fell down the hole by accident and nobody noticed the gun falling out, and both were covered up?" I said in a rush. "So nobody was guilty of anything other than carelessness? And the fact that it resurfaced now was completely random, and some stranger saw Carnell with it and took it away from him and shoved him and

he died," I finished triumphantly.

Marty didn't look convinced. "Well, that lets just about everybody off the hook. You're saying it was just chance that somebody ran into Carnell in a bar and saw he had a Colt whatever stuffed in his pants, and decided to follow him out and take it? I thought we'd tossed out the random-collection-of-coincidences theory already."

"It could have happened that way," I said, but without much conviction.

"Then I'll play devil's advocate," Marty said. "Why did the guy take the time to chat up Carnell and make all buddy-buddy and then leave with him? Once he'd seen the gun, he could have left and waited outside until Carnell came out and tackled him then."

"True," I admitted, "although maybe he just wanted Carnell to trust him."

"And then the two of them headed for Carnell's home, which was in a darker, quieter neighborhood — much better for a mugging."

"Okay," I said. "But, Marty, what's your point? You *want* this to be something other than an accident? You *want* to connect it to the Society?"

"Only if it's true, Nell. Let the police worry about the death. But for me there are

things that just don't add up. And even if the modern death was an accident, I want to know what the hell the gun was doing in my grandfather's lap desk, which wasn't even officially here."

"Fair enough. And since you're on the board, it's on your head that we're devoting a lot of staff time and energy to sorting this out. Not that I begrudge you — the Terwilligers, past and present, have done a lot for the Society. And I'd like to know the truth myself."

I slapped my hands on my desk and sat up straighter. "If we exclude your grandfather as the owner of that weapon, which is fine by me, the list is even shorter. Even I recognize some of those names as bigwigs of the day. I assume your grandfather knew them all, to some extent. Do you have any personal correspondence between them? I know we can check the files here, but if there was anything between friends or colleagues, maybe it never made it to our files. Did they play golf together? Go sailing? Ride to hounds?"

Marty shook her head. "No to all of those. As far as I know, my grandfather hated most forms of exercise, and he spent most of his time here or in his library at the house. Which is long gone, by the way. I can look

through what I've got. I inherited a lot of my father's files when he passed, but I've never gone through them. I've been too busy with the collection here . . . and I guess in the beginning it was too painful, and then I kind of got busy with other things. Maybe some of his father's stuff is mixed in."

"What about other members of your family?"

She shook her head again. "I got all the papers because I was the only one interested. Otherwise they were headed for a Dumpster."

"Do you want some help going through them?"

"I'll ask Rich — he's pretty familiar with the different handwriting by now. And frankly, there's not all that much. We can be done in a day or two. Who knows, maybe we'll find some treasures."

"So that's your assignment. I'll read over what Lissa just gave us, and check with Shelby to see if she can add anything. What do we do now?" I asked.

"Eat lunch," Marty said firmly. "Let's go someplace where nobody knows us and we can talk. How about that cafeteria-type place?"

I looked at my watch and realized it was well past noon. "Good idea." We paused our

conversation until we had arrived and were settled with our food, then I said, "Our main focus at the moment is to figure out who might have owned a hard-to-get gun in 1907 and why he would have wanted to hide it. Our secondary focus is to track descendants of those board members and donors who might fit that description and who also have access to the Society now. If it was in that box in the pit, either somebody knew it was there from 1907, or somebody saw Carnell conceal it and knew what it was. What's the time limit on this?"

Marty swallowed the bite of food she was chewing. "Okay, it's Thursday. I say we gather everybody's reports tomorrow and see what we've got. If nothing jumps out, we go home and spend the weekend thinking it over. I'll go through my father's papers at home. By Monday we can decide if we've done all we can and it's time to get back to our regular business."

"Seems fair enough."

Marty poked at the food on her place. "Nell, if there's a crime that was committed with this gun, don't the police have a right to know?"

It took me a moment to realize what she had just suggested. "Wait — we've been assuming that the weapon was the *motive* for

306

Carnell's death, not the direct cause."

Marty wouldn't meet my eyes. "Think about it. Why would anyone care so much now if it wasn't involved in a crime somewhere back up the line?"

That stopped me cold. "Marty, do you know something you're not saying?"

"No. I'm just guessing. But doesn't it make sense? Why would anyone have hidden it back then, unless they wanted to ditch evidence?"

"So now we're supposed to look for crimes involving a gun between 1905 and 1907?" My head was beginning to spin. I seriously doubted the Philadelphia Police Department had done ballistic testing that early. And why would they share anything from their archives with me? Of course, maybe newspaper records would have something, but would they have named names? Especially if the crime involved individuals of high social standing?

Marty derailed my thoughts. "So, why do you know so much about guns?"

If this had been a cartoon I would have done a comic double take. Marty could change subjects with lightning speed, but she never lost sight of what she wanted to know. And I kind of felt like I owed it to her to answer her question.

"My father and I used to shoot together when I was in high school." That much was true. "He was kind of a gun aficionado, and I was trying hard to impress him, so I did my homework."

"Did you? Impress him, I mean?" Marty asked.

"Maybe. It's too late to ask him now."

"Oh. Sorry."

"Don't be. I know a lot more about your family than you do about mine, so it seems only fair to tell you a little about mine. But that's why I know about firearms. I certainly had never anticipated that the knowledge would come in handy years later."

I sat up straighter. "Let me think about the idea of an old crime, okay? We've got enough going on already, and maybe that will shed some light. Lissa and Shelby are tracking the donor families, and we know Lissa's a good researcher. Okay, maybe she won't be able to get certified copies of birth certificates and the like, but there are other ways of following kinship that are public. Wills. Property transfers. Newspaper articles, especially obituaries, which tell us a lot about family connections, as I don't need to tell you. I'll bet Lissa can have a rough cut by tomorrow."

"That works for me," Marty said firmly.

"But keep thinking about the other thing."
As if I had a choice.

CHAPTER 23

Once back at my desk, I called Lissa on her cell phone. She answered quickly.

"Where are you?" I asked.

"At the library, and I've got a class at three. Why?"

"Have you made any progress on tracing the families of those former board members I e-mailed you?"

"Some. When do you need it?"

"Soonest. Look, I know it's asking a lot, but could you have this roughed out by tomorrow morning? It's important, otherwise I wouldn't ask."

"Sure, I'll just give up sleeping. Seriously, I did make a good start, so I can definitely finish extracting what I can from public records and give you that in the morning." She hesitated. "It sounds like you have a pretty good idea of what you want to find."

Should I tell her to stick to only those families who have living descendants? I

decided not to. "I don't want to bias you. If there's any question about what to follow, concentrate on descendants who stayed around Philadelphia. If they headed for California, put them on the back burner. Does that make your job easier?"

"Much. You want, uh, legal proof?"

"No, just the general descendant tree will be fine. Oh, and if you get done early, e-mail the results to my personal account, okay?"

"You really must want this! Will do."

"Great. See you tomorrow."

One more thing checked off my list. I thought for a moment, then decided to call the bank, the same one the Society had used for the last hundred and whatever years. After five minutes of explaining who I was and what I wanted, I finally reached a knowledgeable human. "Hello, Ms. — uh, what was your name?"

"Esposito. What can I do for you?"

I explain my bona fides once again and could hear the woman tapping at her keyboard, no doubt calling up the Society's information. "Yes, I see your account. Everything appears to be in order. Are you concerned about a particular transaction?"

"I'd like to know about whatever transactions took place between, say, 1900 and 1907."

That startled her into silence. Then she chuckled. "Well, I can tell you that our records go back to the founding of the bank in 1853 but are not part of our electronic database. Let me check with my superior and find out where and how they might have been archived. Can you hold?"

"I will."

I listened to canned music as I made yet another list on a pad in front of me. At least some items were inching their way forward, although I couldn't claim that anything had been resolved on any of them. I wondered idly how many bank ledgers we held at the Society, for banks that had ceased to exist decades or even centuries before? Philadelphia boasted an impressive history in the banking sphere, starting with the first bank in the country. While I waited for the people at the modern bank to get back to me, I noodled around our Society database to see what records we actually possessed, and was pleasantly surprised by the scope — but "our" bank was not among them. I sighed and resumed waiting.

Finally someone came back on the line, a man who introduced himself as Jacob Keefe, the Society's account manager. We went through the whole "who are you" rigmarole again, until he finally accepted who I was

and that I had a right to the information. "Thank you, Ms. Pratt. I know the process is tedious, but I'm sure you understand and appreciate the lengths we must go to, to protect the integrity of our clients' accounts."

"Oh, I do, believe me. But all I wanted was a simple answer: Do you have the records for the Pennsylvania Antiquarian Society for the first decade of the twentieth century, and can I see them?"

"The answer to both questions is yes, but they remain in paper form — they have not been digitized, largely because there has been little call to do so, and they are presently stored in a remote warehouse. I can order them up for you to be here sometime next week."

I didn't want to wait, but did I have a choice? I summoned up my chief-executive-but-really-nice-lady voice and said sweetly, "Is there any possible way you could get them any more quickly? I hate to bother you, but it's really important." I lowered my voice. "There's a police investigation involved." Not exactly a falsehood, was it? When he started sputtering, I hurried to say, "Oh, it's nothing that your bank has done. In fact, I'm hoping that your records will help us establish someone's innocence."

I hoped he wasn't going to ask me how a bank record from that early era was going to make that happen.

He didn't. "Well, of course we'll do whatever we can to expedite their retrieval. After all, you're one of our oldest and most respected clients. I'll make a few calls, and if we're very lucky, they could be in Philadelphia by, say, tomorrow afternoon? Will that be satisfactory?"

"Oh, yes, more than satisfactory. I can't thank you enough, and I'll be sure you get the recognition you deserve for assisting in this matter. Please call me when you know when they'll arrive. And I hope you'll take the time to visit the Society — we have some wonderful original documents here pertaining to the early history of banking in Philadelphia, and I'm sure you'd be interested." I was laying it on with a trowel.

"I, er, um — that sounds delightful. I'll be in touch." He hung up, and I sat in my seat, smiling at how my silly, sexist strategy had gotten me what I wanted.

Would the bank records show any unlikely inflows of cash? It might be instructive to compare the bank's details of the cash flow in the construction account with Shelby's contributions records. Or it might yield another big fat goose egg. Still, I could cross

one more thing off my list.

There were no further revelations that afternoon. James picked me up at five thirty. I let him navigate Philadelphia rush-hour traffic before I said, "May we have a hypothetical conversation?"

"You mean a conversation about something hypothetical. Certainly."

"Excellent. Say, hypothetically, that we may have knowledge of an old crime, and all the parties involved are long dead, so they don't care. And say we have a new crime, which may or may not be related. And we think it is possible that we have a weapon that may link the two. Except that we don't actually 'have' it, but we think it exists. What should we do with this hypothetical information about the hypothetical crime or crimes?" I ended sweetly.

James's mouth twitched as he tried not to smile. "Could you be more oblique if you tried? More to the point, does this involve anything confidential or proprietary?"

"Not right now, as far as I know."

He sighed. "You've found something more about this recent death, haven't you?"

No wonder James made such a good agent: he could read between the lines. "Marty and I think so. But we have little hard evidence."

"Then go ahead and tell me what it is you're thinking."

I presented him with Henry's new information about the gunpowder residue, and added my discovery of the cartridges in the pit, which I thought established the existence of a weapon — a specific weapon whose current whereabouts were unknown. I laid out our theory about the removal of the hypothetical weapon from the Society, Carnell Scruggs's putative possession of it (if briefly), and the alternate scenarios for its seizure, which had resulted in his death. I pointed out which details I had given the police, and which I hadn't. And then I sat back, shut up, and let James mull it over for a few miles.

His first comment was, "The recent death — the only one the police care about — could be no more than a string of coincidences."

"We acknowledge that, which is why I haven't gone back to them with this. I really don't want the Philadelphia Police Department to see me as a crazy lady who keeps bothering them with wild theories."

"So what were you planning to do next?"

"I'm holding another meeting with the inner circle of staff members tomorrow morning, where we will pool the results of our

latest research. Marty and I have agreed that if we don't turn up something of substance, we'll cut it off. It's not right to waste the Society's time chasing wild geese."

"Will Martha let it go?" James asked.

"I . . . don't know. You know how she feels about her family, and this hits kind of close to home."

"I know. She was close to her father — he was a good man, and so was his father, based on all I've heard. I'm sure she doesn't want to see his memory tarnished by finding that he was involved in a serious crime or a cover-up."

"You have any suggestions?"

"Off the top of my head, only one: Have you tried contacting any gun collectors?"

That hadn't occurred to me. "No, but it's a great idea. You know any?"

"I might," James said. "Let me make a call tomorrow."

A collector might know who'd be interested in that kind of antique weapon, I thought. *Or who might buy one, if it turned up on the street. But then again, it might not be relevant.*

"You're familiar with that weapon, right?" James asked.

"I've never handled one, but I've seen pictures. Why?"

"Because to someone like Carnell, it

would look a lot like a modern weapon," he told me. "I doubt that an unskilled laborer would look at it and say, 'Ah, a rare and valuable antique!' He'd be more likely to think, 'Bet I could get some quick cash if I can find a buyer.' Right?"

"Good point, James," I said. "Although whoever took it might still go to a dealer, if *he* recognized it for what it was, so it's worth looking into local dealers. Can I ask, would it be valuable enough to kill for?"

"It may be rare, but it's not that important," James said.

That was what I had thought, but it was nice to have confirmation. "Which brings me back around to our hypothetical crime. Carnell found it by accident and took it because he thought he could sell it, but whoever stole it from him more likely wanted it to disappear again, for reasons not connected to its value. Otherwise, why would he have taken the escutcheon, too? You think our story hangs together?"

"It's possible, even if it's a stretch. You're going at this in the right way: you and your staff are looking at the earlier event, assuming it exists, where you have details that no one else would. What happened then may or may not be related to what happened last week, but that's not your business. Let the

police handle that."

"And that's exactly what I told Marty. But we could be helping by providing a motive."

"And Martha accepted that?"

"I think so. For now. She kind of defines her own boundaries, doesn't she?"

"She is a force to be reckoned with," James said solemnly.

I allowed myself a small giggle, and then we lapsed into a comfortable silence. I felt like I'd cleared one hurdle in working out the ebb and flow of our relationship.

I really hoped my Society staff and Marty and I either caught a break with our research efforts or ran into an insurmountable brick wall, because I was getting heartily sick of devoting so much of my time and energy to figuring this out, not to mention that of a large portion of my administrative staff. Was Detective Hrivnak good at her job? Reasonably. Would she solve this one? I had no idea. Last time we'd talked, at the beginning of the week, she'd been all but clueless — and I meant that literally. We'd handed her the information about the escutcheon, which unfortunately tied some part of the event to the Society, but the man in the blurry bar video who had shown interest in it could have been practically anybody. At least any slim, white, able-bodied thirty-

something male. Which narrowed it down to a few thousand people in Philadelphia.

But which one of those people had a motive to kill Carnell Scruggs? Was I relying too much on motive? Was it as simple as a mugging gone wrong? Not that Mr. Scruggs had looked like he had much on him, but maybe he'd flashed his wages at the bar. How much money was worth mugging someone for? Was there a minimum, or did it depend on how desperate you were?

"Were you going to get out of the car?" James's voice broke into my racing thoughts.

I looked up to find we were parked in our own driveway. "Oh, are we home already? I was trying to work something out in my head." I pulled myself together and gathered my things, then climbed out of the car. He already had the back door open when I reached it. "Thank you, kind sir," I said as I brushed past him.

A short while later, I sat admiring James as he prepared dinner and I enjoyed a glass of wine. "Have you caught any new cases lately?" I asked. "I mean, that you can talk about?"

"Nothing major. I think I've told you before, usually each of us has between ten and thirty open cases at any one time, so there's plenty to keep us busy. Some drag

on because we're waiting for one more piece of evidence, or a lab report — and you know how backed-up the labs are — or a piece of information from a different agency. Make haste slowly, as the saying goes. Not unlike your place."

"I guess I have a different perspective, since we think in terms of centuries. Funny how we keep things because we believe they matter — that something someone did or said in 1823 would mean something to a researcher today. I can't believe I and my staff are trying to solve a killing that took place last week based on something that happened more than a century ago."

"That does sound unlikely," James replied amiably.

"And it's intriguing how perspectives on history, and which bits are important, keep changing."

"Could you see yourself doing something else?" James asked as he chopped something.

"Like what? Academia? I think that boat sailed a while ago, and I'm not sorry. A corporate position? Politics? Or maybe I could become an antique dealer so we could finally furnish this place at a cost we could afford?" I laughed. "Please don't tell me you're thinking of moving to Bora Bora and

opening up a beachfront bar."

"What? Oh no, nothing like that. I work for the government, and that's about as stable as a job gets these days. But if I want to leave the FBI, I'll discuss it with you first, I promise."

That hadn't come up before, which was surprising given some of the situations he had found himself in recently. "Do you think about it? I mean, are you prepared to keep running around wrestling with bad guys and getting shot at for the next twenty or thirty years?" I wasn't sure how I felt about that idea myself.

"Those are relatively rare events. I typically spend far more time on paperwork. As you do," James said, now sautéing what he had finished chopping.

"True. But poor Carnell has been dead for a week now, and if there's a way I can help solve this, I want to try to find it. Whether or not it involves the Society. Because it's the right thing to do."

"I know. And I love you for that." James turned down the heat under the pan and proceeded to demonstrate how he really felt. It took a while.

CHAPTER 24

Friday morning, as we drove toward the city, I mentally reviewed what I hoped we would have uncovered since yesterday. How much longer would it take us to find an answer — or to declare defeat and go on about our business? I felt like somewhere there was a clock ticking.

There were times that I had to remind myself that things didn't always move as quickly as I'd like. As the custodian of an historical institution I should be all too aware of that issue, but when someone died and that death cast a shadow on the Society, I became impatient.

My little band of researchers and I were moving forward by inches, one small fact at a time. I was fairly confident that we had answers somewhere in our files, or maybe in Marty's files, but they were well buried, and who knew how long it would take to unearth them? Some ancient Greek had

once said (in Greek, I assumed), "The millstones of the gods grind slow, but they grind exceedingly fine," whatever that meant. I took it to mean that there was no hurrying the process, but you'd get it right at the end. Or at least have the flour to make breakfast.

The staff collaborators trickled into the downstairs room at nine, with less energy than they had shown the day before. Going back over the same stacks of dusty documents to see if you'd missed something could be draining. Even coffee wasn't helping.

By seven minutes past nine, we were still short a couple of people. "Has anyone seen Rich or Lissa?" I asked.

"I kept Rich working late at my place last night, going over the family papers with me," Marty volunteered. "He looked like he was dragging by the time he left. Maybe he's trying to find one last bit of information."

"I asked Lissa to take on a lot," I added. "She's thorough — she could still be searching, too. But since most of us are here, we'd better get started. We're all throwing our little pieces into the pot and hoping that they magically come together to make a stew, er, sense."

Looking at the still-blank faces, I realized

that Marty and I were the only people who knew *all* the details. Each of the others knew some parts; most of them had done what I'd asked out of obedience or loyalty, but without knowing their purpose. But if we were ever going to bring all this together, I needed to tell them *everything* we now knew.

I cleared my throat. "I'm sorry. I owe you an apology, because we haven't given you all the available information. In part that was to avoid giving you any preconceptions about what you were looking for. In part it was to keep this whole thing as quiet as possible. A man is dead, and maybe selfishly I didn't want that to be laid at our door. But keeping the details from you hasn't been fair to you, and it's getting in the way of putting together a coherent story. So this is what we know." I proceeded to outline what I'd learned from Detective Hrivnak and from Henry Phinney, and I told them about the possible existence of a gun, and sketched out what Marty and I thought might have happened. But it was obvious there were still some gaping holes in the story, and I was hoping against hope that the people in front of me could help fill them. "Any questions?"

Ben, who had been listening intently, spoke quickly. "That's a pretty unusual

weapon, a real collector's item now. But it wouldn't look like an antique — if you don't know weapons, you could easily think it was modern, not a century old. And it would probably work just fine, if it was cleaned up."

"Thank you, Ben. That's what I was thinking. I've been wondering if Carnell Scruggs saw it and figured he could sell it on the street easily. Any other questions?"

There were lots. Marty and I managed to answer all the easy ones, but it was Shelby who offered the biggest piece of the puzzle.

"Let me make sure I've got this straight. Our theory of the moment is that there was an old gun in the box in the pit. Carnell found it and made off with it, someone saw him do it and followed him, and somehow Carnell ended up dead. Sound about right?"

"Yes, in a nutshell. But —

She held up a hand. "I'm not finished. So for the last several days you've had all of us hunting down old records of this, that, and the other thing, I assume in the hope that something will point to someone who had a reason to have such a gun back in 1907 *and* a reason to hide it, and picked this place for some reason that made sense to him. The lap desk shouldn't have been here at all, at least on paper, and you've made it clear that

the only way that gun could have ended up in our basement was if it came in with someone who had pretty close ties with the Society at that particular time. That's a short list." Shelby's smile was still in place. "And you asked me to see what we had in our files about the people on the short list, so that we could put the gun that I didn't know about until three minutes ago into the hands of one of those people. Right?"

"Right again, Shelby," I said impatiently. "Well summarized. Do you have a point, other than complaining that I kept you, if not in the dark, then at least in the shade? I've already apologized for that."

"Well, I think I've got something." With a dramatic flourish, Shelby picked up a sheaf of photocopies and handed them around the table. "You do remember that we're a collecting institution? And that our collections just happen to include microfilms and digitized records of Pennsylvania newspapers going back to before the Civil War?"

"Shelby, if you don't tell us what you've found," I growled, "I will have to strangle you, in spite of all these witnesses. We're short on time. Can you please get to the point?" I wondered for a moment if she was going to stick out her tongue at me, but she decided to take the high road. "Read," she

said, pointing at the papers she'd handed out.

I read. I read about the tragic death of Mrs. Harrison Frazer and her sailing instructor, one Thomas Westcott, both shot to death at the Frazer summer home on Long Beach Island, New Jersey, in August of 1907. (From the grainy newspaper photos, it appeared that the sailing instructor was significantly younger than Mrs. Frazer.) Mr. Frazer had arrived at the beach house unexpectedly, having caught an early train from Philadelphia, and discovered the bodies. He blamed an armed intruder — Mrs. Frazer had been wont to travel with her nicer jewelry, for all those yacht club dinners, so the house was a likely target — who was never identified, much less located. No weapon was ever found, which was one reason why Mr. Frazer, the most obvious suspect under the circumstances, was never arrested.

The later paragraphs of the newspaper article made it clear that Mr. Frazer was an important man in Philadelphia and served on many boards, including that of the Pennsylvania Antiquarian Society. A second, shorter article reported that he was so devastated by the death of his beloved wife of twenty-seven years that he took his own

life a few months later and was found hanging in the carriage house behind his home in a nearby suburb. He left his letters and memorabilia to the Society.

I noticed that Latoya nodded, no doubt recognizing the Frazer gift to the collections.

I looked up from the page at Shelby. "This is amazing."

"Aw, shucks, ma'am, it weren't nothin'." Then her expression sobered. "Seriously, it was the only crime that I could find that was linked to any of the people with connections at the Society at the right time. And that was *before* I knew about the gun."

I looked at Marty, but she was staring into space. "Marty?" I said.

She was slow to focus on me. "What? Oh, right, the Frazers." She stood up abruptly. "I've got to go." Then without another word she turned on her heel and left the room.

"What was that about?" Shelby said.

"I have no idea," I told her.

I'd have to chase down Marty as soon as we wrapped up this meeting. In the meantime, I picked up Shelby's thread again. "All right, then. We have a new hypothesis to add to our string of hypotheses: that Mr. Frazer was the owner of the gun, and he used it to kill his wife and a man we can

infer he assumed was her lover. If that's true, how did he manage to conceal the weapon from the police?"

"Just how thorough do you think they were in 1907?" Shelby asked. "I mean, the man was wealthy and respected. The shootings took place at his summer house, which was probably one of those hulking, big places on the beach, so the local police were first on the scene. You think they searched very hard? Besides, back then nobody would have blamed him for shooting his wife and her lover, at least off the record. Hell, there are countries today where that's still considered a legitimate excuse for murder. The article is pretty evasive about where the bodies were found, so maybe we should infer that they were in bed together — this paper wasn't so much into gory details as we are today."

"I wonder if the original files on the murder are available?" I said, mainly to myself. To the group I said, "From what I understand, there is no statute of limitations on murder, so if no one was ever tried on this, it should theoretically still be an open case."

"Yes, in New Jersey," Latoya said, throwing some cold water on my thinking. "Isn't there a problem of jurisdiction? Are you go-

ing to go to the Shore and ask the police there if you can see the files? You don't exactly have any standing there."

Latoya had raised a good point. We still needed more information before we could take any of this to Detective Hrivnak. If we could convince her, she might be willing to approach the New Jersey police and gain access to whatever remained. Maybe. All we had to offer her at the moment was a pretty weak string of conjectures and very little evidence.

This was getting ridiculous — castles in the air built on straw, or some other, equally mangled analogy.

I realized that everyone else was waiting for me to say something. "Latoya's right. We have a series of assumptions but little more. What can we find that will support our theory, that Frazer killed two people and got away with it? And how did the gun end up here? We need to know more about the man. Was he a banker? A lawyer? A businessman along the lines of John Wanamaker? Or just a member of the idle rich? Maybe he belonged to a gun club."

"Why didn't he just pitch it in the ocean?" Shelby asked. "Or bury it in the sand until the police had checked the house? There is sand at the shore, isn't there?"

"Yes, Shelby, there is," I said patiently. "Lots of it. Why don't you check exactly where Mr. Frazer lived — or rather, summered — at the shore? There must be a record somewhere. For that matter, find out where he lived in this area, and how active he was here. I mean, was he primarily a donor, or was he an historian?"

"Will do," Shelby said. "And we'd better find out if Mr. Frazer knew Mr. Terwilliger, right? I know you hope to keep Marty's family out of this, but if there's any evidence that her grandfather was involved, it'll have to come out," Shelby said.

"Yes, please look into that, too. You know Marty — she's honest, and she respects the facts of history. If her grandfather turns out to have been part of any kind of cover-up, she would want to know. Find out anything you can." Privately, though, I wondered if Marty already had or knew of some evidence of his involvement, which would explain her abrupt exit. I turned to Latoya. "Can you check what was in Mr. Frazer's donation to the collections? He could have left almost anything, or nothing of value. Let's find out."

"Of course," Latoya said. "I can have that quickly."

I had almost forgotten my request to the

bank. "One more thing — yesterday I got in touch with the Society's bank, which has been the Society's bank from Day One. I asked if they could retrieve the records from the period we're talking about. If we're lucky they'll be available today. If not, probably early next week. I want to see if there are any unexpected contributions. I'll share whatever I find with you, Shelby, since you've already looked at the development records for the construction projects. We can compare those to the bank records, and look for any odd timing, or an unexpected late contribution. I'll let you know when the bank receives them and I've had a chance to look at them."

"Nell, I apologize if this is a dumb question, but what do you hope to learn?" Ben asked. "I don't know how your donor records work."

"Sorry, Ben — I keep forgetting you haven't been here long. Assume the lap desk went into the pit no later than 1907, when the building was completed. If a donor contributed a significant amount around or after that time, we would take a harder look at him. If his contribution is way out of line with any prior or later contribution of his, then we look even harder."

"You think it would be something like

hush money?" Ben persisted. "Someone here who knew what was going on said, 'Ante up and I'll keep quiet'?"

"It's a possibility. It probably would have looked like an ordinary contribution to most people who knew about it."

"I'm way ahead of you, lady," Shelby said. "I've already pulled together a list of the Society's contributors from that particular period. Here, I made copies for everyone." She tossed another stack of stapled copies on the table, and everyone helped themselves to one. "I included both regular operating contributions and special campaign contributions. I haven't really had time to digest the results, so if anything pops out at you, tell me and I can look for more detail."

Nobody volunteered any comments immediately, so I went on, "Thank you, Shelby. I asked Eric to look for additional financial reports from the board records, and he came up with a few. I have to say I'm appalled at how sloppy the board's records were back then. There are a few treasurer's reports from that decade, but it's not like they're monthly, or even from every meeting. That doesn't mean they aren't somewhere in the records here, but they could have been filed — or misfiled — almost

anywhere. But if we can find them, they might bolster whatever you come up with, Shelby." I looked at the people seated around the table. "Anything else?" I asked, and got no response. "Thank you all for your efforts. I know you're doing this on top of all your regular duties, and I appreciate it. Okay, that's all, folks. Back to business."

However, before anyone could leave, there was a rapping on the door, and Lissa poked her head in. "Sorry I missed the meeting this morning, but I found something you've got to see."

Chapter 25

We all settled back in our seats. "Pull up a chair and tell us what you've got," I told Lissa. "But before you begin, there are some new details you need to know." When she sat, I gave her the short version that I had presented to the group at the beginning of the meeting and added the bits and pieces that had come up along the way; when I got to the part about the missing weapon, I could have sworn that Lissa grew paler.

When I was finished, Lissa took a moment to digest what I'd said before speaking herself. "Since we're trying to find out why anyone would want to . . . harm that poor man who died last week," she began, "and you believe there's some link to the Society, you asked me to look at anyone around now who might be related to the people who were in charge back around 1900 through when the new building was finished in 1907. Since I didn't have time to get over

here and go through your records, I used online resources like Ancestry.com as much as I could, though sites like that don't list living people, so I could go only so far. We're talking two, three generations, tops. So then I went looking through obituaries and wills and newspaper articles after that, to get as close to the present as I could. I had the names of maybe fifteen board members, an equally short list of high-dollar donors, and the pitifully few staff members they had at the time, all of whom would have had access to the dark corners of the place. I managed to track down something for all of them, though I didn't look at the Terwilligers, since we've got plenty of info on them already. Several lines petered out — either the family members are all deceased now, or the last few moved away and haven't been heard of locally for years. I could have missed a few female lines who married and changed names."

"Understood," I agreed. "Let's start with the obvious ones and see what you found."

Lissa looked around. "Where's Marty? And Rich? They really need to hear this, too."

"Marty had to leave. She said she thinks Rich might still be researching something. But go ahead — we can fill them in later."

Lissa looked at the uniformly somber expressions on everyone in the room. "You really are taking this seriously."

"Yes, we are," I said. "Show us what you've put together."

"All right." Lissa started dealing out papers in stacks on the polished oak table. "Ten members of that original list still have descendants living in the greater Philadelphia area. I can't give you their financial status back around 1900, but you can infer some details from the addresses and professions, I think. I've sketched out the line of descent from each of the early Society members to anyone currently in the greater Philadelphia area. Take a look." She stepped back so that everyone could look at what she had assembled.

I recognized the surnames of a few modern-day members and realized that, like Marty, they were now third- or fourth-generation within the same family. I suppose there were other cities — and other societies such as this one — where the same was true, but it still sort of thrilled me to be looking at it in tangible form.

But I came to a screeching halt in front of one stack of papers.

"What is it?" Lissa asked.

I placed a finger on the nearest page, the

one with the descendant tree on top of one of the piles. "You're kidding," someone whispered. I couldn't tell who because I was still staring at the page.

Rich Girard. Our intern for the past two years. Marty's right hand in the cataloging of the Terwilliger papers. Nice guy. Easygoing, funny, hardworking, meticulous with details. And a descendant of Harrison Frazer.

I turned to Lissa. "You're sure?"

She nodded. "I double-checked. You didn't know?"

I recalled something about a family connection when he'd originally been hired a couple of years earlier, but it hadn't registered with me. Marty had vouched for him, and that was all that really mattered then. I took my time in choosing my words. "Lissa, while you were putting this together, we arrived at — well, I guess you'd call it a strong suspicion that former board member Harrison Frazer was involved in the fatal shooting of his wife and her probable lover in the summer of 1907. Nothing was ever proved, and no weapon was found. Shelby told us about the Frazer murders this morning. It seems likely to me that there was a gun that somehow ended up in the Terwilliger lap desk, at least at the time it was tossed in the

pit, and that this gun was probably the missing Frazer murder weapon. We also believe that the discovery of this gun by Carnell Scruggs is what led to his death, and someone must have seen him conceal it and take it out of the building. As far as we know, the police have no suspects, but the only visual evidence — the recording from the bar where the man ate dinner — shows him in the company of a young white man."

Lissa looked stunned. "So this other man at the bar, you're saying you think it could've been Rich?"

I nodded. "The bar video isn't conclusive, but there's nothing in it to eliminate Rich. It's just a suspicion, but this whole mess has been rife with coincidences, and they keep adding up. Marty was with Rich last night, but she didn't tell us if they'd found anything of interest. She stayed at this meeting long enough to hear about the Frazer murders, but then left in a hurry. She may hold some of the answers." In fact, I suspected she might have left *because* of those answers.

I stopped and thought for a moment, then said, "I'm sorry if this sounds, well, procedural, but let's take a moment and see if we can we put together a timeline for where we all were last Wednesday night, when Carnell

Scruggs was hit by that car."

"I assume you mean whether and when we saw Rich?" Shelby asked quietly.

"I'm afraid so. If one of you can tell me that the two of you were together at the dentist at the time Scruggs was killed, I'll feel a lot better."

Everybody sat silently, scribbling notes on pieces of paper. Latoya finished first. "I'm afraid this won't help much — I spent the afternoon in my office. I did not go to the basement. I might have seen Rich in the processing room, but only in passing — we didn't speak. He wasn't working on anything in particular for me. You'd do better to ask the others who spend time in that room."

I wasn't surprised; her recollections were no better or worse than my own.

"Ben?"

He was shaking his head. "Rich wasn't around the processing room that day. Of course, that doesn't mean he wasn't in the building somewhere."

I nodded. "Shelby?"

"More or less the same as Latoya. I was working in my office all day," Shelby said. "I didn't talk to Rich. If I saw him at all, he would have been trailing after Marty, but I see them a lot, and I couldn't swear to what day it was."

"Does Rich ever look in the development files?" I asked her.

"Sure, although mostly at the Terwilliger stuff. But he probably looks at the people who knew the various Terwilligers . . ." Shelby's voice trailed off when she realized what she had just said. "He could know as much as we do about any connections between the Frazers and the Terwilligers. More, in fact. He's had a couple of years to work on it."

Maybe. I had worked with Rich for all that time. He was a nice guy, a competent cataloger. Marty had been pleased with his work. How could he go from that to shoving a man to his death? Why would he do that? I wasn't ready to believe it. I wanted to hear what *he* had to say. I wanted to know why Marty had left so fast. I wanted to understand what the heck was going on.

Since everyone was now staring expectantly at me, I struggled to pull myself together. "Okay, people, let's focus. We're looking for anything to do with the Frazer family, whether it's in collections or development or board records. And I will try to track down Marty and see what she knows." I was pretty sure she knew something. Maybe even a lot. "And if any of you see or hear from Rich, let me know."

"You really believe he's involved?" Latoya said.

"Honestly, I don't know. I hope not. Anyway, thank you all for your work on this."

We straggled out to our various offices. On the way, I noticed the lobby was empty, so I stopped to talk to Bob. "Did Marty leave the building, Bob?"

"She did, maybe half an hour ago."

Well, that saved me hunting through the stacks, where she might have hidden herself like a wounded animal retreating to her den. "What about Rich — have you seen him today?"

"Not that I can recall, but he could have come in early."

"Thanks, Bob." The lobby was a bit too public to ask Bob about where Rich was on the day of Carnell's death. Surely the police had already talked to them both. Maybe they'd done all of this already.

I trudged back to my office. Eric was back at his desk. "You look like you need more coffee, Nell. And Rich Girard is waiting for you in your office — said he really needed to talk to you."

CHAPTER 26

I didn't have time to wonder how Rich had escaped Bob's notice, but he knew the place well. Had he come to confess? No, that seemed ridiculous — he didn't even know we knew about his Frazer connections, or that we had reason to care. Had Marty sent him to me? One way to find out. "Hold off on that coffee, Eric. I want to talk to Rich first."

I squared my shoulders and marched into my office, shutting the door behind me. Rich was wandering around looking at the framed engravings on the walls, but he turned quickly when I came in. I held my tongue until I had walked around my desk and sat down.

"Eric said you wanted to talk to me? Why don't you sit down and tell me what's on your mind." *Like, have you killed anybody recently?*

Rich dropped into one of the antique visi-

tor chairs in front of the desk. "I don't know where to start. I'm sorry to bother you when I know you're busy, but I found something in the Terwilliger papers yesterday, and I didn't want to show it to Marty until I'd had time to think about it, and I haven't seen her yet this morning, so I figured I'd better bring it to you. I ducked out of that meeting this morning because I didn't want to face Marty before I talked to you, you know?"

"I understand, Rich. Marty left our nine o'clock meeting in kind of a hurry, and Bob says she left the building. Do you know anything about that?" I asked him.

He shook his head. "I haven't seen her since last night."

"What was it you found, that you think was so important?" *And that you couldn't share with Marty?*

He pulled himself up straighter in his chair. "Last night Marty and I were over at her place going over the family papers, the ones that were personal rather than historical, so they never went to the Society. Her grandfather was careful with his record-keeping, you know? Her father, not so much. He kind of saved everything, but he didn't organize it very well. So it took some time to sort through what he left, even

though Marty's been through most of it before, and a lot of it wasn't relevant. I even found a love letter her father wrote to someone who wasn't her mother. Didn't seem to upset her, but that stuff didn't get us any further. And then I found this. I made a copy of it and printed out one for you."

Rich opened a folder he had brought and slid a copy of what appeared to be a hand-written list across my desk. "This is the inventory for Marty's grandfather's gift of the Terwilliger papers and artifacts to the Society. It's the one in your records."

I recognized it. "Yes, we've all looked at this before. Why are you showing it to me now?"

"Marty probably told you that her father ended up with most of the papers from the extended family because he was the only one who wanted them, and then she inherited them from him. When we were going through them, I found this." Rich pulled out another sheet and handed that one to me, then sat back and stared at me, waiting.

I looked at the two pages. The handwriting appeared to be the same, although I was no expert. The second one looked very much like the first, and both seemed to enumerate the same sequence of items in

the collection.

And the second one Rich had just given me included an extra line in the middle: "lap desk made by Benjamin Randolph ca. 1778." Just to be sure, I looked back and forth between the two pages a few times. There was no corresponding line on the "official" list.

I took a deep breath. "So there *was* a Terwilliger lap desk, and it was part of the collection that Marty's grandfather gave?"

"Looks like it," Rich said.

"You know Marty's been looking for something like this for a couple of days now. Why didn't you just give it to her?"

"Because after everything I've been hearing, I knew it would upset her. She's really into the whole Terwilliger name thing. I didn't want to be there when she read the two."

"Why not just leave it where she would find it? Did you think Marty would hide the truth?"

"I don't know. Okay, I chickened out. But I brought it to you, didn't I? I mean, I could have destroyed it and nobody would ever have known."

"You know, Grandpa Terwilliger could have changed his mind about donating that one piece and held it back," I pointed out.

"But it was found here in the basement," Rich said stubbornly.

I considered that. "You think he *did* give it to the Society, but changed the list afterward?"

"Maybe. There aren't dates on either list, but you can tell the handwriting's pretty much the same. So he was the one who changed it, and filed the revised one at the Society — that list we've both seen."

"And why would he do that?" I asked.

"Because he knew the lap desk was gone."

"You're saying that Grandpa Terwilliger knew the lap desk wasn't going to be part of the Society collection. Who dumped it into the pit? Did he? Was it someone else?"

Rich looked distressed. "Nell, I don't know! Either he did it, or he knew who was responsible. But now we know that he knew, and he deliberately kept quiet about it, and he changed the record himself."

I sat back in my chair and studied Rich. What did his "find" add to our information? Apart from the fact that the Terwilliger family was involved somehow, which had been likely from the start.

Maybe it was time for a new tack. "Rich, was your grandfather Harrison Frazer?"

He looked at me, startled. "Yeah, well, great-grandfather. How do you know that?"

"I asked Lissa to check family histories of the board members and donors just after 1900, with particular attention to the ones who have descendants still in the area. She found your name."

"I never hid the connection. That's how I met Marty, a while back. She knows about it."

"Your grandfather Frazer may have killed his wife and her lover. Did you know that?"

"Sure. It's a family story. Nobody talks about it much, but a snoopy kid can find out stuff like that, if he keeps asking. So?"

"Did you know that there's a good chance there was a gun hidden in that lap desk when it was tossed into the pit?"

Rich looked bewildered. "What? Why would I know that?"

"Somebody may have. We think Carnell Scruggs found the gun in the pit, in what was left of the lap desk, and took it away from the Society. And that may be why he died."

"So that's what it was!" Rich said.

"What?"

Rich leaned forward eagerly. "Look, that day last week, I was in and out of the basement — Marty wanted me to keep an eye on the Terwilliger stuff so nothing got misplaced, so I kept double-checking. I was

afraid the boxes would get shuffled around or stuck in some corner somewhere and we'd have to waste time hunting for them, you know? I was in one of the rooms across the hall when I heard the guys talking about this hole in the floor they'd just uncovered, and they were, like, kidding around with each other about what might be down there, and daring someone to go down and see what was in there. Finally they figured out how to send the smallest guy, Scruggs, down with a ladder. And he went, and he was there for, oh, maybe ten minutes? I was standing by the hall door listening by then. I mean, it didn't mean anything to me, but I was curious. So first he called out for a bag or bucket or something, so he could dump whatever he found into it and someone could haul it up. There wasn't a whole lot of stuff — maybe two buckets' worth. And then he climbed out, all dirty. The other guys were joking about it, calling him things like a mole or a worm, or worse. And it was by accident that I noticed he was adjusting something in his waistband or his back pocket. He was turned away from the other guys, but I could see it from the hall. I figured he had found whatever it was in the pit, and that meant it wasn't his. It was the property of the Society, right?"

"So what did you do?"

"Well, I didn't know this Scruggs guy, so I told the foreman, Joe Logan. I just said, I thought Scruggs might have picked up something and taken it with him. Logan said he'd take care of it. He thanked me for letting him know."

Funny — Joe Logan hadn't mentioned anything like that. "Did you tell that part to the police?"

"I said I thought Scruggs had taken something, and I'd told his boss. Then when I heard what you all had come up with, I figured he'd pocketed one of the escutcheons. Isn't that what he showed the guy at the bar later?"

The police had known Scruggs took something, but they hadn't known what. I hated to ask, but I had one rather important question for Rich. "Do you have an alibi for the time when Scruggs was hit by the car?"

Rich's eyes widened. "What, you think I killed the guy? No way! I was at a bar over near Penn with a bunch of my friends, watching a basketball game until it ended. That's what I told the cops."

I felt a spurt of relief. If the cops had checked out the alibi, then there was no way Rich could have been responsible for Scruggs's death. I was glad, because I liked

Rich, and I really couldn't see him as a killer. "Rich, you don't know how happy I am to hear that."

"You really thought I was a killer? Wow!" Now he looked almost pleased.

My relief was short-lived: Marty burst through the door. "There you are, you little weasel," she said to Rich. "What'd you do with them?"

"Nice to see you again, Marty," I said mildly. "I assume you mean these? The mismatched inventories?" I held up the copies Rich had given me.

Now Marty was glaring at both me and Rich, alternately. "Yes, those."

"When did you discover them?"

"A few days ago."

Interesting: she hadn't hidden or destroyed them. Had she been waiting for Rich to find them? Or hoping no one would? "Were you planning to share this information with me? Or anyone else?"

Marty dropped into the other guest chair, looking deflated. "Yeah, but I wanted to think about what they meant. Heck, if I was going to hide them, I could have destroyed them, right?"

I shook my head. "You would never destroy historical documents, Marty. Even

ones that put the Terwilliger family in a bad light."

"You're right." Then she turned on Rich. "So you found them, but instead of coming to me with them, you sneaked them out when you thought I wasn't looking? Why didn't you say something?"

"Because I knew you'd be upset. Like you are," Rich said. "But I brought them straight to Nell."

Marty rubbed her hands over her face. "Oh, crap, crap, crap. This just keeps getting worse."

"You want to explain why?" I challenged her. "We now can prove that your grandfather owned that lap desk, and that he knew that something had happened to it." Another thought struck me. "You left the meeting right after Shelby reported on the Frazer murders. What's the connection?"

"You know anything about the social scene on Long Beach Island, back in that era?"

"Not really. Why?"

"In some ways it was a summer enclave for the Philadelphia elite — that's why you see so many of those big Victorian hulks there. They'd just transfer their families and staffs to the summer house and keep up with their usual social schedule, throwing in

a few events at one or another yacht club. The men with jobs came down by train for weekends, just as that news article described. Just like Harrison Frazer did."

"I take it the Terwilliger family had a house there?"

"Yup. Right next to the Frazer house. The one where the shootings took place."

Like Marty had said, *oh, crap.*

CHAPTER 27

We sat in an uncomfortable silence for a few moments. Finally I took the lead. "Okay, now what? Rich here says he saw Carnell Scruggs take something from the pit, and that he told Joe Logan."

"And I told the police about that," Rich added quickly.

"And he has an alibi for the time of Scruggs's death. What does this new information about the lap desk change?"

"Other than depressing me?" Marty asked. "Not much. According to Henry, there was a weapon in the lap desk. We've figured out that it may have been used to commit a crime, and my grandfather probably knew something about it. Nothing we can take to the police. Rich, you didn't tell Logan what Scruggs took away?"

Rich shook his head. "I didn't see it. I just know he hid something and acted kind of furtive after that. Which I also told

the police."

"And they probably assumed it was the brass piece," I said. "If there really was a gun, we don't know where it is now or who has it."

Shelby popped her head in. "Wow, you look like somebody rained on your parade. I was going to ask Nell if she wanted to have lunch, but I'd hate to spoil the gloom. Anything you can talk about?"

"You might as well come in, Shelby. To bring you up to speed, we have just determined that Rich has an alibi for Scruggs's death, that Marty's grandfather owned the lap desk and knew it had gone missing, and that the Terwilligers and the Frazers were next-door neighbors down the shore in 1907."

Rich stood up quickly and backed away, apparently glad to be out of the line of fire, and Shelby dropped into the chair he had vacated. "Wow," she said, "I can't leave you alone for long, can I? What do we do with this information?"

"Got me," I said. "Hey, if Grandpa Terwilliger and Harrison Frazer were friends once, or at least cordial colleagues, he might have cut off all social interactions with the Frazers after this murder. Right, Marty?"

"Frazer killed himself not long after,

didn't he?" Shelby reminded me. "Out of grief for the loss of his wife, or so said the papers."

"That was the public story," I said. "Wonder what the real story was."

"A guilty conscience? But where would Grandpa Terwilliger fit in that? Marty, you have any ideas?" Shelby asked.

Marty roused herself from her funk long enough to say, "Not yet. I'm going to have to go back and look at the more personal papers, see if there are any references to the Frazers there."

"Do you happen to know if the Frazers had any other children, Marty? Apart from Rich's grandfather?"

She shook her head. "I can't say — before my time. Shelby, you can find out, right?"

"No problem," Shelby said.

"So, Shelby is going to go back and dig through her files some more. I've got Eric hunting for any board notes and reports that might have gone AWOL, looking for references to Harrison Frazer. Latoya's going to check out the details of his bequest to the Society. You found a contribution to the building fund from Frazer, right, Shelby?"

"I did. Came in early, too — long before his wife's death. The family was rolling in money. What are you going to do?"

"See if the bank records have arrived. If they have, I'll check them to see if there were any odd deposits from Harrison Frazer."

The mass exodus from my office was quick, and I was left with my thoughts. Gun: still missing, unless the police hadn't bothered to tell me about finding it. Suspects in Scruggs's death? We were back to none again, since we had eliminated Rich. I assumed the police had interviewed Joe Logan, and wondered what he had told them. Other guilty parties: Harrison Frazer, who had probably killed his wife and her lover, and Grandpa Terwilliger, who most likely had some knowledge of that. Would confirming that he had leaned on Harrison Frazer for a contribution in exchange for his silence help anything? So far, nothing seemed strong enough to take to the police.

It all came circling back to Carnell Scruggs's death and the missing and still-hypothetical gun.

I called the bank. Yes, the records had arrived, I was told. Did I want them delivered? No, I decided. I needed to get out of the building and clear my head. "Why don't I stop by and look at them there? I'm only a few minutes away."

We settled on one o'clock, which meant I

could get myself some lunch. As I gathered up my things to leave, another thought bubbled to the surface, and I wondered if the Frazer house was still standing, particularly after Hurricane Sandy. If a firearm that had been used in the killing had turned up amid the debris, would anyone have reported it? It was equally likely that if it had been concealed in the house, it had been washed out to sea, and it might reappear somewhere else entirely or not at all. But somehow I didn't really believe it had been hidden in the house. My gut was telling me that it had been in the Society building.

I marched out of my office and stopped at Eric's desk. "Eric, I'm going out to grab a bite. Then I'm going over to the bank to see what the old records can tell us."

"Have a nice lunch, Nell."

"Thanks, Eric."

I couldn't tell you what I ate. I think it was a sandwich, and I managed not to drop it down the front of me or in my lap while I was lost in thought.

Reviewing what I had heard from the others about what they had found, and what I had asked them to look for now, I felt like we were actually getting closer to a solution. The net was closing, the noose was tightening . . . but I didn't like what was in

that net or noose or whatever. *Stop with the metaphors, Nell!* I was looking in the bank records for something very specific, within a short time frame, so it shouldn't take long there.

The bank looked like exactly what you'd hope a nineteenth-century financial institution would look like, with a small staff and discreet electronic devices scattered around. I waited in the wood-and-marble-paneled lobby for Jacob Keefe, our account representative, to come collect me. When he arrived, he escorted me upstairs in a small elevator (also wood-paneled, with polished brass accents) to a small conference room, where several boxes were stacked. "I'd offer you coffee or tea, but I wouldn't want to present a risk to these archives," he said apologetically.

I laughed. "Believe me, I understand. I'm just pleased that you could get them here so quickly. If I want photocopies of anything, should I ask you?"

"Of course. Will there be many copies required?"

"I hope not, but I can't be sure."

"Then I'll leave you to your work. Please let the woman outside the door know when you've finished." He retreated silently, leaving me alone with all the paper.

It took me several minutes to work out the coding system for the files, but in the end I zeroed in on 1907 easily enough. The Society files in that folder were a bit thicker than those of the surrounding years, most likely because of the influx of contributions for the new building, but given the limited number of donors, even those files were relatively slender. I pulled out the earliest one and started skimming.

It was heartening to see the influx of the state funding, all duly recorded and reported on. I wondered what that $150,000 from the state government would be worth in today's money. They'd built our entire building with that amount — I'd settle for a mere ten percent in modern dollars.

I read the files in chronological order, and made notes on Harrison Frazer's payments along the way — he'd pledged early but paid in installments. But in September 1907 he had made another contribution, equal in size to his original one. There was no explanation, and most people (including the Society's then-treasurer) could have presumed it was due to a surge of enthusiasm for the project, then close to completion. But I had my suspicions, even if I couldn't prove them: Had Grandfather Terwilliger known or learned about the murder weapon

hidden in his beloved society — worse, in his own lap desk — and rather than expose his colleague, had he exacted a payment to the Society from Frazer? Had he demanded what amounted to hush money? It wasn't a pleasant idea, and I was sure that Marty wouldn't welcome anything that raised questions about her grandfather's integrity. The bank record wasn't exactly evidence, but it was one more brick in the . . . Shoot, I couldn't find any metaphor that fit. Fine. Taken in combination with various other facts, it was suggestive and it confirmed my suspicions.

I stuck my head out the door and asked the staff member outside if she could copy that page for me. I didn't need to read any further, because I knew that within a couple of months of that gift Frazer would be dead. His last donation to the Society was the bequest of his library and his papers.

It was now past three, and I wanted to tell Marty what I had found at the bank. I tried her phone, but she didn't pick up. But she'd said she was going to dig deeper into her family's personal papers. I was only a few blocks away from her home, so I might as well see if she was there.

Normally I would have enjoyed the walk to Marty's townhouse. She lived in an at-

tractive, long-settled neighborhood, and her house was lovely, filled with a mishmash of antiques and eclectic personal acquisitions that were uniquely Marty. When I reached the house I walked up the steps, and rapped the polished brass knocker. No response. I laid my head against the door, hoping to hear some sound from inside: nothing. Was she really not there, or was she ignoring me? I looked around the quiet street. There was no one in sight, not even a dog walker. I had nothing to lose.

I pounded my fist on her solid paneled door. "Martha Terwilliger!" I shouted. "You'd better open the door! I'm going to stand here and keep pounding until you do!" To emphasize my point, I pounded some more, hard enough that the ground-floor windows rattled, which was some kind of achievement with a brick building. "Open up!" I yelled. I was making so much noise I half expected a police car to pull up to the curb, and I wondered how the heck I would explain myself.

But I didn't have to. I heard the sound of footsteps inside, accompanied by what I took to be muttered curses, and finally Marty pulled open the door.

"Did it ever occur to you that I didn't want to see anybody?" she demanded.

"Of course it did. But you should know that if I make a fool of myself like this, I have a good reason. You going to slam the door in my face?"

Without answering, Marty turned away and walked down the hall — but at least she'd left the door open. I entered, then closed it behind me and followed her down the long hall. In the living room beyond, she had dropped into a well-worn chair and was avoiding my eyes.

I sat in a second overstuffed chair opposite her. "I'm not going away, so you'd better talk to me. I've just come from the bank. Harrison Frazer made a whopping big contribution to the Society a month after the killings at his summer house."

Marty didn't look surprised. "It figures. What you're not saying is that it means that my grandfather kept his mouth shut about whatever he knew about the Frazer shooting in return for money for the building."

"That'd be my guess. Does that mean the murder weapon was in the lap desk at some point?" And had Marty's grandfather known? When?

Instead of answering my question, Marty changed course. "Philadelphia society was different back then," she said, almost to herself. "Class made a real difference — not

that it doesn't now, but in a very different way. In the early 1900s, the 'right' people all went to the same schools, belonged to the same clubs, supported the same worthy causes. It was expected — it came with the status. You want something to drink? Tea, coffee, something stronger?"

"Whatever's easiest," I said, afraid to break the mood.

"Coffee, then." She went to her kitchen, where I could still see her, and kept talking as she filled a kettle with water, spooned coffee, and so on. "Do you see what that means?"

"That your grandfather and Harrison Frazer played by a different set of rules from most of the rest of the world?"

"Sort of. Their loyalty was to their own kind. Matters were settled between gentlemen, without the intervention of the police, unless it was absolutely necessary. And most of the judges back then were from their class anyway, so maybe justice was a bit skewed. The men would probably have argued that what they did was for the greater good, and of course they knew best what that was." Marty returned with two mugs of coffee.

"Why are you telling me this?"

"I guess so you'll understand how those founders of the Society thought in those

days. Gives you a better sense of them than a bunch of names and a list of contributions."

I could see what she was trying to say. "Okay. What you're getting at is what might have happened when one of those men, Frazer Harrison, did something unthinkable, like killing two people, one of them his wife, in cold blood?"

"Yup." Marty didn't add anything.

So I was going to have to pull the story out of her? "The two men knew each other. They summered next door to each other. Are both the houses still there?"

Marty was laying back in her chair, staring at the ceiling — and not looking at me. "Sure are. I used to spend a couple of weeks each summer at the Terwilliger place — all the cousins took turns. It's not right on the beach, but sits on as big a rise as there is out there, so there are still sea views. Lost a couple of porches during Sandy, but unlike the houses closer to the water, which are pretty much trashed, the rest of ours is holding together just fine. One of my cousins owns it right now." Her eyes were unfocused; she was lost in happy memories.

"And the Frazer house?" I prodded her back to the point.

"Yeah, it's there, too. I think it's a B&B

now. It had like eight bedrooms, not counting the servants' quarters in the attic."

"So presumably it's been remodeled, probably more than once," I said mainly to myself. I was pretty sure it didn't matter: the gun hadn't stayed in the house long. Time to cut to the chase. "Marty, what do you think happened?"

Finally she looked at me. "I think you can guess, you and your merry band of researchers. Harrison Frazer caught an earlier train than he expected and walked in on his wife and some summer stud going at it at the house. He got mad and shot them both, with a weapon he just happened to have handy — we may never know how he came by it or why he had it then. Maybe he had just picked it up in the city and hadn't had time to leave it at his house because he was in a hurry to get away for the weekend. Anyway, then he panicked. Did you know he was a lawyer? He might have gotten away with it in court, under the circumstances, but he didn't want to count on that. So there he was, literally holding the smoking gun, when my grandfather, his nearest neighbor, knocked on the door and says something like, 'I thought I heard a shot.' " Marty lapsed into silence.

It made sense. "Marty, did you know any

of this from your family? Or from the Frazer family?"

She shook her head vehemently. "No. I'm just spinning a tale out of what little we do know. Were Grandfather and Harrison Frazer buddies? Did they hate each other? I have no idea. I don't know how Frazer explained anything. Did Grandfather tell Harrison Frazer to go straight to the police and turn himself in? If he did, we know Frazer didn't do that. Instead he told the police that some unknown person had killed his wife and another man, and nobody even mentioned they'd been in bed together — the upper crust closed ranks on that. The police took Frazer at his word — in part because they didn't find a murder weapon. I don't think they would have tested Frazer's hands for gunshot residue, the way they do now. They believed him."

"But there's more, isn't there?" I prompted.

"Sure there is. Where did the gun go? That's the big question. I see a couple of alternatives. One, Frazer went over to my grandfather's house and hid the gun when he wasn't looking, in the first thing he could find — the lap desk. My father told me years ago that his father liked to carry important documents he might need when

he went on vacation, and the lap desk, with a lock, might have been what he used for them. The other choice is that my grandfather helped Frazer cover it up. They made up a convincing story, and most important, my grandfather took the gun away from the house, back to Philadelphia."

"Then why did it end up in the lap desk?"

Marty turned to face me. "How the hell should I know? Maybe he thought no one would ever look in that. Maybe one of his kids walked in and it was the first place he could find to hide it, and he forgot to take it out again. Maybe Frazer handed him the gun and said, 'Help me,' so he carried it home with him, and *then* it went into the lap desk. Maybe the movers came too early or too fast to pick up the collection items he was giving to the Society and took it out of the house before he could retrieve the gun, which would get it into the building."

"Why didn't he retrieve it from the lap desk, then?" I asked.

Marty gave me a humorless smile. "Maybe he couldn't find the damned desk, once the movers brought it into the building. We're still hunting for things we know are there somewhere, but it's not easy to track them after a hundred years. You know that."

I did indeed. "We could probably find the

exact date for the arrival of his materials —
if it was before the Frazer shooting, your
story falls apart. But say it *was* with the
Terwilliger collections at the Society — then
what?"

"Nell, how are we supposed to know, this
long after it all happened?" she demanded.
"Maybe after the dust settled Frazer wanted
to make sure it disappeared permanently.
Did they do forensic stuff with bullets back
then?"

"Damned if I know. I could ask James."

"Don't bother. Someone — Frazer or
Grandfather himself — pitched the desk,
contents and all, into that convenient hole
in the floor, and there was no point in
retrieving it. They both would have known
that the hole would be covered and the finish work would go on, and it would never
surface. They were right for over a hundred
years, but in the end they were wrong." She
sighed. "I'm being stupid. My father never
said a bad word about any family member.
I mean, if somebody had a drinking problem
— and believe me, that happened a lot —
then he'd say something like, 'Our cousin
Chauncey is indisposed again.' We all knew
it was code. He wasn't a prig or even
squeamish — hell, he'd fought in a war, and
it wasn't a desk job. But I guess in the world

he grew up in, you just didn't talk about unpleasant stuff, particularly in front of the kids. But what I can't get my head around is, why would my grandfather cover up a double murder?"

"I think you've already explained it," I offered. "They were friends, or at least social peers, or had been until then. There was some sort of code of honor involved?"

Marty didn't look convinced. "Thanks for trying to make me feel better, Nell. You can take your pick of the alternatives. I do know that he loved that collection. From all I've ever heard, he cared deeply about the Society and his role there. I don't know what his relationship with the Frazers was like, beyond being neighbors and colleagues, or if he felt any need to protect them, but I'd bet he would have wanted to protect the Society. Having a sordid scandal about a prominent board member come out at that particular moment would have done real harm, tarnished the reputation of the place, maybe even cost the Society some financial support. I'm pretty sure he wouldn't have wanted that."

That was a motive I could understand. "Marty, I've got one more piece for this puzzle that I think supports your theory — that's what I came to tell you. I had our

bank pull the records for that time period, and I looked at them on my way over here. Frazer had made a substantial pledge to the building campaign early on, and he'd fulfilled that obligation. But in September 1907 he made another one of the same size. My guess is that was one of your grandfather's conditions for keeping quiet about what happened."

Marty didn't speak immediately, but finally she said. "That fits, I think. Grandfather may have promised to say nothing, and he was a man of his word, but he made sure that Frazer paid for it. But we'll never be able to prove any of it."

We sat in silence for a few minutes, and I turned over the new facts in my mind, fitting them into the puzzle, whose picture was becoming even clearer.

I looked at Marty. I'd known her for several years, and for the last couple I'd come to see her as both a friend and a staunch supporter of my role at the Society. But there was still a gulf between us: she was Old Money (whether or not there was any actual money anymore) and I was a middleclass outsider when it came to old Philadelphia society. In the eighteenth century my people had been farmers, while hers had been managing the Revolutionary

War, at least in part. It wasn't personal — she wasn't a snob, she didn't throw her weight around, and she was a very down-to-earth person. But still, the divide was there.

I couldn't begin to interpret the social relationships that those board members shared back at the turn of the twentieth century. Would all this really have been enough to persuade Marty's grandfather to look the other way if he knew one of his colleagues was a murderer? And worse, if that colleague had asked him to help conceal the killings? Was this about money or honor, and where did they cross?

Marty began speaking again. "Obviously I never knew my grandfather — he died before I was born. But my father talked about him. He described him as a stern old man who always wore a suit. Who tried to be kind, but who really wasn't comfortable with children. My father said he lived by the old rules — he had, after all, been born in the Victorian era, and he was a gentleman, back when that term meant something. Social class mattered to him. If a friend or colleague — someone he considered a peer — was in financial trouble, bad enough to actually admit it, then he would have tried to help. I know that's not in the

same league as covering up a murder. But as far as I've seen in my research, and from what my dad said, he was a man of his word, an honorable man. It must have hurt to do what he did. Assuming he did it."

"Since we know he changed the inventory, as Rich discovered, he must have known *something,*" I said. "You didn't happen to find any documents signed by Harrison Frazer among your family papers, did you?"

"No, or not yet at least. Maybe Latoya will turn up something," Marty shook herself. "Okay, I'm over my snit about protecting the proud name of Terwilliger. If Grandfather covered up a crime, it's too late to hurt him, or any of his descendants until you get to me, and I can live with that knowledge. I'm sure he had good intentions."

"On the topic of descendants, I forgot to tell you: Lissa found out that Rich Girard is Harrison Frazer's great-grandson."

"Yeah, sure, I knew that — we talked about it when I interviewed him for the internship . . ." Marty started off in a dismissive tone, until she realized what she had said. "Is that important?"

"I don't think so, now. Lissa said he's the only current or recent person attached to the Society who's connected to the board

and donor list from 1907. But Rich came to me this morning and told me that he saw Scruggs pocket something when he came out of the pit. He said he told the construction foreman, Joe Logan. Plus Rich has an alibi for the night of Scruggs's death, and I'm pretty sure the police have confirmed both facts. Besides, can you see Rich laying hands on anybody?" I noticed that Marty swallowed a smile at that idea.

I heard my cell phone ringing in the depths of my purse, and when I fished it out, I saw that it was James calling. I held up one finger to Marty. "Hey," I said when I answered. "What's up?"

"I wondered if you wanted a ride home?"

"Uh, sure, I guess, but I'm over at Marty's. Can you pick me up here?"

"Sure. Half an hour?"

"Great. See you then."

"Your ride, I assume?" Marty asked as I put my phone away.

"Yup. The bloom is still on the rose."

"Does he know about all this?" Marty waved vaguely at the stacks of Terwilliger private papers.

I considered. "Only bits and pieces, and I may never share the whole story. In any case, it's not his problem, it's ours."

Marty didn't look surprised but coun-

tered, "It's James's family, too."

"Yes, but he doesn't feel quite the same way as you do. *Most* people don't feel that way about their families. Heck, most people can't trace their families any further back than their grandparents."

"I know," she said glumly. "That's why it's hard to explain to anyone else. Like the police."

CHAPTER 28

I was startled when my phone rang again. Had James changed his mind? I looked at it and realized it was a Society number. When I answered it, it turned out to be a rather breathless Eric.

"Nell, I'm so glad I found you!" he said in a rush.

"Calm down, Eric. Is something wrong?"

"Well, not exactly. Or I don't think so. That Detective Hrivnak called, looking for you, and I couldn't tell her where you were. I wasn't sure if you wanted me to give her your cell number, so I said I'd track you down if I could. Where are you?"

"I'm at Marty's. Am I supposed to call the detective back?"

"Yes. She didn't sound happy. You need her number?"

"No, I've already got it. Thanks, Eric. If I don't make it back today, I'll see you Monday."

"Call if you need bail money," Eric joked, then hung up quickly.

I tried to collect my thoughts before I made my next call. Maybe Detective Hrivnak had found the killer and this whole thing would go away. Unlikely, I thought. I knew a lot of things she didn't know about what might have led up to Scruggs's death, but I doubted she would have paid much attention if I had tried to share them with her. I realized Marty was staring at me. "What?" I demanded.

"You planning to call the detective any time soon?"

"Of course. I'm just trying to figure out what's going on, or what I can say, or shouldn't say, or — you know what I mean."

"Just call the woman, will you?" Marty snapped.

I did and was put through to her quickly. "I've got something that might interest you," Detective Hrivnak began.

It was unlike her to be coy. "What would that be?"

"A weapon. An *old* weapon."

Alarm bells started ringing in my head. It could be anything — or it could be Harrison Frazer's missing gun. Should I play dumb? I decided against it; I wanted this whole mess to be over. "Let me guess: it's a

1905 Colt pistol."

My statement was met by a long moment of silence. "Bingo. We need to talk. Can you come over here?"

"Can I bring Marty Terwilliger?"

"If you have to."

"See you in fifteen minutes." I hung up. I could be abrupt, too.

Marty and I stared at each other wordlessly, but I was pretty sure we were thinking the same thing. Our silent communication was interrupted by a knocking at the door, and Marty leaped out of her chair. "That should be Jimmy — I'll let him in." She went down the hall toward the front door, and returned a moment later with James, while I was still puzzling over what Detective Hrivnak thought we should talk about. James looked at me quizzically.

"Change of plan," I told him. "We're going to police headquarters. Now. Can you give us a ride?"

James's demeanor changed in an instant, and he morphed into serious FBI agent. "Why?"

"Because Detective Hrivnak asked. Almost nicely, for her."

"I'm coming with you," James said.

"So am I," Marty added.

I wasn't about to object. "Then let's get going."

We were standing in the lobby of the Roundhouse in less than fifteen minutes. Detective Hrivnak came down to collect me, took in my escort without comment, and said only, "Follow me."

We did, up the elevator, down a hallway, down another hallway, until she opened a door to a small conference room and said, "In here."

We went in and sat around the bare table. In the center of the table there was a cardboard box that I knew was the kind used for evidence; inside the box was a firearm that I recognized as a 1905 Colt semiautomatic pistol.

"Have you seen this before?" the detective began.

"No, but I know what it is. Where did you get it?"

"That's the odd part. We pick up a lot of weapons in this city — old, new, working or not. Nothing unusual there. This one was brought to us by a guy named Joseph Logan. He says he's been working on your building over on Locust. You know him?"

"Yes, we've met. He's the foreman of the construction crew that's working on our renovation there." This was beginning to

feel like a game of Ping-Pong, but I was reluctant to volunteer any information. "Where did he get it?"

"He *says*" — her emphasis on that word was troubling — "he found it outside the Society building a couple of days ago. You might remember that we searched that area pretty well after Carnell Scruggs was found dead. Mr. Scruggs worked for Mr. Logan, right?"

"Yes. You talked with Mr. Logan at the time, right?"

"We did. He said he'd paid Scruggs what he was owed at the end of the day, and told him he didn't need him again."

The detective paused, as if waiting for me to spew forth a confession of . . . what? I stayed mute.

Hrivnak continued, unperturbed. "Now, Rich Girard, who works for you, told us that he saw Scruggs take something with him when he left. He says he told Joe Logan about what he saw, and Logan said he'd take care of it. But Logan says he didn't see Scruggs after he left your building. Nothing from your Society was found on or near Scruggs at that time, although the bartender identified the whatsis later."

"The escutcheon," I said. "And you figured that must have been what Scruggs took

away with him?" When Hrivnak nodded, I said cautiously, "Do you have a question?"

Detective Hrivnak chose her next words carefully. "Do you think this weapon was removed by Scruggs from the Society at that time, on the day he died?"

I glanced at Marty, who sat like she was carved in stone. I avoided looking at James, who made no move to interrupt. I took a deep breath. "We believe it was. But it's kind of a long story."

Hrivnak sat back and folded her arms across her chest. "I've got time."

"Marty and I think this all started in 1907, when the Pennsylvania Antiquarian Society building was being finished." And I launched into the whole story that my staff and Marty and I had pieced together, with a few comments from Marty. James sat silent, listening, watching. Detective Hrivnak, to her credit, did not interrupt and let Marty and me spin our tale until we came to the present day — and the death of Carnell Scruggs.

Finally the detective said, "So this gun on the table here was probably used to kill two people in New Jersey in 1907, and one or another Terwilliger knew about it and hid it, and Scruggs just happened to find it last week and take it, and a couple of hours later

he's dead next to your building. What'm I missing?"

"I don't know," I said. Detective Hrivnak looked skeptical. "Seriously, my staff and I have spent over a week putting this information together, based mainly on what's in our files, and we think we can track the gun from that killing at the shore to the day it was found last week, but once it left the building, we don't know anything." And I was afraid to guess.

"So this Logan guy just happened to find it? Pretty convenient, don't you think?"

"I can't say. He has access to the building and the area behind it, because of his job. Where did he say he'd found it?"

"In a corner of the alley behind your building."

"Is it possible it ended up there when the car hit Mr. Scruggs?" I asked.

"Maybe. Can't prove it either way."

"Were there prints on it?"

"Scruggs left prints. Other than that, smudges. It was a cold night — somebody coulda been wearing gloves."

I felt an obscure sense of relief: our shaky reasoning about the path of the gun to Scruggs had been proved right. Which brought us no closer to solving his murder. What did I know about Joe Logan? Not a

lot. He'd been recommended by the architect; he'd worked on museum jobs before. He had every right to be where he said he found the gun. "When did he say he found it?"

"Yesterday. He brought it in this morning. It was kinda dirty, but it didn't look like it had been sitting out for a week or more."

Might as well face this head-on. "You doubt his story?" I asked.

She studied my face, and I wondered what she was thinking. Would I have any reason to protect Joe Logan? No, I'd barely met the man. Now, if she'd accused Rich or Bob or even Scott the architect, I might have felt some responsibility, but in this case I didn't have any knowledge to share with her. I didn't know Joe personally, and I didn't want to guess what he might have done.

Finally she answered, "Let's just say I'm keeping an open mind. You have anything else to add?"

Marty spoke for the first time. "We told you, that gun might have been used in a murder in New Jersey in 1907. Is there any way to find out if the police kept the bullets back then, and see if they're a match?"

"You kidding? You want the Philadelphia Police Department to waste time and money on something like that?"

Marty held up her hands in defeat. "I was just asking. Forget about it."

Detective Hrivnak stood up; apparently our meeting was over. "Thanks for coming in. I'm not sure what to do with what you told me, but if I have any more questions, I'll be in touch."

"One more thing," I said before she could leave. "Who does that weapon belong to now?"

"What, you want it back?"

"Well, it was found in our building. If you can't identify an owner, does that mean it's ours?"

Hrivnak snorted. "I'll look into that. Let me take you to the elevator."

We followed her mutely down the hall, descended, went outside to where James had parked his car. "Martha, can I drive you home?" James asked.

Marty sighed. "Might as well. I'm tired — it's been a long week. And I've still got some thinking to do. I guess that's the problem when you look into your family history: you never know what you're going to find. And it's not all pretty." She was silent for the rest of the trip to her house.

When we'd dropped her off and she'd gone inside, I turned to James. "What do we do now?"

"As far as I can see — unofficially, of course — you don't have to do anything. You don't know anything more than you told the detective, do you?"

"No, I do not. Which is not the same as saying I don't have suspicions."

"Joe Logan," James said bluntly. "You don't believe his story?"

"I don't know," I said slowly. "Scruggs's death still could have been a random mugging — somebody attacked Scruggs on the street, maybe followed him from the bar, where he was a little too free with his payday cash, and mugged him, and in the process shoved him into the street. Which doesn't explain why the escutcheon was gone, or how the gun ended up so far from the street. Wouldn't a mugger have taken the gun?"

"If he knew about it. Maybe he couldn't find it in the dark, and when Scruggs got hit by that car, the mugger panicked and ran. That will probably be the official story."

"And that means the case is closed, right?"

"Yes. You have a problem with that?"

"I guess not. We need to get back to our business as usual. We've already spent too much time on this."

"So we can go home now?"

"Yes. Please."

The ride home passed quickly, despite the Friday traffic, but it was dark by the time we arrived home. James pulled into the driveway and turned off the engine, but then I grabbed his arm and pointed. "Look."

He followed my finger toward the front steps, where a man was sitting. The man stood up as soon as he knew we had seen him, and even in the dark I thought I recognized Joe Logan. Maybe the story wasn't over yet. "That's Joe Logan."

James the agent was back again. "Let me get out first and see what he wants." He opened the door on his side and climbed out — and I noticed he kept one hand close to where I knew his gun was. I wasn't worried that Joe meant us any harm, but it was nice to have James run interference for me. I watched as the two men faced each other but didn't see any hostility, so I got out of the car.

Joe looked relieved to see me. "Sorry to bother you folks at home, Nell, but I really need to talk with you, and I didn't want to do it at the Society. I won't take long."

I glanced at James, and he gave me a barely perceptible nod. "That's all right, Joe. Come on in and you can tell me what's bothering you. Oh, have you met James Morrison?"

"Special Agent Morrison," James said, although his tone was mild. I wondered if Joe paled, but it was hard to tell in the dim light.

I entered first and went ahead turning on lights. "You guys want something to drink? Coffee?" Susie Homemaker, that was me, about to chat with a possible murderer accompanied by my FBI agent lover. How had my life come to this?

Both men declined. I hung up my coat, then said brightly, "Let's sit in the parlor," although we had barely enough seats for the three of us. When we were settled, I said, "What's this about, Joe?"

"I assume you know about that gun I turned in to the police?" he began.

"Yes. We just came from there. Did you tell them the whole story?"

"Not exactly. Do you mind if I tell it my own way? It's hard enough without interruptions. I'll answer any of your questions after."

"Go on," I prompted.

He nodded, looking relieved. "You already know that I hired Scruggs for short-term jobs. I had known the guy slightly for a few years, and I felt sorry for him, so I tried to throw some work his way. He'd always been honest and worked hard. Last week his part

of the job at the Society was done, so I paid him for his work for the day, and he left. Then this other guy who works for you came to me and said he might have seen Scruggs pocket something and thought I should know.

"I knew where Carnell hung out after work — he lived over past Spruce, but he had a favorite bar on Chestnut — so I went looking for him. I didn't plan to accuse him, just ask if maybe he'd taken something accidentally. I found him where I expected to and we talked. Turned out he *had* picked up something he found — he thought it didn't matter if he took it along, because it seemed like trash to him."

"The escutcheon," I said.

"If that's what you call that brass thing," Jose said. "I told him I wasn't sure what it was or if it was worth anything, but he'd been wrong to take it. You know he was kind of subpar mentally? He wasn't angry. He apologized, and he gave it back to me. I thought we'd settled things. I bought him a drink, and we left maybe half an hour later. He started walking toward home, and I tagged along because I'd left my car parked near the Society.

"So we're walking along Locust Street and I see he's got something else tucked in his

waistband, something bigger. So I asked, 'What's that?' And he gets all defensive about it. Says, 'Nothing.' But he's acting odd, so I ask him again. And he tells me it's his, and finally he pulls out this gun he was hiding. Now, I'd worked with Carnell for a while, and he's not a violent man, and he had no reason to have a gun. So I look closer and realize it's kind of dirty, and not new. So I ask, 'Where'd you get that?' And he wouldn't tell me — he tried to walk away. And by then I was really suspicious, so I asked, 'Did you take that from the job today?' And he tries to lie, but finally he said, 'What if I did? Somebody threw it away. I found it. So now it's mine.' And I told him, 'You have to give it back,' and I held out my hand for it."

Joe stopped and swallowed hard. "And he started backing away, shaking his head, and then he was in the street and this car came along . . . and you know what happened then."

"Joe, why did you leave?" I asked gently. "Maybe you could have helped him."

He shook his head. "That car hit him head-on, and he must've flown about twenty feet through the air. I can still hear that *thud.*"

Was it illegal to leave the scene of the ac-

cident? I had no clue, but I had a feeling it was. "And the gun?"

"When Carnell was hit, he was holding it in his hand. It went flying right over my head, but I saw where it landed and picked it up."

"Did you call nine-one-one?"

"I could see the woman in the car had her phone in her hand, and I think there was someone else coming from Locust Street. Nobody noticed me, so . . . I kind of left. I'm sorry. I should have stayed. But I swear, I never touched the guy!" Logan protested. "It was his own fault! He just backed straight into the street without looking."

"Why'd you turn the gun in?" James asked quietly.

"I didn't want the damn thing. It was what got Carnell killed."

"But you just dropped it at headquarters and left, didn't you?" James added.

Joe looked away. "I told the cops that I'd found it, and that was true. I kind of changed *when* I found it, is all." Then he looked at us squarely. "Look, I could have dumped it in the river, or left it in a Dumpster somewhere, couldn't I? I'm not a bad person. I've never been in trouble with the police. I was trying to get back something that Carnell stole, that wasn't his. I never

meant to hurt him." He struggled with himself for a moment before asking, "You going to turn me in?"

I looked at James, who finally spoke. "I would urge you to go to the police yourself and tell them what you've just told us. If they have no evidence against you, they'll probably be lenient. But if they find out you're covering something up, it'll only get worse."

Joe sighed. "I guess that's what I expected you'd say. I know it's the right thing to do." Joe stood up. "Thanks for listening to me, and I'm sorry for any trouble I've caused. I'll be on my way now."

James escorted him to the door, and I thought I heard the murmur of voices from them before I heard the door shut. When James came back to the parlor I said, "Is today over yet?" I felt exhausted.

"Close enough. I'm guessing you need food and drink, not necessarily in that order. Follow me to the kitchen."

I followed.

In the kitchen, James doffed his jacket — and his gun — and set about making sandwiches. I was content to watch, and he had food on the table in no more than five minutes. As he worked, James said, "You did a good job with this."

"High praise indeed," I countered, spreading more mayo on my sandwich. "Aren't you glad you stayed out of it? Although your imposing if silent presence was invaluable."

He shook his head. "You put the information together in ways I never could. In all honesty, I will admit that the atavistic — or do I mean Neanderthal? — part of me wanted to jump in and protect you, but you didn't need it. Professionally, I had no place in this investigation."

I put my hand on his. "Thank you. For letting me do this my way. And for listening. And for so many other things." I paused. "Do you think Logan is guilty of anything? And will he go back and talk to the police?"

"Maybe. There's little evidence of anything. Of course, it's easy for us to say that he should have gone straight to the police and told them the whole story, but even the police know that people can panic and do stupid things. I told him I'd back him up if there was trouble, but I do think he's basically honest. He's a good guy who got caught in a bad situation."

"You are a kind and decent man," I told him — and meant it. "Isn't it ironic that a whole bunch of us waded through over a hundred years of documents only to find

out in the end that this was a simple theft that had nothing to do with anybody's history? And along the way we may have solved a pair of 1907 murders?"

"Sometimes the simplest solution is the right one. Now eat."

I ate. James was right: I felt better after eating. "You want to go upstairs and investigate that Neanderthal side of yours a bit more?"

"What about the dishes?" he protested in mock dismay.

"Tomorrow's Saturday, and the dishes aren't going anywhere."

As predicted, the dishes were still sitting there the next morning when we ambled downstairs in our weekend grubbies, and James made coffee while I washed up. We were just ready to sit down with some breakfast when we heard what sounded like a piece of heavy equipment lurching its way up our driveway. I peered out the kitchen window and saw a large truck parking in the driveway next to the house. "Are you expecting anyone or anything?" I asked James.

"No." He joined me at the window in time to see Marty climbing out of the passenger side of the cab. "Uh-oh."

I went around to the front door to intercept her. "Good morning, Marty. You're out early. What's this all about?" I waved vaguely at the truck.

"I have a little surprise for you two. Come on." She led me to the back of the truck, and when the driver climbed out I recognized Henry Phinney.

"Yo, Nell," he greeted me with a grin and then unlocked the back doors of the track and swung them wide. The interior was stuffed to the ceiling with bulky items wrapped in quilted moving blankets.

By now James had wandered out to join me. "Good morning, Martha. What's going on?"

Marty looked smug. "You two need furniture to fill this Victorian barn. I've got furniture. Well, no, not me — but the Terwilliger family sure does. And before you protest, this is all stuff no one is using and doesn't want — call it the family rejects collection. Henry and I have been gathering it up for days now. You can take your pick."

"Wow." I couldn't think of anything else to say.

James could. He cocked an eyebrow at Marty. "No strings?"

"Nope. Well, somebody in the family might be miffed it you started a bonfire with

it, and family gets the right of first refusal if you want to get rid of it. Otherwise, do with it what you will."

James eyed the bulging contents of the truck with a critical eye. "That's a lot of stuff to move."

Marty waved his objection away. "I've even taken care of that. I hired a couple of local football players to do the heavy lifting. They should be here by ten. With all of us, I think we can manage."

James and I exchanged a look, and I think his mouth twitched. "Marty, this is amazing," I said. "Can I offer you coffee? Or breakfast?"

"Sure. Henry, come on in — you can drool over the original woodwork in the house."

"Happy to. You still got knob-and-tube here?"

"Uh — you tell me," I said happily. I felt like a kid at Christmas, wondering what might be lurking under all that padding in the truck.

"Thank you, Marty," I told her as we walked toward the house. "You okay?"

"Sadder but wiser, I guess," she said. "At least we know what happened last week — and in 1907. And I'm glad of that, even if I

don't like it much. So let's go fill up your house!"

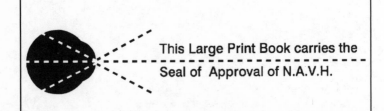

This Large Print Book carries the
Seal of Approval of N.A.V.H.

PRIVY TO THE DEAD